KEEPER OF THE FOREST

D.K. HOLMBERG

ASH PUBLISHING

CHAPTER 1

$\mathcal{E}$ris stormed through the palace, hands gripping her dress so it didn't flutter about her as she raced to the garden. Today she would find a flower to satisfy Lira. What did it matter she'd failed every day for the last few months?

"Another wasted day?"

Eris looked up with a flash of annoyance. Her sister Jasi stood in a doorway leading toward the center of the palace, blue eyes blazing with condescension. She wore a gown of light blue and held her back straight and stiff. Her golden hair, so like their mother's, shifted in the soft breeze.

"Mother send you on another errand?" Eris asked.

Jasi frowned, barely a shifting of her lips, holding all her disappointment in her eyes. She was like their mother in that as well. "I'm going for a few perisals for my arrangement. Perhaps, if you would find your flower, you will be allowed to learn what we do."

Eris bit back her first reply. Jasi would never understand she didn't want to be like her. "And that's all you do?" Jasi could have any one of her handmaidens run for the flowers. Why would she come herself?

She shrugged. "Mother asked me to check on you. She worries about your progress. Especially since you chased off another hand-maiden…" At nineteen, Jasi was permitted more freedom than Eris, even though only two years separated them.

"I progress just fine." Eris hadn't wanted someone following her around. It was fine for her sisters, but she had no interest in such things.

Jasi tilted her head, turning it slightly to the side in her attempt to look dignified. "Indeed? Is that what you want Mother to hear?"

"You'll tell her whatever you want anyway."

Jasi shifted her hands, moving them from where they were clutched behind her back to hold them in front of her. "You should worry as much about Lira. How much longer will she have patience for you? At some point you will fall so far behind us that you cannot keep up with the lessons."

Eris looked away. "How do you know what Lira will do?" But she feared the same.

"Well. Perhaps today will be better for you." Jasi paused. "You know, you *don't* have to be so difficult. I mean, the Sacred Mother knows you're so much like Aunt Rochelle!"

Eris glared at her. Jasi didn't say it, but Aunt Rochelle had always been odd. Even when she'd lived with them in the palace, she never really fit in, always disappearing for days at a time before she finally disappeared for good. Worse, Eris looked more like Rochelle than her own mother. Yet her aunt always had made her feel special, like being different was a good thing rather than a curse. Since she'd been gone, Eris no longer felt the same way.

"Really, Eris, just ask Master Nels for help. He knows the garden quite well. Finish this foolishness of picking your flower and join us in lessons."

Jasi studied Eris for a moment more before nodding and

sliding past her. Eris watched as she hurried down the hall and out into the garden. Annoyance churned her stomach. Her sister had made a point of coming just to taunt her. Typical of her. And she always knew where to prick Eris to have the greatest effect.

Eris sighed before following Jasi down the hall.

As she neared the doors, the booming voice of her father drew her attention. She hadn't seen him in a few days, though he often left the city of Eliara to visit other parts of the kingdom. Eris glanced at the massive garden visible through the doorway, knowing she should begin her search for the day. The sooner she attempted to find her flower, the sooner she could fail and move onto something else.

"The north hasn't pressed an attack in *years*," her father said. There was urgency in his voice she hadn't heard before. "Why would they move now?"

Eris frowned and made it to the cracked door before she knew what she had done. Peering in, she saw her father sitting in front of his council table, the smooth rivenswood surface gleaming from the bright sunlight streaming through the upper windows. His wrinkled face wore a tight expression, and his eyes flashed from one person to the next.

"Perhaps they simply bided their time while consolidating their position."

Eris couldn't see who spoke, but it sounded like Tholen. The old general had a distinctive rough voice that carried even when he spoke softly.

"But what do they want? Attacking from the east is a fool's game." This from a nasally voice, likely Eldan. "And they haven't the ships to sail south first. My lord, I think this is nothing more than bluster. We have no reason to believe the Kelths and Vardens would even unite, let alone push south together."

"You would risk losing the eastern edge of Errasn because

Eldan doesn't *think* it's anything? Do you know what happened the last time we underestimated Varden? How much we nearly lost?"

The speaker stood off to the side and out of view so it took Eris a moment to recognize the voice. It was deep and rough, different than Tholen, and sounded more like his throat had been burned. A hint of a scarlet cloak could be seen from where she stood, not enough to make out clearly, but enough that she recognized Adrick. Her father's advisory magi often disagreed with Eldan. She didn't know what he meant about country Varden. When had they been a threat?

"Father—let me take a company of cavalry. What better way to simply see—"

Adrick cut Eris's brother, Jacen short. "We cannot risk the prince, my lord."

"You think I'll be at risk leading men across our lands, Adrick?" Jacen asked.

Eris wished she could see Jacen, but the door obscured him.

"I could accompany him, my lord." Tholen shifted in his seat to face someone at the opposite end of the table. "This would be an opportunity for him to prove himself. You said yourself he needs to gain experience. Something like this would be an ideal way for him to gain it and prove himself to the men."

There was a moment of silence before her brother answered, "I'd never pass on the opportunity to learn from you, Tholen."

Her father slapped a hand lightly on the table. "Just a scouting mission. Nothing more. If you find evidence of northern movement..."

Tholen nodded.

Someone murmured something so soft that Eris couldn't hear, and then chairs pushed back. Most of the men filed out the back of the room, disappearing. Her father sat motionless in his chair. For a moment, Eris considered going in and speaking to him, but Adrick spoke, and she halted.

"Have you considered my other proposal?"

Her father sighed. "I have. And the boy is here. As unusual as that is, I haven't prevented it. Jasi will make up her own mind on this."

"Of course. But you can...encourage...her to see the benefit of this arrangement."

"I can encourage her all that I want, Adrick, but my wife offers her own council. And listens to the Mistress of Flowers."

At the mention of Lira, Eris leaned forward. She knew Lira had her mother's ear, but counseling her as well?

And an arrangement? Had she managed to overhear plans for marrying her sister off? Eris knew it was time for Jasi to marry, but always before her father had delayed. What had changed?

And what did it mean for her?

"You think it wise to let Lira have such influence?"

Her father laughed lightly. "If I value my safety." He laughed again. "She has proven herself useful many times over. Surely you can see that."

Adrick sniffed. "I see the mess she's made of the courtyard since she's come to Eliara. That is the extent of what I've seen."

"A mess? I think it quite lovely. Other than needing to move the barracks outside the palace yard, it hasn't really created any inconvenience. And Elayne finds it pleasing that she added onto what my sister started. My wife is not always so easy to please. Besides, Lira needs the garden for her instructions with my daughters."

"Perhaps their time might best be used in other ways," Adrick said. "Especially if this arrangement is accepted. Jasi, at least, will have much to learn. She shouldn't waste so much time learning about flowers that won't even grow—"

"I leave the education of my daughters to Elayne. As should you."

Silence held for a moment. "Of course. I was just suggesting—"

"I know what you were suggesting. Besides, what harm is it

that they are distracted by pretty colors? After Jasi, I'll have to start planning for the others. Finding a match for Desia is easy, and if this business in the north isn't what you fear, she would make a suitable match for a high lord of Varden. Perhaps even Haenish. His land abuts ours and would strengthen any alliance we can craft."

Eris tensed, waiting for what was next.

"What of the other?" Adrick asked.

Eris noted he didn't say her name.

Her father smiled. "Eris will be challenging for many reasons."

Adrick huffed loudly. "Not the least because she's—"

She turned away before listening to the magi finish. She didn't need any reminders of what she was not. She was not like her sisters—golden-haired and pretty. She was not like her mother—regal and proud. Eris didn't fit in anywhere in the palace. Not even in her classes. Unlike her sisters, she hadn't even managed to find a flower Lira accepted. Always so different, just like Jasi said.

She hurried away from the door without looking where she was going and ran into Jacen.

Her brother wore deep blue pants with heavy embroidery down the side. The pattern made Eris think of their mother, which she suspected was Jacen's point. His green shirt buttoned up to his square chin. A few days of growth covered his face. Brilliant blue eyes smiled at her as he caught her.

"Better be careful they don't see you spying on them," he said.

She shook him off and looked toward the council room. She didn't want her father—or Adrick—to realize she'd been listening. Jacen catching her was no better, really. "I'm trying to reach the garden before Master Nels disappears for the day," she said. Eris didn't really expect Jacen to believe her, but as long as he didn't question her more, it didn't really matter.

A wide smile split his mouth. "You think the gardener has someplace to be other than the garden?"

Eris stood and planted her hands on her hips. "And where are you heading?" She wondered if he would admit that he was going north. Or would he think to protect her and not share the information?

His eyes narrowed. "Serving the realm, of course. Isn't that what the crown prince is supposed to do?"

"Well...yes. That's exactly what you're supposed to do."

Jacen shrugged. "Then it's what I'm doing. Father wants me to head north. There's a concern about the border with Varden. Probably nothing, but with the damn northerners, you never really know."

"We haven't had trouble with the north since before I was born. Why would they start now?" She realized she sounded like her father, but like him, she couldn't understand what the north would gain by attacking. Maybe if she'd paid more attention in her studies she might better understand the intricacies of politics.

"Who knows with Varden? Or Kelth." He said the last with a hint of contempt that surprised Eris. "But you shouldn't worry about it here, Eris. We're protected by the eastern range. It would take...something significant...to cross over and be a threat to us."

"What kind of something significant?"

Jacen took a deep breath and ran his hand through his long golden hair. "Not sure. That's why I'm going north." He patted her arm gently. "Don't let me keep you from playing in the garden."

He said the words kindly—Jacen always supported her, regardless of how odd she might be—and she slapped his hand away. "Careful, or I'll make sure your room is covered in thorns."

Jacen laughed and turned away. "See you when I return, little sister."

Eris watched with envy as he made his way down the hall, a purposeful stride in his step. She'd never have quite the same purpose as Jacen. Even if her father managed to marry her off, as he apparently intended, she'd never have the same sense of urgency or responsibility. And marrying some distant lord wasn't what she wanted. Would she spend her days trying to look pretty, like Jasi? Or would she turn to collecting tapestries and paintings like her mother?

Eris sighed. Nothing suited her, but there wasn't anything she could do to change it. It would be one thing if she knew what she wanted. Instead, she wasted her time trying to work with Lira.

She turned back to the garden. At the least she could find her flower. But then what?

CHAPTER 2

*T*he great garden stretched out before Eris, hundreds of flowers mixing their scents, all turning toward the bright sun shining overhead. Some even seemed to turn toward her as she passed. Each day the gardeners added new flowers. What would happen when it inevitably overgrew the walled yard?

Eris inhaled, tasting the mixture of fragrances on her tongue: the sweetness of the lilacs and roses, the bitterness of the blue tarasc, the foulness of the stipel—almost like a sickly sweet rot. A cornucopia of scents filled the garden, drifting up and into the soft breeze to create a cloud of hovering aromas . Each day the smells changed, sometimes rapidly shifting throughout the day.

Colors abounded. Flowers arranged perfectly, the colors complementing each other. There were obvious formations, simple separations, but over time she noticed subtler patterns, such as how flowers alternated in rows in what had seemed irregular at first.

Yet, as much as the flowers drew her attention, she couldn't help but think about the conversation she'd overheard. Had her father actually arranged for her sister to marry? All these years she'd spent annoyed at Jasi—soon she'd be gone. And, from the way it sounded, Desia, too.

After that?

After that was her. As a princess, it was her duty. If not for her sister Ferisa, she might have been given to the Sacred Mother. Now she was a middle daughter and her role was marriage.

Eris shuddered at the thought.

"Can I help you, my lady?"

The master gardener stood alongside a nearby path. A spade rested on the ground; he held a small rake in his hand. His fingers were stained black from years spent digging in the dirt, and his weathered face watched her with a neutral expression, but his pale eyes betrayed annoyance at her presence. A brown hat tilted on his head to shade him from the sun.

Eris smiled and shook her head, brushing a strand of her coiled black hair away from her face. It never stayed pulled back as it should, leaving her looking constantly mussed. So different than the manageable golden hair her sisters had inherited from their mother.

"A lesson is all, Nels."

"Each day is the same," he remarked neutrally.

She nodded. "It is the same lesson. But today will be different." She smoothed her dress, the bright colors nothing that any of her sisters would ever choose. They preferred the subdued blues and yellows favored by their mother. Eris couldn't stand the boring colors—probably why she enjoyed wandering the garden—and the seamstresses managed to find fabrics of much bolder colors for her.

Nels sniffed. "Many young ladies are satisfied with lilacs or corinths."

Eris smiled and nodded. They were some of the first she had

tried and the first Lira told her would not work. "I've been told lilacs do not suit me. Not bold enough."

Nels almost smiled. "And corinths?"

"Too pale."

"So what does the mistress think you should find?"

The questioning surprised Eris. Nels rarely spoke this much to her. Usually he simply watched her, standing along the paths while pretending to ignore her. Eris learned he would follow wherever she wandered as long as she remained in his garden, never leaving her fully alone, as if he tended to her as he tended the flowers.

Eris shook her head. "She says I must find my own flower."

"And then?" the gardener asked.

Eris shrugged. "Then I can continue with my lessons."

Nels harrumphed softly.

"Until then, I search."

Nels looked out over his massive garden. Eris couldn't remember a time when there weren't flowers everywhere. Surely before Lira had first arrived in the palace—and she too young to remember, barely old enough to roam the halls without a hand-maiden. With Lira's arrival came the garden, a magnificent creation of color used to create her arrangements.

"Currently there are two thousand and forty-one different species within this garden," Nels went on.

Eris knew the numbers were well into the thousands, though most were variations on similar strains. So far, she had tried over two hundred without success.

"When the gardeners return from Baylan next week, I will have two thousand one hundred," Nels continued.

At the rate the gardeners collected flowers, she could spend years searching before she ever found the right flower. If she ever did. How many more months would Lira let her simply wander aimlessly? How much longer before she was deemed too slow to teach? And then what would she do?

"It would help if you knew what you sought," Nels suggested.

Eris sighed as she nodded agreement. "I wish I did."

"Hmm," Nels said, narrowing his eyes as he looked over the garden. He swept his hat from atop his head and cupped it over his eyes. "If color is what you seek, then there are some bright orange celias in a bed over there." He turned. "Or, for something a bit more bold, my lady, I might suggest a brasy tolia? They have thick petals with many different, brightly colored flowers, some red, some blue, some pink..."

Though Eris nodded, any he suggested would be unlikely to work. She'd tried following suggestions at first, asking others in the palace what she should try. Each flower suggested was beautiful in its own way, but Lira quickly rejected them. She seemed to know when Eris did not search on her own.

As Nels seemed to consider the flowers in his garden, one of the assistant gardeners ran up to him. Younger, and with brown hair hanging long and tucked behind his ears. It slipped out as he ran. The assistant glanced at her a moment, his eyes lingering a half second longer than appropriate, before he looked back over to master Nels.

"Master Nels," he huffed as he approached. "There is word from Baylan, sir. There is a problem with the..."

Nels's face twisted and he started grumbling loudly. He shifted his hat, rolling it in dirt-stained fists, and pulled it back down atop his head so hard it strained the fabric.

Eris didn't stay to listen. Waving briefly to Nels, she slipped away. He didn't even bother to look at her, which Eris found surprising, but she had no doubt he would follow. It was the same every day.

She wandered down one of the cobbled paths and passed flowers of gold and red and orange. Some, like Jasi's parisal, were striped, others speckled. She considered a dozen different flowers with thorns. The sharp thorns suited her irritation better than some of the softer leaved flowers, but nothing really called to her. So many seemed too similar to flowers she had brought back to Lira in the past. Eris continued on, ignoring the flowers in this part of the garden.

Eventually, she reached a shadowed area. She couldn't remember if she'd been here before. After this many months wandering, she no longer found many parts that surprised her, but at this point, everything looked much the same. It was hard to believe there might be a part of the garden she *hadn't* visited.

Here in the shadows of the wall was an area where the sun didn't quite penetrate and struggled to reach beyond the tall walls surrounding the palace and its garden. The flowers were different. Some seemed subdued, their colors faded compared to the bright red or yellows she saw in the more sunny parts of the garden, but as she leaned in to look at them, she realized the colors were deeper, as if somehow thicker. The shapes of the leaves were different as well; some were nettled and thorny while others were velvety. Others were vines unlike anything she had seen before. The scents here were different, subtle and rich and tinted with a heavy earthen odor.

This far in the garden, nearly complete solitude surrounded her. Other than her wandering, nothing moved. In most parts of the garden, bees buzzed around flowers or the occasional bird dipped toward the petals as it pulled up hidden nectar. Even Nels or one of his assistants, ever present, moved along the paths. Not here, though, not where the shadows grew.

A few of the flowers seemed promising. One had two, large, blue-green petals, each with jagged edges and cupped like some devious mouth just waiting for a bite. Eris considered plucking one of those. If nothing else, she might scare Lira. Seeing her unsettled might be worth the time she had already spent in the garden. But as Eris reached for the spiny stem, the flower shuddered, as if twisting itself toward her. She jerked her hand away.

Another flower had petals which bowed out before rolling back in, colors in vibrant shades of red or blue with a hint of bold green mixed in. The stem felt more like tree bark than part of a flower. Eris reached to pluck the flower until she realized only one such flower grew in this part of the garden. The idea of destroying the only flower of its kind bothered her, so she left it where it was and moved on.

The air cooled as she moved deeper into the shade. Not just cooler, but damper as well, carrying more than just an earthy smell, like that of leaves piled up and rotting, so thick she nearly tasted it. The fragrances coming from the flowers changed; the more shadowed the garden became around her, the more she noticed a mix of bitter and spice, less of the sweetness that at times overpowered her in other parts of the garden.

With a start, she realized she'd reached the palace wall. Had she really reached the end of the garden?

The wall was different than she remembered. Now raised beds set into the side, wooden boxes set atop thick stone almost like stepping stones twisting toward the top. Eris had never really seen the flowers here—had only really reached the outer wall once during her searches, and then the garden had stopped nearly fifty paces shy. Either this was new or just a section she had never visited.

Vines dangled over the sides of a few beds, thin creepers of green working down the wall coming off a thicker stem. Small buds grew on the nearest vine, barely different in color than the vines they flowered from. They smelled bitter, almost tangy, and reminded her of the ale her father's men preferred. Near the top of the wall, a small, painted white bed worked into the stone. Only a single strand of green hung over the edge.

As she squinted at the vine, she realized it was not a single strand but many, all twirling about like a braided rope. Unlike the others, no flowers hung off the vine. Eris considered ignoring it, but something about the way it twisted drew her to take a closer look.

Carefully she climbed onto one of the lower level beds, wondering if the narrow ledge would hold her weight. When satisfied it would, she jumped to the next ledge, then the next, careful at each one to step over the wooden box and mindful not to step into the still damp earth the vines sprung from.

When almost to the top, she looked down and felt a moment of dizziness. A fall from where she stood could be dangerous. Worse than the broken arm her brother Jacen suffered after falling from his horse during a hunt three winters ago with their father, she could break her leg or neck falling from this height. Had Nels seen her, she suspected he would demand she come down. Thankfully, the gardener had stopped following her today.

The small box holding the braided vine rested on the last ledge, nearest the top of the wall. The distance between it and where she stood was enough that she would have to jump. Even then, she wondered if she could make it in her dress; the widely flared gown would likely catch her feet and trip her when she jumped.

Eris considered climbing back down. She could take one of the small flowers off the lower vine and bring it to Lira for her day's attempt, but they weren't right. The buds were too small, not decorative enough even for her. Besides, the bitter aroma was too simple for her flower.

More than that, she felt curious.

Bunching up her dress, rolling it up along her legs, she stood carefully. Had Nels followed her, he would have gotten a shock at this. Eris could only imagine the look of horror on her mother's face if she learned how Eris stood atop the wall, dress rolled up exposing leg and thigh for any passing beneath. *Very* unladylike.

Of course, maybe then her mother would decide her lessons with Lira could stop. Eris didn't expect much out of them anyway.

Only, that meant she'd lose her excuse for wandering the garden, and she wasn't ready to give that up.

Taking a deep breath, she jumped.

And did not jump nearly far enough.

In a panic, she scrabbled for grip along the ledge, nails painfully attempting to dig into the stone before she managed to grab the ledge tightly.

With a heave, she pulled herself up, and stared at the painted white box. It was made of rough wood and nailed loosely together. She managed to crawl onto the ledge. She lay there for a moment, catching her breath, steadying breathing that came out in a pant.

Pain bloomed in her hand, and she pulled it up to her face to see that she had scraped much of the flesh from one of her palms. Blood blossomed across her palm. Eris squeezed her hand shut to keep from bleeding on her dress. That, more than anything, would draw the ire of her mother.

Now having reached the ledge, she looked over the top of the wooden box, curious what she would see. The braided vine started as many individual shoots, each stretching from the soil and growing toward the center. When they joined in the middle of the box, they twined together, twisting about each other. The vine coiled a few times in the box before hanging over the edge.

Along the vine were seven flowers. Each petal was a different color, as if made from one of the different shoots, but all of the same shape. Petals grew long and narrow, overlapping just enough so they curved together and spiraled outward, almost like a reverse of the braided vine.

Eris smiled. This would be the flower she chose today.

She looked down, wondering how she would manage to reach the next ledge. From there, she thought she could manage, but the distance was more than she had gauged at first. She was stuck.

What had she been thinking jumping to this ledge? Just to see a flower? From below, Eris had not even known there would be any flowers along the vine. Now atop the ledge, she was stranded.

So she sat along the ledge, bare legs dangling. The cool air was a welcome sensation along her skin, stealing some of the heat the dress generated. As she looked out over the garden, the swirls of pattern to the colors were even more impressive from this vantage. Eris pushed the dress down as best she could, careful not to rub her bloodied hand on the fabric, and realized she had torn the dress as well.

She sighed. Nothing to do but wait.

She did not pluck one of the flowers, not yet. She would wait for Nels or one of his assistants to find her and help her down and deal with her mother's irritation as best she could.

Thankfully, she did not have to wait long before one of the gardeners found her. Had it been Nels, Eris did not know how she would be able to return to the garden and face him again. She could very well imagine the look on his face, stern and admonishing. Much like her mother. This gardener was younger and not schooled well enough to hide the smirk upon his face.

"Don't just smile at me," she said. "Fetch me a ladder."

Eris couldn't tell how old he was, only that his sandy brown hair hung down near his shoulders, covered only by a hat similar to the one Nels wore. He might even be the same gardener who had run up to Nels earlier, though from where she was perched she couldn't be entirely certain. His gardener's jacket, green and stained with dirt, appeared a size too small.

"My lady?" he asked. His smile faltered.

It would be just her luck to find a gardener with wits like Ferisa. "I can't climb down," she explained, choosing her words carefully as she was forced to do with her sister. "Please fetch whatever ladder you use to plant these beds."

His smiled returned, stretching wider. Much like Ferisa, at least he was pretty, his smile turning his otherwise plain face into something quite handsome. Once Eris made it down from the wall, she would have to make sure Ferisa and he met.

For a moment she feared he would simply watch her sitting along the wall, but then he turned and strolled off down the garden, his wide back clearly visible. It would have been nice, she decided, had he hurried just a little.

As she waited for his return, she could not help but look over toward the flower. The petals looked soft, almost silky, yet the flower grew from the sturdy single vine. One of Lira's tasks would be preserving the flower. Without much of a stalk, she would have a difficult time keeping it watered. Something like that would wilt quickly.

Perhaps she had made a mistake. As different as this flower was from the others she had selected over the past few months, at least she had some idea what those were and how to manage them. Likely as not, this flower would wilt before she even reached Lira.

Eris stared at the flower, deciding it didn't matter. For the first time in weeks, she had no idea what Lira would tell her about her choice.

CHAPTER 3

*E*ris saw Jasi first.

Jasi stood in the hall just inside the palace. Dressed differently than earlier during their first encounter, in a long light red dress with pleats the only decoration, her golden hair pulled tight in a twisted bun atop her head. Jasi stood as if trying to mimic Lira but it only came off as mockery.

"What were you doing?" Eris asked.

Jasi came from the main wing of the palace. Eris frowned. That meant she'd been visiting her father.

Jasi tilted her head, looking as if she debated answering. "I was —" She cut off as she shook her head. "Never mind. You'll know soon enough."

Eris almost said something about the conversation she'd heard, but held her tongue. Doing so would only bring more questions. After what had happened with her in the garden, she had no interest in asking more questions.

Jasi shook her head and waved her hand. "I hate to ask...but was it another wasted day?"

Eris hid the surge of frustration she felt, careful to keep her hand clenched. Had Jasi seen her torn up palm, she would run to their mother to report. She glanced down at her dress, worried about the tear from the jump, but it wasn't visible.

"Not entirely. I got to see you twice." She held Jasi's blue eyes for a moment before looking away and glancing at the line of tapestries hanging from the marble walls. None really captured her eye, and she turned back to Jasi with a disinterested gaze.

The comment set Jasi off. "You think this to be some kind of joke, but you are already so far behind. And you stopped your other lessons. I think even Mother knows you haven't been working with the seamstresses." She lowered her voice as she said it. "Even Ferisa has moved through the earliest arrangement lessons, knowing which colors are complementary. Now we have moved on to learning which flowers to choose for each arrangement to convey a message." She shook her head and sighed. "I really wish you would try harder, otherwise, what will become of you?"

"I'm sorry I can't be more like you."

Jasi's mouth tightened into a thin line. "That's not what I mean. I can't help it Lira thinks we all might have the gift."

"The gift of snobbery?" Eris could not hide the hurt she suddenly felt. Even at this, something she thought she might like, using the flowers to create a hidden language, her differences from her sisters prevented her.

Jasi fought to keep her face serene, twisting her head and trying to stand like their mother. "An eye for color, dear sister," she said, running her gaze over Eris's dress. "It is too bad you have little of the gift. I mean, you have spent what—months?—searching to even begin the lessons? I took less than a week. Desia less than two…"

"And Ferisa found her flower in days. What of it, Jasi?"

Jasi cleared her throat, clearly annoyed at the reminder Ferisa had done anything better than her. "Yes. Right. So have you found something today?"

Eris took a deep breath, clenching her hand, thankful she'd tucked the flower into her pocket. "I find something every day."

"Something useful?"

Eris didn't bother telling Jasi that she enjoyed the time she spent wandering the garden. Jasi would never understand anyway. Everything was a competition to her, something to win. Sometimes it was better to just *be*. "I am going to Lira now, if that is what you ask."

"You had better find her quickly. The last I saw, she'd come from a meeting with Nels. She was going to her quarters, and once she is there…"

Eris thought it strange she hadn't seen Lira in the garden with Nels. But she needed to hurry to find her. Once Lira went into her quarters, there was no telling when she would come back out, and all were forbidden entrance. Even their mother dared not disturb Lira's rooms without her permission.

"Don't worry about me, Jasi. Soon enough I will rejoin you in classes. Then you can remind me every day how far behind you I am."

Jasi pursed her lips. "Perhaps. And that would be a welcome change. I see Mother's disappointment every time we bring her one of our arrangements and you aren't there."

As usual, Jasi had no idea how much that would bother Eris, how close to her own thoughts the comment struck. It almost made the words harder to hear.

"Truly, Eris, if you cannot do even *this*, what else is there for you?"

"If I can't learn the art of arranging flowers, maybe I'll just have to serve as your handmaiden. Oh, I do so think the Sacred Mother has blessed me."

"If you can't even manage something as simple as finding a

flower, how do you think you'd be qualified to be my handmaiden?" She smiled politely. "If I were you, I'd hope that Father finds you a suitable match."

"Good thing I am not you."

Jasi huffed. "Maybe you will be lucky and marry some northern lord where it is too cold for flowers."

"And maybe you will prick yourself on one of the thorns and grow too sick to rule. Then I would only have to contend with Desia," she suggested.

Jasi's mouth opened in horror at the suggestion. "You know, it has been positively pleasant learning from Lira while you waste your days in the garden. I fear what will happen when you finally manage to find your flower."

Eris smiled. "It is only pleasant because Desia dares not upset you, and Ferisa is too kind to speak up."

Jasi narrowed her eyes briefly. "And at your rate, I should not have to worry for another year or more. And then it will not matter. By that time, you will have little hope of ever catching up to us." She smiled. "Always the little sister."

She turned and strode down the hall, moving with a practiced glide where her dress barely moved as she walked.

Eris watched her, angry at herself for letting Jasi upset her, before hurrying through the palace, hoping to reach Lira before she disappeared for the evening. If even a moment too slow, she would be left to keep her flower from wilting through the night. More than once, Eris had returned to the palace too late, making a waste of her chosen flower.

The first time it had happened, she brought a faded and wilted flower to Lira in the morning. The look of disgust on the master of flower's face told her everything she needed to hear. The next time she'd tried to preserve the flower in water, but had not taken the same lessons as her sisters and did not manage to keep it looking quite as fresh as Lira preferred.

With this strange and beautiful flower, she at least wanted credit for finding something unusual. Many times Lira commented on her lack of vision or lack of insight. This flower promised a better response.

Eris found Lira in the corridor just outside her quarters.

The hall was empty, only a small lantern glowing at each end giving light. The soft runner of carpet worked in the patterns and colors of the western province; Eris could not think of the names —she didn't spend hours studying the politics of the realm. Such things would never be of use to her. A tall oak table stood on either side of the dark stained door. The flowers in the squat ceramic vases on each table created a pattern Eris almost recognized from the garden.

"An interesting choice."

The words brought her attention back to Lira.

Eris felt fortunate that she'd found Lira at all. Standing just outside her door, she wore a long, slender, violet-blue dress that flared along the floor, like an inverted petunia—another flower which had failed to fit Eris. The doors to Lira's quarters were closed as usual, but the master of flowers reached for the door right before she arrived. Another moment, and Eris would have been too late.

She wished she had at least had the opportunity to see behind the door. Maybe another moment would have helped. The last few weeks she had made a sort of game out of trying to see inside Lira's room, but Eris still had yet to even catch a glimpse.

"There are not many flowers quite like this. You actually worked to find this, didn't you?" Lira asked. A note of surprise and something else—could it be she was impressed?—mixed into her voice. Her accent thickened her words more than usual today, a lilting to the way she spoke trailing each word upward. Lira brought the flower so close to her nose that the petals nearly touched.

23

Eris had been uncertain how to pick the flower from the vine safely so the vine went undamaged. When the assistant gardener had finally returned with the ladder—and taking his careful time as he went, she noticed—she had brought the entire flowerbed down with her, tucking it safely along the wall until she knew what Lira would decide. She would let one of the gardeners return it to its ledge later.

"How would you characterize its fragrance?" Lira asked.

The question took Eris aback. Lira never said anything more than the flower was unacceptable. "I...I don't know how I would describe it."

"Try."

Eris swallowed. Lira always made her nervous. "The flower seems bitter, though there are soft, sweet notes buried deep within the petals." It was unlike any of the other flowers she had brought to Lira.

Lira tipped her head. "That is a fair start. Simplistic, but not incorrect."

"How would you describe it?" Eris asked. Lira had never bothered to teach her anything to make her descriptions anything *but* simplistic.

Hazel eyes narrowed. Lira's thin lips pursed slightly, just enough to convey a sense of annoyed disappointment. "Hints of bay and chantral, perhaps even a touch of chamomile, though there is something smoky and complex to it as well."

She inhaled again, more deeply this time and then, surprisingly, touched her tongue to one of the petals. The bright yellow one, Eris noted.

"Yet," Lira went on, head tilted in the strange way she had that Jasi had tried and failed to mimic, "the nectar tastes nothing like its aroma." She pulled the flower away from her face and handed it to Eris. "That is how I would describe its fragrance."

As Lira described it, Eris knew she had been right. Her own

description *had* been too simplistic. Now that Lira offered hers, the different layers of the aroma became clearer. It only served to frustrate Eris more that Lira continued to refuse to teach her.

"You think this to be your flower, Eris Taeresin?"

Eris looked at the flower. Of all the comments she'd dreamed Lira might say when she returned with the flower, this was not one of them. Always before, she made it clear that Eris had not tried hard enough or had not considered her choice deeply enough. She had the sudden impression that this was different.

She suddenly wondered—was this her flower? After months spent searching and failing, Eris had a hard time believing any flower could be hers. The only reason she'd brought this one to Lira was because it was unique.

That, and she had nearly broken her neck to get it.

What would happen when she found her flower? Her lessons would change, she knew. She would have to sit with Jasi—at least until she was married off and left the palace—and learn about arrangements, about the message the flowers could be used to send. Much better to spend time wandering in the garden.

She considered saying no, it was not, anything to be left alone so she could continue to have afternoons free to wander the garden.

Lira tilted her head, and her dress shifted, sliding just above the tile. Hints of color mixed into the chestnut hair pulled into a swooping spiral atop her head. Piercing hazel eyes waited for an answer.

"You do not answer. Shall I take that as an answer?"

She started to turn, as if to return to her quarters. Once she entered her quarters, there was no telling how long until Lira emerged into the rest of the palace. It might not be until the next morning.

"I'm not certain," she said.

Lira hesitated, waiting for her to say more.

When she still said nothing, Lira turned back toward her quarters. As her hand reached the wide, dark-stained doors, Eris tentatively touched the flower with her tongue, mimicking what she saw Lira do. She paid no mind to which colored petal she tasted.

Suddenly her head swam. Colors shifted in front of her vision, becoming more intense. Dark spots streamed upward, as if she would nearly faint. Sounds changed, the muted sounds of the hall becoming something deeper, richer. Even the way the dress fell on her body, the way the fabric rubbed along her skin changed, becoming heavier, as if she could feel the individual weaves. She felt a deep connection, a sense of hidden strength all around her that she could touch if she only knew how.

Then it faded and was gone.

Eris blinked, wondering if the sensations were only imagined or were something different, something real. Perhaps the flower had medicinal qualities; some of the herbs the master healer used caused visions when taken. But what she experienced seemed different.

"Yes," she whispered. Even if it wasn't, she *wanted* this to be her flower.

Lira paused near the bronze handle on the door. She turned slowly, her dress flaring for a moment as she did, her eyes narrowed in an unspoken question. She waited for Eris to say more.

"This is my flower, Lira," Eris said with more confidence.

Always before, there had been no real expectation that she'd found her flower. Always, her search had been half-hearted or driven simply by the need to bring something—anything—to the Mistress of Flowers or risk angering her mother for her lack of trying. Saying it today felt different.

Lira's face changed. She almost smiled. "Very well."

Eris waited for Lira to confirm that she had found her flower, knowing Jasi, Desia, and Ferisa all were told that they had indeed found what she asked of them.

But confirmation did not come.

"Your next assignment is to learn about your flower: what is its name, where it comes from, what does it take to grow. This information is critical now that you have claimed your flower. Find out all you can and then report back to me."

"I don't understand," she said, shaking her head. "Don't I get to join the lessons with my sisters?"

Did Lira not want her around the others? After months of searching, maybe the others really did have the gift while she had...nothing. Had Lira preferred she keep failing, that she stay away from her sisters? And now when she thought she had finally succeeded, Lira found a new reason to keep her away.

"Is that what you would like, Eris Taeresin?" Lira asked, always so formal with her full name. "Would you prefer to rejoin your sisters as they sit inside each day, learning the basics of the proper care and arrangement of pleasing flowers?"

She sensed a different question hidden within what was asked. "I would like to learn the language hidden in flowers." Of all the things her sisters were taught, that, at least, seemed useful.

Only then did Lira truly smile. "You think that you would like the lessons your sisters sit through? Does that suit you, truly?"

The lilting inflection to her words left Eris with uncertainty. "But when will I get—"

"Discovering your flower is about the journey. Like each flower is unique, each journey must be unique. No one shares the same experience. But if you nurture it well, you will end up with something lovely and very much your own. Just like your flower."

Eris thought about her flower, about how it seemed to grow in the shadows and the shade, unlike most in the garden that seemed to prefer bright sunlight. What did it say about her that she would claim *this* flower her own?

"Now," Lira went on, as if everything had been decided, "find me when you have learned all that you can of your flower."

"Tomorrow?"

Lira tilted her head. "Will you have learned everything that you can by tomorrow?"

Eris shrugged. "I don't know how long it will take." She knew where she would start. If anyone in the palace knew anything of the flower, it would be Nels. Even though he could be sour at times, the master gardener was still a wealth of information about everything in the garden. His garden really, regardless of what Lira had to say about it.

"You will find me when you have learned all you can." Lira watched Eris for a moment, almost as if waiting for her to challenge her again.

Eris only nodded. "Yes, Lira."

Lira turned in a swirl of her dress and opened the door to her rooms, sweeping inside and quickly closing the door. Eris saw a flash of color, almost as if a garden grew within, and then the door shut in front of her, leaving her with just the memory of colors.

Eris stood outside the door for just a moment, one hand clutching the strange flower she'd found—her flower—the other gripping her dress. Finally, she turned to return to the garden.

She made a point of not thinking about why Lira seemed determined to keep sending her away, almost as if not interested in teaching her. Her sisters had been allowed to quickly choose their flowers. As much as they might suit them, none of them were unique and none had taken a daring climb atop the wall to find. Now they were able to learn from Lira, learning what she knew of flowers, turning arrangements into a type of language Eris did not understand because she was not allowed to participate.

Even now, even after finding a flower Lira did not deny was unique, she still wasn't allowed to rejoin her sisters.

Lira's message was clear—Eris was not welcome in her lessons.

CHAPTER 4

*O*utside, the sun hung just over the wall, spilling a reddish orange light onto the garden. Eris smelled the scents swirling around her but didn't feel the same meandering sense she'd felt earlier. Now she came with a purpose. She hoped to find Nels.

Instead, she came across the same assistant gardener who had helped her down from the ledge earlier. He looked at her with a bemused expression—likely remembering finding her with her dress rolled up to her knees, legs exposed, as she dangled off the ledge. Princesses did not behave in such a manner.

Dressed in his poorly fitting green jacket squeezed over the top of brown pants, he wore a hat atop his head much like Nels. His face was round and soft. Not fat, like some of the boys in town, rather simply smooth and natural. His long brown hair was brushed back from his head and now knotted in the back. Streaks of black dirt smeared across his cheeks and hands. She'd not seen him before today—at least, she didn't think she had.

He smiled as she stopped in front of him, blocking his path. Up close, his smile was more lopsided than handsome.

"My lady," he said. He tipped his head, as if debating bowing or sweeping off his hat and choosing to do neither. "Will your search require another ladder?"

The question caught her off guard, and she barked out a laugh. "I can't say that it won't."

The gardener smiled more deeply. "Should I summon Master Nels?" he asked. "He's much more skilled with ladders. And ladies."

"That won't be necessary." She pulled the flower out of her pocket and held it out to him. To her surprise, it still hadn't wilted even a little. The delicate appearing flower was sturdier than she would have expected. "Can you tell me the name of this flower?"

He held out his hand and waited until she set the flower into his palm, as if afraid to touch her hand. Then, much like Lira, he pulled it toward his face, twirling the flower between his dirty fingers as he stared at the multicolored petals. Unlike Lira, he did not smell its fragrance or try to taste the leaves.

"Ah...I wondered what it was you found on that ledge. When you wouldn't let me look in the flower bed..." He trailed off, still staring at the flower, before shaking his head.

"Do you know what it is?"

"It looks familiar. Something I've heard about before, but it wouldn't grow here." He looked up at her. "I've only been here a few months. There's still much to learn. For something like this, you should ask Master Nels."

"What is it?" Eris asked.

He flicked his gaze over to her. "Like I said, I've only heard of one flower that looks like this, but I don't know with certainty. If you need a definite answer, you'll need to speak with Master Nels. Or the mistress?"

Eris shook her head. "She wants me to learn on my own."

"Then, my lady, what are you doing here?"

"Trying to find out on my own."

The gardener smile widened. "By asking me?"

"Is that not how I should learn of the flower? I should think the gardeners would be well suited to help."

His expression changed slightly, a quizzical look coming to his face as he watched her, as if waiting for something. When it didn't come, he shook his head. "I have never seen one myself, but it's said to grow within the Svanth Forest. As far as I know, none have ever grown outside the forest."

"What's it called?" she asked again, holding her hand out and waiting for him to return her flower.

Eris knew little about the Svanth Forest. It grew on the borders of the kingdom, a vast expanse of trees separating the northern edge of the kingdom from the wild lands beyond. Jacen would know more than she did. Of course, he was expected to know all about the realm he would someday rule.

The gardener looked up at her. He had blue eyes deeper than the sky that, surprisingly, did not hesitate to meet hers and hold her with a piercing gaze. "That one's called a teary star, my lady. But this can't be it. They don't grow outside the Svanth."

A teary star. A strange name for a flower, but the only one she had at the moment. "What can you tell me of it?"

He shrugged, pulling off his hat and wiping it across his brow. Dirt smeared on his forehead. "Beyond what I already have?" he asked and then smiled. "Not much else, I'm afraid. I'm still an apprentice. I have a stack of books with different plants and flowers I haven't even started learning about. I grew up near the Svanth and never saw one."

"Then how do you know of it?"

The gardener shrugged. "My grandfather used to speak of rare plants. A hobby of his, you might say." He glanced around before meeting her eyes again. "Perhaps Master Nels could be of more assistance?"

Eris was surprised to know gardeners had to study as much as they did. Now that he'd said it, it made sense. Nels was expected to grow and care for anything brought to him.

"And where might I find Nels?" Eris had not seen him since this assistant interrupted them earlier in the garden.

The assistant gardener smiled, balling his hat in his hands. "Check the greenhouse. Last I knew, he was preparing the beds for new arrivals from Baylan. An exotic delivery, with canubells and divanis and..." He trailed off, as if realizing he had nearly started rambling. Pulling his hat back atop his head, his smile faltered for the first time. "Apologies, my lady. You don't need some gardener telling you all about these things." He tipped his head again and slid back a step, eager to disappear.

She hadn't been in the greenhouse before, just wandered past it during her searches. She nodded to the gardener and started off.

He coughed and cleared his throat. Eris turned to see him pointing down a different path than she'd been taking. "Middle of the garden. Might be hot this time of day." He eyed her up and down and then flushed. "My lady," he stammered.

Eris suppressed a smile. Usually it was Ferisa or Desia who had boys looking. Even Jasi, for all her practicality and the fact that she would only be married off for just the right arrangement, had her share of suitors, though they were usually neighboring lords. "I suspect I will manage just fine. Besides, maybe I'll just roll up my dress again."

He had already seen her perched atop the wall, but the red rushing to his face nearly made her laugh again.

The gardener started to stammer something else, but Eris strode away in the direction he'd pointed, not looking back.

She followed the paths set between the large beds, their colors less vibrant in the fading light, almost as if they settled in to rest for the night. Some were damp, the soil smelling earthy and wet, as the long pipes running throughout the garden pumped water to them. A few had markers identifying what grew in the garden, but most did not.

Eris recognized the lilies and roses of the nearest bed, having tried to select varieties as her flower. According to Lira, they were not unique enough for her. As if Jasi's perisal was unique in any way!

A clump of trees up ahead marked the middle of the garden. Once, the ancient flowering elms were all that occupied the palace lawns. That was before the gardens, before Lira. In the half dozen years or more since she'd come to the palace, the gardens had grown into something substantial. The beauty was undeniable, but not the only reason her mother pushed to continue expanding the garden each year. The queen prized the arrangements Lira made with the flowers.

A flash of bright sunlight bounced off glass behind the nearest elm. The greenhouse.

She never came to the heart of the garden, always staying away from the elms. No real flowers grew around the trees. The greenhouse was small and squat, large panes of glass set into frames to let light in. Peering inside, rows of boxed beds like the one she had pulled off the wall lined tables and the floor. Small spaces between the boxes allowed access. Tiny buds emerged from some of the beds, just the early beginnings of new strains of flowers. Most were empty, little more than empty beds of dirt.

She didn't see Nels inside.

Curious, Eris worked her way around the greenhouse until she found a small wooden door and pulled it open. The heat and humidity hit her first. She nearly staggered back but remembered what the assistant gardener said and pressed forward, determined not to let him be right.

Sweat immediately began running down her back. Much longer in the greenhouse, and her dress would be soaked. Eris smiled; she could just imagine her mother's horror if she saw her standing in the greenhouse, sweat streaming off of her. Nothing ladylike about that.

She peered at the nearest bed. The barest, topmost of a green bud erupted from the damp dirt. A small sign next to the plant marked it as widow bloom. A strange name for a flower, but many had strange names.

Eris reached down, curious.

"Don't touch that."

She stood up quickly and turned. Nels watched her, a strange expression on his face. Sweat glistened on his dirt-stained cheeks.

"Master Nels. One of your assistants suggested I might find you here." With the way he looked at her, as if not at all pleased she'd invaded his greenhouse, she decided on formality. "Might I ask you a question about—"

He shook his head, cutting her off as he grabbed her by the arm and shuffled her from the greenhouse. Eris didn't even have time to be surprised at the way he treated her. Once back outside, the change in temperature came as a welcome relief.

Nels let go of her arm, and she pulled it away. A smudge of dirt remained where he had gripped her sleeve. She would have to wash it out before one of the servants reported it to her mother. No use getting Nels in trouble.

"Greenhouse has to be the right temperature, or they will all fail," he said. "You go bustling through there, tripping over the beds, killing off all the seedlings—might as well start over." He was gruffer and more annoyed than usual. Nothing like he had been the last time she had seen him. Now he seemed truly angered by her presence.

"I didn't know," she answered.

"Need to be careful with your ignorance, my lady."

The comment sounded like an insult. "I just came to ask what you know about a flower." She would find out what he knew, and then leave him alone. Something clearly bothered Nels today.

He glanced at the greenhouse, and then looked around the garden, shifting on his feet. "I am sorry, my lady. It is just that too many of my flowers have been failing lately. Those which should grow well are weak. Those that are difficult to grow do not even bud. In all my years..." He shook his head, letting out a sigh. "I don't know why the garden suddenly struggles."

"I'm sorry, Master Nels. I don't want to disrupt your work." If she did, she would hear of it from her mother. Probably Lira as well. "I didn't know the garden struggled. The flowers still look so beautiful."

"The established flowers continue to grow well. Only the newer flowers don't grow as they should, if they make it here at all. Those from the north especially." He shook his head, his brow furrowed. "My lady, I shouldn't take my irritation out on you. I know you simply enjoy looking."

She didn't bother correcting him. She'd tried doing more than just look but had failed for as many months as she had been wandering the garden.

"You said you seek a flower?" he asked, steering her away from the greenhouse.

"A particular one." She pulled the flower from her pocket, cradling it carefully in her palm. "Your assistant called it a teary star and said it was from the Svanth Forest."

Nels eyed the flower carefully. He reached for it. "Where did you find it?"

Eris pulled it back, and he dropped his hand slowly. There was something about the way the master gardener looked at the flower that left her wondering if he would return it to her. Always Nels tolerated her intrusion into his space—accommodating even—but the suspicion in his eyes was new.

"Why?"

Nels shook his head. "Was it Terran you spoke to?"

She shrugged. She hadn't gotten the assistant gardener's name and felt a moment of shame she hadn't bothered to ask.

"Long hair pulled back? Muscular?"

She nodded. It was what Lira would call a simplistic description.

"No teary stars here. Never heard of them growing outside the Svanth." He looked up at her. "You said you found it in the garden?"

She straightened her back and tried to look every bit as royal as her mother managed so effortlessly. Eris was afraid she only ended up looking as foolish as Jasi. "Along the wall. There are several of those beds placed along ledges." She pointed into the greenhouse toward where the boxes lay upon tables.

Nels frowned. "Along the ledge?" he asked.

Eris nodded.

"You must be mistaken, my lady. The beds along the wall only contain simple vines. Decorative greenery only designed to crawl along the wall and hide the stone. There are no flowers. And certainly not this one. Besides, as you may have seen, most of the flowers the mistress prefers do not tolerate the shade anyway."

"I did not realize Lira cared which flowers you grew."

Nels frowned. "Of course she does. Have you not noticed she has a particular taste?"

Eris did not admit she had not, looking at the flower again. Of course, now that she thought of it, there were particular colors more prevalent within the garden. "Is there something wrong with this flower?" She carefully placed the flower back into the pocket sewn into her dress.

"It appears to be quite healthy," Nels said. "Like I said, as far as I know, teary stars have not been grown outside of the Svanth Forest. If someone has managed to grow one, I would very much like to study it."

Eris decided to try a different tact. "How does it take on the color?" She already thought she knew the answer but wanted to see if what she suspected was the same as what Nels told her.

His brow raised briefly. "Unusual, that. From what I know, the vine grows as thin tendrils, shoots grow together into a braid."

She nodded, remembering seeing up close as she had nearly fallen off the wall how the vine grew. One of the more unusual features of the flower. The description matched what she'd seen, making it likely this *was* a teary star.

Nels motioned toward the flower. "It appears each shoot is responsible for only one of the petals."

"Are there other flowers like this one?"

"My lady," Nels said. His expression changed, softening. An almost concerned look came into his eye. "I receive seeds and shoots from all over the realm. Most I manage to grow into the flowers you see here, even cross them with others, creating new flowers never before seen. All of this I do for your mother and the mistress." He paused and nodded toward the flower. "I've never successfully managed to grow anything from the Svanth. Often they start out well enough, shoots of green and the occasional bud, but I've never managed to keep anything alive long enough to grow anything useful."

"But if what your assistant says is true, then *this* is from the Svanth Forest." She again pulled the flower out of her pocket.

She glanced down at the petals, fearful it had already begun to wilt. She needed to spend more time with it before the color drained from the petals and it dried out. How else would she learn what she needed? How else would she ever catch up to her sisters?

Nels nodded. "And possibly it is. But as I said, it should not be here. Few enough have even heard of a teary star let alone seen one flowering."

Eris didn't understand. "It was growing in one of your beds!"

"Teary star is a strange flower, my lady. Growing in the heart of the Svanth, it blooms only every seven years. Even were I to have one of the vines, many seasons would have to pass before one would flower." He shook his head. "Besides, there is something different about the soil at the heart of the Svanth I can't replicate. I can't believe that flower grew here."

Eris looked from the flower to the long, painted, wooden flowerbed boxes in the greenhouse and realized something. "Are all the boxes like those?" She pointed through the glass of the greenhouse.

"Like what?"

"Those." She walked toward the greenhouse and moved as if to open the door.

Nels hurriedly stepped in front of her and blocked the door, a surge of protective annoyance flashing across his face she had seen earlier. "The narrow beds are all manufactured similarly. Allows ease of configuration. Their shape allows them to be set together within a larger bed if needed."

"Or along the ledges in the wall."

Nels tipped his head in acknowledgment.

Eris stepped back, and Nels relaxed, moving his foot away. The box the teary star grew in was different than the others, more crudely made. "Regardless of how the flower came to be on the wall, what can you tell me about it?"

"How it came to be on the wall is the better question, my lady. Not only should it not have grown, but it should not be flowering. Not unless it's the seventh year of growth, possibly longer. I don't know enough about the flower to say with much certainty. And I have certainly not had that vine growing here during that time."

"What are you saying, Master Nels?"

He shook his head. "I am saying nothing, my lady. Only that I was not the one who grew the teary star. Someone else has cared for this plant."

She didn't ask how. Nels was responsible for the entire garden, and the vine had most definitely been growing in his garden, even if it had been along the wall. "Why would someone grow this flower without informing you?"

Nels took his hat and squeezed it between his dirty covered hands. A look of consternation darkened his face, wrinkling his brow. "My lady," he continued. "Would you be so kind as to show me in which bed you found the teary star?"

Eris agreed. She led Nels quickly through the garden. The sun had fallen farther in the sky, leaving orange and red streaking overtop the wall. Clouds threatened overhead, growing thick and grey. Distantly, she thought she heard thunder. She stepped as quickly as possible, trading grace for speed, not wanting to get stuck out in the garden in a storm.

They reached the wall and the small ledges she'd climbed. The simple vines grew from the small boxes, only the tiniest of buds visible. "Here."

Nels nodded at the white painted boxes. "Those are hopis vines. They will not flower, at least not well. They are decorative only."

Eris glanced up the wall. At the top, where she had found the teary star, there was another white box. It appeared the same as the others lower down on the wall. Shoots of green draping over the edge did not twist and twine together. Not the teary star.

"Well...it was up there."

Nels glanced from her to the ledge. "Might I ask how you reached the bed?"

Eris smiled. "You can ask."

Nels frowned when she didn't say anything more. "Those are also hopis."

"I see that," Eris said.

"My lady," he began, "if this was your idea of humor, I will inform you I do *not* find it particularly funny. With the way the garden has struggled, I have many other uses for my time. There are sprouts I should be attending and seeds needing my care, especially since the shipment from Baylan—"

"It is not a trick," Eris said, wandering down the wall to look for the narrow bed of teary star. Since she was out here again, she might as well harvest another flower to study.

She looked along the edge of the wall for the roughly made white bed she'd brought down when she climbed down the ladder. She'd left the box tucked up against the wall, thinking Nels or one of his assistant gardeners would return it to its ledge. Instead, they had placed something different.

Stranger still, was that the box was nowhere to be found. The teary star was gone.

Nels looked at her, waiting.

For once, Eris didn't know quite what to say.

CHAPTER 5

*E*ris hurried through the palace hall. She passed white-clad servants all scurrying along, none paying her much attention. She rarely demanded attention from servants, certainly nothing like Jasi, but once in a while it might be nice to have them at least acknowledge her. Even Ferisa demanded more respect than Eris.

She clutched her long dress, keeping the pleats from trailing along the ground as she hurried toward the throne room. A summons from her father came rare enough that she didn't want to keep him waiting. The timing made her a little anxious, especially after what she'd overheard a few days ago.

The last few days had been frustrating for her. In the week since she'd found her flower, she hadn't learned anything more than what she already knew. Which was to say, nothing at all.

As she rounded the corner leading to the central part of the palace, a line of people waited outside the door. A more formal summons than she realized. Nearest her, Desia stood with her back to her. She wore a long dress of a pale yellow. Her golden hair twisted into layers held atop her head with a slender silver pin. She barely glanced over as Eris approached.

"You're late."

Eris suppressed a sigh as she looked at the people outside the door. Ferisa stood a few paces from them, looking radiant in her delicate yellow dress. Jasi must not have come yet, or perhaps she'd been allowed into the throne room. A few handmaidens waited alongside Desia and Ferisa.

"I only now received the summons."

Desia sniffed. A row of pale yellow corinths were woven into her dress. The color seemed to make her glow, making her more lovely. "If you'd been in class—"

Eris glared at her. "If I'd been in class? You think I don't want to be there with you?"

Desia turned and looked at her. Deep blue eyes so much like their mother's frowned at her, the expression a mixture of disappointment and sadness. "You would rather waste your time wandering the garden. Don't think the rest of us haven't noticed. Lira might not say anything, but it's time you hear what we think."

"Did Jasi put you up to this?" Usually so soft-spoken, Desia wouldn't say anything if Jasi hadn't already mentioned it. Now it seemed they'd teamed up against her.

Desia shook her head and turned away. "Jasi shouldn't have to."

"Lira won't..." she began, and lowered her voice when one of the guards near the door glanced over at her. "Lira won't let me join your classes. She said I had to find my flower first."

"But you've found your flower. Now you need to join class."

Eris sighed and looked around. First she had to argue with Jasi about this and now Desia? When would Ferisa join in? It shouldn't surprise her they would team up like this against her, but it still disappointed her. And hurt a little. With as much time as they spent together in lessons, they had the chance to bond. Not Eris. Always the outsider. Always so different than the others.

"Well?" Desia whispered. "Don't you want to join us?"

"I will when Lira says I can. Until then, I've been told I need to learn all I can about my flower."

Desia frowned at her, and Eris stepped away, letting Desia's brown-haired handmaiden step between them. She hurriedly began fussing with Desia's dress, smoothing the fabric and laying out the pleats. The handmaiden even applied a dusting of powder on Desia's face. Eris had to admit it made Desia look even lovelier.

A crimson robe appeared near the door. Adrick. He glanced at each of them before looking away dismissively. The guard nodded to Ferisa, a wide smile splitting his face, and she started in. Her handmaiden trailed behind her, gripping the back of her dress so Ferisa didn't have to. Desia shot Eris a look before she followed, as if admonishing her to behave while in the throne room. Eris just smiled serenely, unwilling to give Desia the satisfaction of a response. When it was her turn to enter, Eris paused at the doorway before going in.

As often as she'd seen it, the throne room was still majestic. Walls of white granite stretched from the polished stone floor toward the ceiling high overhead. Massive tapestries lined the walls, each decorated with the faces of the kings who came before. Windows arranged around the top let light stream in and caught motes of dust suspended in the air. Two hearths at opposite ends blazed with crackling flames. Lanterns set into sconces gave off more light.

Near the back of the room, high over the throne, hung a painting different than the others, meant to depict the Sacred Mother. Eris noted how Ferisa nodded at it and placed her hand to her lips before looking at their father. Eris just glanced at it before making her way after her sisters, dress bunched in her hands so it didn't drag on the floor.

Her father sat at the end of the room atop the great rivenswood throne. Next to him, in a smaller seat, sat her mother. Dressed regally in the formal colors of the kingdom, navy and green, she eyed each of the princesses as they approached. A smile spread across her mouth as she looked at Ferisa and then Desia. When she saw Eris, the smile faded. She shook her head slightly until Eris dropped her hands to her sides, letting her dress drag across the stones.

Where was Jasi? Eris was surprised that her sister wasn't here. Other than Adrick standing behind her father, no one else was present.

What was this?

Eris turned to the hurried sound of boots across the stone. Jacen made his way toward the throne. A long sword hung at his waist. His long golden hair hung damp and was pushed back behind his head, tied with a simple throng of leather. He wore dark navy pants and a forest green jacket.

"Sorry I'm late, Father. Finishing preparation for the—"

Their father waved him off as Jacen took a place beside him. Her father looked at each daughter in turn. When he got to Eris, his deep brown eyes lingered. "We asked you here today as we make an announcement. As you know, your sister Jasi has been particular in choosing a suitor. Over the last few days, we've been host to Prince Petra. Jasi met with him, and I am pleased to announce she's agreed to wed him. All that remains is meeting his parents. I am told they are to arrive soon?" He glanced over to Adrick.

Eris hadn't known her sister had been particular in choosing a suitor, but shouldn't have been terribly surprised. Wedding the eldest took precedence over the others. Next would come Desia, and then Eris.

Their mother leaned forward on the throne. Her face seemed tenser than usual, the lines around her eyes more strained. "You are to support your sister over the coming weeks." She gave Eris a pointed glance. How much had Lira told her? "And you will do your best to welcome our guests."

"Where are they from?" Eris asked. If Adrick had encouraged the arrangement, she wondered where Petra came from. Did the way her mother looked mean she didn't agree with the arrangement?

Desia looked over and frowned.

Eris shot her a look. "What? I think that's a reasonable question. If she's marrying this Prince Petra, we should know more about him."

"Honestly, Eris," Desia said, exacerbation was thick in her voice. "It's almost as if you don't live in the palace."

Jacen leaned toward Eris. "He's the eldest son of King Danis, ruler of Saffra."

Their father nodded. "And a union between our realm and Saffra will bring great stability for many years. This is especially important given recent unrest with Varden." He glanced at Adrick.

"That is quite correct, my lord." Adrick tilted his head slightly, enough to show the top of his balding head. Not nearly as much as he should bow before the king, but her father took no affront.

Eris tried to think of what she knew about Saffra. Desert land far to the south, beyond the Verilain Plains. From what she remembered, reaching Saffra meant a difficult journey.

"How will this help with Varden?" Eris asked. "It's not as if they can send troops or—"

Adrick frowned at her. "There are many benefits for your kingdom. Errasn feels frequent threats from the north. As the High Seat of the Conclave sits in Saffra, you will find greater protection."

Eris knew she shouldn't say anything more. Especially with the way her mother looked at her, but she couldn't help herself. "And Jasi wants this?"

A warmth crossed her father's face. "Your concern for your

sister is appreciated, Eris, but Jasi welcomes the union. In a few moments, we will meet the King and Queen of Saffra. They will be greeted as honored guests and will remain with us until the ceremony concludes."

She looked over to where Adrick stood, leaning over her father's shoulder and whispering into his ear. Then he stood. The magi's leathery face suddenly tensed, blooms of color coming to his cheek. He frowned for a moment, flat eyes going distant, before smiling a thin smile and looking over at her father. "They will be here momentarily."

Her father tapped the arm of the throne. The dark band encircling his middle finger thumped softly as he did. "Excellent. You will welcome them?"

A flicker of annoyance passed across Adrick's face, almost too fast to be seen. He tipped his head. "Of course, my lord." He made his way to the entry, glancing at the flowers woven into Desia's dress and pursing his lips, before turning toward the doors.

They said nothing. Their father motioned them to the side of the throne. Ferisa was the first to follow instructions, her handmaiden guiding her alongside their mother's seat, giving enough space for Desia and Eris to stand between. Desia moved with precise grace to take her place alongside their mother. Normally, Jasi would stand there, but this ceremony changed everything.

The doors to the throne room opened. Adrick bowed deeply—much deeper than he did for her father, Eris noticed—welcoming the King and Queen of Saffra inside as he stood.

Their clothing looked nothing like anything Eris had ever seen. The king wore a crisp white jacket made of a flowing fabric. Red lines were woven or embroidered into it, sweeping up his sleeves and around the neckline. Pants nearly the same color as Adrick's robe flared up from dark boots. A sweep of fabric swirled around his deeply tanned face. A curved sword hung at his waist.

Eris frowned, surprised her father would let any into the

throne room armed. Custom maintained they would not. She glanced at her father, but he seemed not to mind.

The Queen of Saffra had dark, black hair and olive skin. A series of stones—pale blue and yellow—were fixed to each cheek. A crimson scarf wrapped around her neck. She wore a simple dress of pure white which matched the king.

Adrick followed behind them. Another crimson-robed man walked next to him, barely a step behind. A magi, Eris decided, and probably the king's advisor. She glanced at the king's hand, looking for a dark band like her father wore, and found it on his left hand. A marker of the Conclave. Adrick had one for each finger.

Following behind Adrick came Jasi. Dressed in a heavy gown of purple silk, she kept a tight smile affixed to her face. Her golden hair was carefully swirled on her head. A striped perusal was pinned to her dress. A handmaiden scurried behind her, ducking low as she came.

A young-looking man walked next to her. He had olive skin like the queen. Dressed much the same as the king, the only difference was the lack of red stitching through his shirt. He kept his black eyes fixed straight ahead as he made his way toward the throne, but every so often they flicked toward Jasi.

Eris realized she'd seen him in the palace over the last few days. With his white clothing, she'd thought him another servant.

A tall woman, slender and wearing a plain white dress similar to the Queen of Saffra's, followed after Jasi. She had black hair hanging in loose curls to her mid-back. Black eyes searched the room as she made her way toward the throne. A single, pale blue stone stuck to her forehead.

When they nearly reached the throne, Lira swept into the room. Her eyes scanned the room as she hurried toward them. She wore a deep green dress and her chestnut hair hung loose around her shoulders. A weave of flowers hung around her neck like a necklace. Lira took a place directly behind Desia, standing near enough to their mother to whisper into her ear.

Adrick's cheeks tensed as he looked at Lira. Then he took his place behind their father.

Eris's parents stood and bowed to the King and Queen of Saffra. The gesture was returned in kind. "Welcome to Errasn and Eliara," her father said. "May the Sacred Mother grant you comfort and shade."

The King of Saffra met her father's eyes. "Your welcome is most appreciated. We have traveled a great distance to be here. Your southern hills and the...what do you call them?...Verilain Plains were particularly difficult to traverse. Quite different than the wide expanses of Saffra." He looked around, eyes touching on each of the tapestries hanging around the throne room. "Greener." He said the word distastefully and turned to look at her father. "Petra tells us you have treated him well?"

Her father looked to where the prince stood. Two paces separated him from Jasi, an appropriate distance. She met his eyes and nodded.

"You have raised a respectable young man. Jasi seems most taken by him."

"We had a few moments to speak with her following our arrival. I admit my hesitation. Usually the Sons of Saffra wed Daughters of the Sand. That should take nothing away from your child. She is a lovely young woman," the king said. He turned and looked at Jasi, appraising her as he might a horse. "But Saffra is a different place than your Errasn." He looked away from Jasi and over to his son. The prince nodded once, never looking over to Jasi. "Still, I have been convinced there is merit in the joining of our lands."

"And if this goes well..." her father began, glancing to the woman standing behind the queen.

Eris realized this must be the Princess of Saffra. She looked to

Jacen and was surprised to see him staring at her with more attention than she expected. Usually women of the kingdom chased him, hoping for a chance to marry the prince. Instead, they might see his bed, but little else. If he wasn't her brother, she might be more upset by his behavior.

The King of Saffra tilted his head enough to look at the princess. "She is a Daughter of the Sand."

Her father waited. When the King of Saffra said nothing more, he went on. "We have prepared the west wing of the palace for you. Feel free to consider it home. We will feast tonight, and then we can begin the arrangements for the ceremony."

The King of Saffra nodded. "Our custom requires that it be carried out on the eve of a full moon. It is said to bring prosperity and a healthy child."

Had they not been standing in the throne room, Eris would have laughed at her sister's reaction. Her eyes widened slightly, and she gripped the silk of her dress before unclenching her fingers. Perhaps Jasi was not completely convinced the wedding was the right thing for her.

Her father glanced at Adrick, who only nodded. They whispered something. Eris heard her father say, "that is two weeks away," before Adrick said something to sooth him.

"You think it wise to rush a ceremony?" Lira asked.

Adrick glanced over, his lips pursed as he shot her a strange look. The King of Saffra studied the Mistress of Flowers. Lira paid him no attention, focusing instead on the queen sitting on the throne.

"Two weeks is not much time to make the proper preparations. The Sacred Mother knows we don't want to rush anything or we might—"

"Certainly you can get your decorations ready in two weeks?" Adrick asked.

Lira looked from the magi to Eris's father. He sat watching

them, a curious expression on his face. Eris's mother set her hand on his arm, and he smiled.

"The decorations will be ready. As you are not from this land, you may not know there are other preparations required by the Sacred Mother before a wedding. Some take much time."

Adrick's mouth twisted in a dark frown, but he said nothing, only leaned forward and whispered into her father's ear again. Her father nodded a few times before looking up at Lira.

"Could both customs be accommodated?"

The King of Saffra looked from Lira to Eris's father. Before nodding, his eyes searched over the throne and met Adrick's. The magi's face tightened, and then he looked toward the stone floor. Lira studied them both, saying nothing.

A sense of tension built in the room. Eris's mother broke it, nodding toward the Queen of Saffra. "I'm certain the two mothers can find a way to ensure our customs are accommodated."

The Queen of Saffra glanced at Adrick before looking toward Eris's mother and nodding.

Eris stood watching, wondering why they needed to rush. Another thought troubled her just as much. Two weeks until Jasi was married. Desia would be next. And after that...Eris looked at the floor, suddenly worried what her father might have planned for her.

CHAPTER 6

*E*ris sat at the long oak table in the palace library, a small lamp flickering behind her and lighting the large leather-bound book propped open in front of her, as she searched for some reference to the teary star. Thoughts of her sister kept intruding.

Jasi seemed completely wrapped up in preparations for the wedding to the point where she didn't notice anything else. Eris could not believe how much there was to prepare. Between Lira scurrying all over the garden preparing arrangements, to Eris's mother speaking with the Priestesses of the Sacred Mother—and more than once dragging Eris along with her—to whatever the Saffra delegation did to get ready, there seemed so much pomp.

Having the flower to focus on at least gave Eris something to do. And a place to escape. This way, her mother didn't notice her. No one did, really, though it wasn't the first time she'd felt that way.

But the flower proved difficult to discover anything more about than she'd already learned. After she failed to show Master

Nels where she'd found the flower, he refused to speak more of it. He seemed to think she'd played some sort of prank and began to ignore her altogether. Even when she returned to the garden the next day to search, he set one of his assistants to monitor her—the same brown-haired man who'd helped her from the ledge—but Nels almost pointedly ignored her. Eris did not know whether to be hurt or amused.

The day after the Saffra delegation arrived, Eris spent nearly all morning wandering along the wall, looking for signs of the teary star vine. Mostly, she hadn't wanted to watch Jacen leave. He was the only person who ever seemed happy to see her, and now he was leaving. She'd watched from atop the north tower as the company of men all lined up and prepared to depart, her father saying words to them too quiet for her to hear from where she stood. And then Lira did something Eris found strange, sneaking behind Jacen's mount and slipping what appeared to be a small flower arrangement into Jacen's saddlebag.

So far, Eris's search had been pointless. All she found were more hopis plants. That afternoon, she'd tried looking in other parts of the garden. With something particular in mind, it became easier to focus her search, but so far she'd come up empty. The next few days had gone no better. Eventually, she abandoned searching the garden.

She turned to the next place she could think of—the library. The palace had an expansive collection, and the elderly Master of Books had been more than happy to show her around the library.

"Can you show me where you keep your books on flowers?" she asked.

Billiken, the Master of Books, shook his head. He had a wild shock of white hair and a face covered in wrinkles. "There are many books on flowers in our collection," he said, sweeping his hands along rows of shelves.

Some shelves stretched as high as the ceiling arching high overhead. Ladders ran along the lengths of shelves, giving access to the highest rows. The library had no windows. Light came from small lanterns. The air held a distinctly musty odor.

"Is there a particular book you seek?" He led her down the rows, the thick carved cane he carried tapping along the ground as he went, before he stopped before a tall shelf only slightly less dusty than others. Most of the spines were old and of various sizes, tall and short, thick and thin. A few even had lettering worked into the leather.

Billiken stepped closer to her and leaned on his thin cane, looking at her through filmy spectacles. He wore a shirt nearly as musty as the library itself. The pale lantern light made his face look ruddy.

"I don't know of a particular book," she admitted. "How many could you possibly have about flowers?" All this time she had spent wandering the garden, she had never thought to stop and try to learn more about what she saw.

His eyebrows rose slightly. "Ah, as you well know, it is a topic of much renewed interest, especially since *she* arrived. As such, I have made a point to procure as many tomes on the subject as possible. Best to be prepared for any interest." He pushed his glasses back and tapped his cane on one of the nearby shelves. "The top shelf has books on native flowers. The next," he said, tapping the shelf below it, "contains descriptions about plants outside the kingdom. Below that…"

Eris felt her heart drop. There had to be hundreds of books. "How are there so many?"

"As I said, I procured as many books on the subject as was possible. There are a surprising number of works on the subject. Some authors are quite prolific, writing several volumes. I admit I did not understand the interest at first, but after seeing her work…" He smiled and shrugged. "I imagine there are others like her studying the art of the flower, though few enough mention the proper arrangement. In fact, most of these are nothing more than a description of plants and where they are found. Some describe their care and breeding, subjects the master gardener has found most helpful." He stood taller and tapped his cane on the stone floor. "There are probably few collections quite as complete as this. And more work is added each month. Your mother has been quite pleased with me."

"That makes one of us," Eris said.

Billiken only frowned. "I am sorry I cannot be of more help, my lady. If only you knew what you wanted?"

She shook her head, eyes searching the shelves, just imagining the next few months spent combing through the books for a reference about the teary star. Her heart sunk; just as she'd finally thought she would be able to make some progress. "I do not know which book I need."

"Well...if not a book, is there a particular region you have in mind? I could narrow your search."

Finally, Eris smiled, touching a loose coil of her dark hair. "Wonderful, Master Billiken." His ruddy face seemed to grow even redder with the complement. Why had he not told her that at the beginning? "I am looking for information about flowers native to the Svanth Forest."

Billiken pursed his lips as he considered the stacks. He tottered down the row of books, the cane smacking off the stone as he moved. "Svanth? Lucky for you...not many books on the Svanth." He huffed heavily as he walked and reached the ladder and pushed it down the row. Setting his cane to the side, he started up the ladder.

Eris could easily imagine him falling. "Master Billiken—can I help you with anything?"

He glanced at her, pale blue eyes sharp and piercing. "I may be old, but I still manage quite well, my lady."

He turned and climbed toward the top shelf. Eris had to admit that for his age, he really *did* move quite well. Billiken shuffled through a few books, pulling them out and glancing at covers, shaking his head with a tremor of white hair when he found the wrong one, until finally finding what he wanted.

When he reached the bottom of the ladder and grabbed his long cane, he handed her a thin book with a tall cover. Embossed lettering in the old style marked the faded and cracked brown leather. Eris could make out the word *Svanth*.

"This is not quite the one I sought," he said, "a brown leather bound tome by Feliran, but this should get you started."

"Thank you, Master Billiken!" she said, taking the book from him.

"If I may be of further assistance..." He nodded to her before leaving her alone. Unlike Nels in the garden, the Master of Books had no interest in watching her read.

Now the book lay open in front of her. Pictures of different flowers were drawn on the page in incredible detail. In some, Eris could make out the veins in the leaves, the striations of color along the leaves. The author had taken painstaking care to draw with as much detail as possible. Alongside each flower were lines of text, all written in the old style. She struggled with reading them. The words were the same, but the meanings were sometimes different, especially when referring to different flowers.

The book consisted entirely of flowers found in the Svanth. Eris was surprised to learn there was a wide assortment of flowers, much more than she ever would have expected. Anything from wide-petaled, blooming flowers that apparently were members of the rose family to long, needlelike flowers the author named *spinus loras*. She found records of venomous flowers and carnivorous flowers. Flowers that looked like leaves and others no larger than an insect. Apparently, the Svanth Forest was home to many strange and exotic plants. But so far, Eris failed to find any reference to the teary star.

She closed the book with a frustrated sigh. Nearly a week since she had first discovered the teary star, she still knew no more.

The flower had held up surprisingly well. She kept it moistened, floating it in a bowl of water in her room, kept away from the sun and light, thinking that since it had grown in the shade that perhaps it preferred dark. The colors faded a bit as the week had progressed, but the petals had not dried like others she'd tried to preserve.

Eris stood from the table. She decided she could not sit staring at books any longer.

She passed Billiken on her way out of the library. He gave her a cursory glance and nodded as she passed him tottering down one of the long aisles—the aisle with books on flowers, she noted—carrying a basket of books hanging on one arm. Briefly, she wondered who they might be for; she had not seen anyone else in the library other than Master Billiken during her time in the library.

The library was in the western most wing of the palace. Wide stone steps swept down and out of the library, leading past small windows set into the walls giving glimpses into the garden as flashes of color. At the bottom of the steps, she hurried out the wide wooden doors and into the courtyard.

She wandered along the first rows of flowers, only veering away when she came across one of the assistant gardeners. The smells and fragrances slowly cleared her head. Before long, she found herself walking along the palace wall and into the shade to trail a hand along the cool stone.

As she rounded a curve in the wall, she heard hushed voices up ahead. Eris was in no mood to speak to any of the gardeners, not interested in explaining her interest in a flower they claimed did not actually exist in the garden.

The tone to the voices caused her to stop, a voice Eris almost recognized. The speaker had a rough timber. Even hushed, his voice carried, drifting above the flowers, destroying the silence of the garden.

"Another season, and we will be too late. Already this garden resembles Elaysia. You would do well to remember the energy we expended clearing those gardens."

"But the queen—"

"You said the queen thinks these little more than pretty flowers."

"And you're certain they're not?"

The speaker sniffed, annoyed. "I cannot be certain. When she first came, I thought this only for decoration. The gardeners were gone, disappeared to the north and east."

"The north. The Kelths shelter too much there. And there is more than just decoration here. They gain influence, whether the king sees it or not."

"I recognize that now."

"Had we not come..."

The other grunted. "I don't know why I haven't done anything sooner. Blasted flowers."

"You grow blind and lazy here in the north. The cool nights are too soothing. Perhaps we need to bring you back south."

"Not blind. And you know what I've been working on. Had it not been for me, you would not be here."

Eris shifted around the flowers, wanting know who was speaking. She was surprised to see Adrick as she slid around one of the beds. She should have recognized the voice, so distinct and rough and so much like her father's generals with the course way they spoke. Only the top of his leathery head—now nearly completely bald—was visible, but there was no mistaking his scarlet cloak, worn even on the hottest days, pulled up around his neck. She could not see who he spoke to and did not recognize the other's voice.

"We're still not certain of this plan."

"We or you?" Adrick asked.

The other laughed. "Does it matter? We serve the same master."

"I don't know if the queen will believe the power the gardener stores within this garden. I can try explaining to the king, but in this he defers to the queen. And she does not see it."

"You must convince? Perhaps your position is weaker than we thought. You need to make certain they understand the threat."

"The unrest to the north has been noticed. The prince was sent."

"That is good. They should hold them back long enough for us to clear this infestation."

Eris frowned. Did the magi mean the garden was somehow tied to the Kelths in the north? But how? And for what reason? Before Lira, they'd never had a garden like the one that was here now. For years, they'd known nothing but peace. What did it mean that the north suddenly became unsettled? What did the magi know?

She turned her attention back to the magi.

"What would you have me do? Poison the garden? The two of us might be able to accomplish that, but it will drain me."

The other laughed. "That I have to explain to you tells me plenty."

"Do not think to lecture me. I have been here too long for that."

"You think you serve at your leisure?"

There was a pause. "I will take care of this garden," Adrick said.

"Without knowing more, I fear it is nothing but a waste."

"Can we not simply burn the garden?"

"If you think you truly are powerful enough, you should try. Perhaps that might impress the High Seat. I do not think that you will be successful."

"No. I don't think it will." Adrick turned and glanced at the garden.

Eris ducked down to stay out of view.

"So you sense it."

"Sense what?"

"The protections around the garden." The other magi paused and then laughed. "You *have* been here too long. I thought you playing some dangerous game where you allowed this garden to flourish, but that's not it at all, is it? You're just ignorant."

Adrick tensed. The top of his head flushed a deep red. "What protections?"

The other magi laughed again. "There is more than just this garden to fear from this gardener. I can feel it."

"Another garden?"

"It would explain much."

"Such as?" Adrick asked, looking around again.

"We must be like her. We must be subtle."

"You said you had another season," Adrick said.

Another season for what? Before attacks in the north really became an issue? What did that mean for Desia, destined to marry some Varden lord? Or her? What would happen to her if she'd been married off and the north attacked?

"Another season at most," the other agreed. "Possibly less. In the time I have been in this blasted land, I can tell how she presses forward. Even the skies feel her presence."

"The skies?"

"You *are* a fool."

"Do not continue to abuse me, or you will learn first-hand what I have been doing during my time in this land."

The other magi laughed. "Such empty threats. You would attack the emissary of the High Seat?"

"Is that what you are? I thought you served as an advisor, like me."

"An advisor to the King of Saffra," the magi agreed. "Where the High Seat of the Conclave sits. Do not mistake our places in the order."

"Tell me, then. What have you seen about the skies?"

"When was the last time you saw clouds? Or a typical northern storm?"

Adrick laughed this time. "They come nearly daily. The rains may not be as heavy as legend would have you believe, but the downpours can still be severe."

"And do the legends speak of rains coming only at night, leaving cloudless days for the flowers to flourish in the sunlight?" When Adrick didn't answer, the other magi continued. "I see you haven't made the connection."

He leaned forward and placed his palm on top of Adrick's head. Adrick tensed but didn't move. A sense of pressure built around Eris, and she almost coughed. Then the sense faded.

The magi laughed softly. "She is subtle, that one. Impressive."

"What?" Adrick asked.

"It's not only the skies she touches."

"Me?" Adrick sounded disgusted, practically spitting out the word.

"I have burned off the effects of whatever she did to you."

Adrick turned, a deep frown on his face. Eris pressed low between the flowerbeds, hoping the flowers would keep her hidden.

Adrick let out a soft grunt. "I see it now. I thought the destruction of Elaysia weakened whatever gardeners remained."

"And they didn't scatter far enough. Most went north. How many have reestablished their gardens? What sort of threat will we face the next time? How many of the Conclave will fall then?"

"The Conclave has grown strong. Look at how much Saffra has changed since the destruction. How much power we're able to draw now."

The other magi laughed. "Saffra hasn't changed nearly as much as it should have."

Adrick's eyes widened briefly. "But the source..."

"Oh, we access more of the source than ever before. But had the gardens been fully destroyed, we would already have moved beyond Saffra."

"Such stubbornness…I hadn't counted on it."

"None did."

"I have never met a flower mage who is anything but delicate. Brittle. This one…" Adrick said it this time with a hint of grudging respect.

"Perhaps she still touches you."

"No, but you are right. She must have a hidden store of power. Or we were incomplete with the destruction of Elaysia."

"I thought you saw the gardens after the emissary passed through. It's how you gained this post."

"I did," Adrick agreed. "I also saw the bodies of the order. This, too, I showed to the Conclave. With so many of us dead, the remainder of the Conclave feared pressing into the forest, but they cannot feed a garden in their forest."

"They should not be able to." The other magi held something in front of him. His narrow body and the draping of his cloak obscured Eris' view. "This tells me we all underestimated them."

"It is but a single flower," Adrick said.

"They are like rats. Where there is one, there will be others." He paused and plucked a flower, holding it up to the light. It slowly shriveled and turned to ash. "I sense this garden is nearly complete. And too close to Saffra. Too close to the palace."

A soft sound like that of steps on dry grass caused him to stop. Eris looked around, keeping her head low so Adrick would not see her. She did not understand what he feared, but recognized the fact he planned something against Lira.

"Keep vigilant." He paused. "What of this garden? Have you spoken to the gardener? You know the High Seat will be here soon."

Adrick grunted. "I have taken all I need from Billiken. I do not need Nels to tell me what I can easily read."

The other laughed. "Even after what I've shown you, you remain arrogant." Eris was surprised it came off as a compliment. "It is good you remain confident. The High Seat will like to see so when he arrives."

Adrick tensed. "How much time do I have?"

The other grunted. "A week? I cannot know his mind."

"Then I will do what I must."

"You think to go to Svanth?"

Adrick nodded. "If that is what the High Seat commands. I will join the king's men, find her source, and return."

"And then?"

"And then I will destroy it."

CHAPTER 7

*E*ris stayed low until she was certain the magi were gone. She didn't realize until she was alone that she had been gripping the nearest flowerbed tight, her fingers squeezing so hard the blood blanched from them. The palm she had skinned climbing the wall to find the teary star suddenly screamed, and she eased her grip, only to find she had broken the flesh open again.

She didn't know what to make of what she'd just heard. The magi meant Lira—of that she had no doubt—but they accused her of having some sort of power she would use against Errasn.

It made no sense. Everything Eris knew of Lira told her so... but what did she really know of her? She'd come to Eliara when Eris was very young. Since then, she'd gained the ear of the queen. And she *did* have a strange way of speaking. Was her accent a northern accent?

She shivered. Could Lira be working against her father? Against the magi?

The idea seemed too insane to be real, but Adrick and the other magi seemed convinced. And there was the movement in the north for the first time in years, just when the magi thought Lira's garden was nearly complete.

She had to say something. She knew she did, but to who? Her mother was so busy with the wedding planning that she wouldn't have time for her. And her father...he never really had time for her.

If only Jacen hadn't been sent from the city. Then she might have someone who would listen. Her sisters certainly wouldn't. Desia would ignore her while Ferisa would offer a prayer to the Sacred Mother for guidance.

No...that left Eris.

But how would she find out if something was up with Lira?

She needed to be close to her. And that meant getting into classes.

Of course, none of this mattered if it weren't true. What if it were simply idle fear from her father's advisor, worried now that the High Seat of the magi planned to come for the wedding? Maybe Eris had to do nothing at all. Besides, what could *she* do, really?

"Are you well, my lady?"

Eris stood quickly and spun. The assistant gardener watched her with a look of concern, though she wondered if there wasn't a mix of annoyance added in.

"I'm fine."

"You're bleeding," he noted, pointing toward the streak of maroon on the wood of the flowerbed.

Eris shook her head. "It's nothing. An old injury. I must have scraped my hand as I was looking at the flowers." She glanced to see what flowers she'd stopped in front of.

Pink langines and purple brightnams. Perfect, she decided.

"They are lovely," he said, sweeping off his hat and tilting his head slightly as if just remembering to bow before her. "Some might find them a bit bland."

Eris looked at him, meeting his soft brown eyes, and furrowed her brow as she stared. His eyes widened, and he bowed more deeply.

"I meant no disrespect, my lady," he started.

Eris could tell from his tone that he was trying not to smile. It made it very hard for her to hold onto her stern expression.

"Only that from what I've seen draw your attention in the past, it seems you don't care for the bland and the common."

"And what do you know of what I've looked at in the past?" she demanded.

The assistant gardener stood. Traces of his lopsided smile still tilted his mouth. "Only that you seem to be drawn mostly to more interesting flowers. Especially like the one you showed me the other day…"

Eris thought about it for a moment. "What happened to the flower bed?" The question had been plaguing her since she first showed Nels the teary star. Did it have something to do with Lira? Had she hidden it from her because she didn't want to teach her?

"The flower bed, my lady?"

"The one I was holding when you were staring up my skirts as I climbed down the ladder?"

He tried to avert his gaze, but just like the first time he was too late. His face flushed a bright red. "I don't remember any flower bed, my lady."

Eris sighed, shaking her head. Likely as not, he had been so focused on getting her down from the wall he had not minded she carried something with her. She remembered placing the box along the wall, thinking one of the gardeners would simply replace it atop its ledge. She didn't know who was more surprised when she found that it was missing. Nels seemed distressed that she played some kind of joke on him, pointing to the hopis vine growing along the wall. Eris was simply shocked the box with the teary star had gone missing.

Now, she had nothing but the slowly drying flower to remember. Much longer, and she would be left with nothing.

"Do you help care for the flowerbeds along the wall?" she asked.

He nodded quickly. At least chastising him seemed to remind him she was a princess, even if she didn't always act like Jasi.

"Do all the beds contain hopis vine?"

"Hopis," he said, correcting her pronunciation, saying the word more like 'hope'.

As she glared at him, she realized she acted more like Jasi than she intended. All she wanted was to get information, not make him cower from her. She softened her gaze.

The gardener shrugged, twisting his hat in his hands much like Nels did. The green jacket he wore today seemed a better fit than the one she'd seen on him the day they first met. Dirt still stained his face, smeared further across his brow as he wiped his arm across his head.

"Hopis," she repeated. "Do they all grow hopis vines?"

He shrugged. "I think most of them do. Master Nels only wanted decorative plants along the walls, and the hopis can creep along the stone."

"Aren't *all* of these plants decorative?"

The gardener's face changed, losing some of the softness. "Are they?" he asked. "This many flowers seems more than simple decoration. They are quite beautiful, of course, but the master of flowers had a specific pattern she wanted Master Nels to achieve. It seems more than simple decoration."

Eris thought about what she had overheard. Adrick had accused Lira of storing power in the garden. That must be how she did it, but Eris had never heard of such a thing.

"Is that not what you are learning? My lady?" he added hastily.

Eris had learned nothing. And maybe it was for the best. Especially if what her sisters were learning could be used against the kingdom.

Suddenly, Lira's annoyance at the arrangement with Saffra made more sense. If Lira worked on behalf of the north, did she try and sway her sisters, too? Now that Jasi was soon to leave, would she do the same to her?

He watched her carefully. "I didn't mean to offend you."

Eris shook her head. "No offense. I don't truly know what I'm learning." She laughed. "How to wander the garden. How not to choose flowers. How to get stuck on the wall."

He smiled. "There aren't many who wander the garden quite so well as you. I don't know about how you choose flowers, but from what I've seen, you have interesting taste. And about the wall…" His face bloomed red again, and he looked away. He managed to get himself under control fairly rapidly and looked back at her. "Is there a particular reason you ask about the hopis?"

"They are not all hopis," she said, shaking her head.

The assistant gardener watched her for a moment. "Well, it is a large garden. Certainly the largest I have ever seen. It is entirely possible there are places along the wall where other plants can thrive."

Thinking of what she'd read in the library, she asked, "Are there many plants that thrive in the shade?"

He looked around, cupping his hand over his eyes as he looked over the garden. "Most of the garden is in direct sunlight. The flowers Master Nels and the Master of Flowers choose prefer bright sunlight." He looked back down to her, wiping his arm across his forehead. "Though there are some strains preferring the shade and shadows we keep along the perimeter of the wall."

"Any others from Svanth?" She started toward the wall, hoping he would follow.

"Others?"

She shook her head slightly. She had *not* imagined the teary star vine. The flower she kept carefully protected in her pocket was proof of that. "Any from the Svanth Forest?" she asked. If Lira *was* some sort of flower mage, was she using the garden here? Maybe that was why Lira refused to teach her—she didn't know if Eris could be trusted yet. But what did that say about her sisters? Her mother?

Her looked at her with a helpless smile and shrugged. "I'm just an apprentice. I know there are flowers native to the Svanth region, but have not learned enough about them. Master Nels has tried to grow what few we have received, but has failed. Even if they sprout, they do not survive for long."

It was the same thing Nels had told her. "Something about the soil," she said.

But the gardener shook his head. "Not the soil. At least, not only the soil," he started. "Several of our plants were transported in pots full of fresh Svanth soil, some even fully grown. Even they eventually fail." He shook his head again. "No. There is something else." He smiled ruefully. "Maybe they do not care for the weather or perhaps there is too much sun? I wish I could tell you more, but I don't really know."

Eris wondered about this as they neared the wall, wondering if Adrick had anything to do with the failure of plants native to Svanth being able to grow in the garden. What had he said? Something about attempting to poison the garden in the past?

She sighed. There was more going on than she understood.

Eris made her way to where long shadows stretched nearly a dozen paces from the wall. The air was cooler too, smelling more damp and earthy than it did farther from the wall. The heavy aromas off the flowers were more muted here, mixing more deeply with the earthen scent. The effect was pleasing.

Eris looked along the wall, staring at smooth stone set carefully together. Vines of the green hopis grew and stretched along the wall. Thin tendrils—creepers she thought Nels called them—

worked their way up the stone. She wandered around the perimeter of the garden, occasionally reaching out a hand and touching the vines, as she paused to look at a flower or an arrangement.

The colors of the flowers in the bed, particularly here along the outside of the garden, here where the shade held the longest, were bright. Each bed had flowers of a single color, but the beds alternated colors, slowly slipping from pink to purple to blue then orange. Eris had never quite noticed it before. The flowers in the center of the garden where the sun shone more brightly didn't seem arranged quite the same way.

"Who set the pattern for these flowers?" she asked the gardener.

He had been following her, keeping a respectably distance behind her. When she paused, he moved to stand next to her and pulled at the sleeves of his green coat uncomfortably. "Master Nels is responsible for all the flowers of the garden."

"But you mentioned he does so at the guidance of Lira?"

The gardener nodded. "The Mistress of Flowers makes suggestions. There are certain flowers she states grow better together or look better in particular arrangements. I don't claim to have the same eye for detail she does, but I can't deny her suggestions always grow better when placed where she recommends." He scanned the nearest flowerbeds with an appraising eye. "I could almost imagine she would have made an excellent gardener were she so inclined. So many from Varden have that talent."

Lira was from Varden? That didn't seem right, did it?

More than that, Eris couldn't imagine prim and proper Lira scrubbing along in the dirt, hands and face stained with soil like Nels and his gardeners so often appeared. Lira always looked so composed. There was an air of elegance about her that even Eris' mother appreciated.

Thinking of Lira like that made it seem unlikely she could be working against the kingdom. It made no sense.

"I suppose to do what she does, she would need to know what grows well together," Eris suggested.

She continued wandering around the outskirts of the garden. Hopis appeared to grow in each box as the gardener said. Intrigued by how Lira had arranged the color, she looked for a pattern to the rows of beds where various flowers grew, with all of the same color bunched together.

The path between the beds twisted and snaked, almost like a vine creeping along the ground. Occasionally, the path simply ended and she needed to turn back, looking for another path to follow.

There was a certain familiarity to the way the garden was arranged in the shadows near the palace wall, but Eris couldn't place it. She hated that her sisters might be better equipped to identify the pattern, especially as they spent so much time studying arrangements and the hidden language of the flowers.

"Is there anything particular you would like to see, my lady?"

Wandering through the garden reminded her of the freedom she'd felt for the last few months. The freedom to simply exist, no demands on her time, certainly nothing like she had before her mother assigned her to work with Lira. Then her life had been more regimented, scheduled with all sorts of classes on how to be a proper lady. Everything changed when Lira assumed their lessons. Eris managed to ignore lessons on politics and sewing and dancing, focusing instead on Lira's assignments. Eventually, even this time would be gone. She'd be expected to follow Jasi's example.

The smell of the flowers soothed her. Birds chirped nearby, a reassuring sound. Around her were the carefree movements of bees darting from flower to flower, other insects crawling along stalks toward the petals. Eris enjoyed the sense of vibrancy, of life, all around her not bound to the confines of the palace and the restrictions placed upon her by birth.

There were other ways to learn, she decided. Things which could not be found in books, at least not easily. There would be time enough to sit gossiping with her sisters.

"I would like to see the most unusual flower you can think of," she told the gardener.

He frowned for a moment, and the lopsided smile returned to his face. An eager light burned in his eyes. "There are many unusual flowers in this garden. It's one of the benefits of having a master of flowers so well versed in the various strains."

"Well?" she asked.

He crushed his hat between his hands. "How unusual would you like me to get? I know many flowers. Master Nels gave me a stack of books." He demonstrated with his hand how the stack would tower over his head. "And some of the flowers are *quite* strange."

Eris couldn't help herself and laughed. "As much as you can."

His smile spread. "I am Terran, by the way. My lady," he hurriedly added. He closed his eyes and shook his head slightly, seemingly annoyed that he continually forgot the honorarium.

Eris smiled. "Seeing as how you've seen more of me than most, you can call me Eris."

Terran's face flushed again, but he shrugged it off and waved her forward. "Come, my lady, be prepared to be impressed."

Terran led her away from the wall, back into the brighter sunlight where the air changed as they passed out of the shadows, growing warmer and lighter. Eris glanced back, thinking she had missed something, a hint of Lira's design just visible as she turned.

As she looked at the flowers, she lost whatever she might have recognized.

Terran waited for her, a curious expression on his tanned face, and smiled again when she started after him.

CHAPTER 8

Over the next week, Eris had mostly forgotten about the overheard conversation in the garden. If there *was* some power struggle between the magi and the mistress of flowers, Eris wanted no part of it. And Adrick already had the attention of her father while Lira clearly had her mother's ear. It seemed to Eris that such a balance might be beneficial. And perhaps they might all leave her alone.

"You look distracted."

Eris turned and saw Terran watching her. He wore his hat pulled down over his ears. Streaks of dirt stained his cheeks and shifted when he smiled, giving her that lopsided smile he always wore.

"Not distracted. Not like the others, at least."

"Your sister?"

Eris nodded.

"The preparations seem to be going well enough," Terran commented. "At least, Master Nels says so. Had we only the flowers from Baylan…"

"What happened?"

Terran shook his head as he took off his hat and wiped it across his face. This only served to smear the dirt deeper into his skin. "Not sure. Shipment damaged. None of the plants we'd been expecting made it. If not for the wedding planning, Master Nels would be much more irritable. At least with that he has to focus on providing the flowers the mistress requires."

"Where's Baylan?"

"Baylan is to the south and far east."

"Near Saffra?" Eris asked.

Terran shook his head. "Saffra is fairly isolated. From what I know, it's mostly desert. Baylan is not quite as far south and borders the sea." He smiled. "I hear it rains most days there. The plants that grow there are said to be quite exotic."

"But they didn't make the journey."

Terran shook his head. "Not intact."

Eris started through the garden. Terran followed behind her, keeping a careful distance. She found she didn't mind his company. He always made a point to remain proper with her, but only when he remembered. How much of that had to do with how he'd found her the first time they'd met? Probably not much. Terran didn't seem to fit at the palace quite yet. Sort of like her.

"What do you have to show me today?" she asked him.

A wide smile crossed his face. "What do you want to see?"

"Impress me."

He laughed. "I will do what I can, my lady."

He grabbed her arm and started down a path Eris rarely traveled. She wondered how it must look for one of the gardeners to hold onto her wrist as if she were nothing more than a commoner, before deciding she didn't care.

Terran stopped in front of long row of twisting yellow flowers with large central pistils pressing out and surrounded by stamens almost as large. She leaned forward and inhaled. The scent was sweet but not overwhelmingly so. The flowers were beautiful. She suspected Ferisa would enjoy them.

"What are they called?"

Terran touched the stem, his fingers working briefly through the dirt as he did. "These are golden ulsens. Found mostly along the rocky slopes of the Yisn Mountains. Master Nels had to carefully create soil for them. Few manage to get them to grow so successfully outside of the Yisn."

The flowers all seemed to point away from the sun, which she found odd, angled so that they opened toward her and Terran. Perhaps that was part of how they grew. "They are lovely. But…"

"You're not impressed."

Eris shrugged. "They look like corinths."

Terran frowned at her. "Corinths? Not at all. Just look at the way the petals curl at the ends with a hint of orange. The stems are much narrower than corinths. I mean, the only thing anything like corinths is the color."

Eris started laughing and turned away just as a bright red flush came to Terran's face.

"You weren't serious," he said.

Eris looked over her head and smiled. "Nope. Corinths are generally a lighter shade of yellow. They have hints of green striations along the petals as well. Even their sepals are longer, with serrations along the edge."

Terran studied her for a moment. "I thought you said the mistress hadn't invited you into her classes yet."

"She hasn't." Eris forced away the irritation she felt at how Lira kept her away. Maybe it was a good thing she had. Whatever was happening between her and the magi, she wanted no part of it.

"If you say so."

"What are you saying?"

Terran raised dirt stained hands as if to defend himself from her.

"Only that you seem to know quite a bit about flowers for someone who hasn't had any formal training. I don't know that I'd have known about the serrations along the sepals if Master Nels asked."

"If you waste enough time wandering through the garden, you begin picking things up," she said. It wasn't as if her time in the garden had been *completely* wasted. She really did study the different flowers while wandering. But that wasn't the reason Lira had sent her to the gardens.

"I'm not sure I'd call it wasted time."

He stopped in front of another bed. This was longer and wider than some of the others and angled toward the outer wall. Like the golden ulsens, the flowers seemed twisted toward them, angling away from the sun. Deep green petals rolled away from the stem, the ends curled a little as they did, revealing a thick pistil with petite stamens punctuated with white. Streaks of deep blue ran along the length of the petals.

Eris leaned in and inhaled. Less sweet than the ulsens, this had a strong note, one reminiscent of oak and deep woods. She found the scent pleasing.

"Where is this from?"

Terran touched the soil, dipping his fingers into it and pinching. He made a face as he did. Eris couldn't tell if he was pleased or not.

"These are hyanlilly. They are only found in the south, near Baylan. There are wetlands there. These need to be heavily watered to survive." He pointed toward a long copper tubing running along the back of the bed. "Most of the flowers only need to be watered a few times each week. Some even less. But these need much more. Master Nels has me water these practically every day."

Eris hadn't considered the different needs of the plants before. Of course some would need more water than others, just like some needed more sunlight. "Did Nels hope to find more flowers like this?"

"From Baylan?" Terran shook his head. "Hyanlillies are fairly common there. What he had shipped were much rarer. Some only grow in specific parts of the Baylan." He shrugged. "A significant loss. Most will be difficult for him to get again this season."

Eris wondered if Adrick had been responsible for the damaged shipment.

"These don't impress you either," Terran said.

"Sorry, Terran. They're lovely. I shouldn't take up any more of your time."

He swept his hat off his head and balled it into a fist, nodding toward Eris in an attempt at bowing. "My lady, it's my pleasure to walk with you through the gardens—"

Eris waved him off, and he stood. "I should see if I can be useful," she said. She'd spent too much time simply wandering as it was. Maybe she should stop acting annoyed with her sister and see what she could do to help. Besides, she'd barely spoken to Jasi since learning of the engagement.

"Of course." Terran sounded disappointed as he said it. He touched the damp soil again before following Eris as she made her way toward the front of the garden. Master Nels caught his attention, and he hurried off, but not before attempting another bow.

Eris bit back a laugh. Doing so would only hurt his feelings, and Terran had only been trying to help find other flowers which might interest her. She reached the palace with the intent to find either her mother or Lira, when she came across Jasi.

"In the garden again, Eris?" Jasi snapped. She wore a long lavender gown. A series of perisals were woven into the neckline, making it seems as if Jasi wore a necklace of flowers.

Eris paused as she glanced up the hall. A single handmaiden followed Jasi but stepped to the side to let them speak, turning her head to look at the floor as if not wanting to get in the middle of the sisters. A few other servants dressed in the palace white hurried down the hall. Some carried stacks of platters and another carried what appeared to be a bundle of fresh cut flowers from the garden.

"I was," she answered. She didn't want to argue with her sister. Not today. "Is there anything I can do to help with your planning?"

Jasi opened her mouth and looked like she readied to snap, but closed it again. "Did Mother send you?"

Eris shook her head. Why would Jasi care if mother sent her? "I've seen the arrangements and know how much you have going on."

The truth was she hadn't seen the arrangements, not many of them anyway, but if she helped Jasi, she might be able to get closer to Lira without having her question her about the flower. Then she might be able to figure out what was going on with the magi. And if there really was more to Lira than how she appeared.

Jasi looked past Eris, her eyes searching down the hall. Eris thought she saw a hint of agitation on her face. "Mother is not as pleased with this arrangement as father. He thinks the union between Errasn and Saffra makes sense. Mother does not."

Eris hadn't realized her parents disagreed on the wedding. Should she be surprised? Adrick had her father's ear while Lira had her mother's. It made sense they would have differing opinions.

"What does Mother want?"

Jasi took a deep breath. "She'd rather see me wed the Varden prince. Unite the north."

Eris tensed. How much influence in the decision did Lira have? "What do you want?"

Jasi pursed her lips. For a moment, Eris thought she might make a snide comment as she often did and readied herself for it. She wouldn't argue with her sister today. Doing so would only risk her getting pushed farther away from the planning. And she *did* want to help her sister. As much as they disagreed, she still loved her and wanted her to be happy.

"I will do what is needed for the kingdom." She pulled her back straight as she said it, and her hand briefly gripped the fabric of her gown.

"But is that what *you* want?" Eris repeated.

Jasi looked over at her, and her voice dropped to a whisper. Her eyes softened, a hint of moisture sweeping over them before she blinked it away. "Does it matter? Father planned to marry me off somewhere. It's my role. Then Desia and you." She nodded, as if coming to a decision. "Yes, even you. Better someone like Prince Petra than others I've met." She looked over to where her hand-maiden had looked up and shot her a hard glare. The woman looked back to the floor and turned so her back faced them. "Pray to the Sacred Mother you or Desia get to choose."

Jasi almost said something more but closed her mouth and turned away, heading back down the hall, her handmaiden following after her.

CHAPTER 9

*E*ris sat in the library, again searching for anything on the teary star.

A question burned in her. Why *this* flower? Why now? What did the flower mean to Lira? She almost wished Adrick hadn't left; then she might have been able to see what he knew.

But she found nothing. If only she could, she might be able to get closer to Lira, to see if what the magi had said was true...but even at this, she couldn't succeed.

Worse, compared to the sweet fragrance of the garden, the musty odor of the library felt stifling. Eris had taken to carrying one of the flowers Terran showed her the day before with her to the library. Doing so seemed to brighten up even the dreary shadows Master Billiken seemed to prefer.

She grew increasingly frustrated with her inability to learn anything more about the teary star. The books she'd found had little to offer. She'd visited with Terran a few more times and he continued to make a game of trying to show her ever more exotic flowers, but Eris didn't think he had anything that would be of any use to her in learning more. Pretending not to be impressed by the flowers he chose lost its fun. Eris sighed and glanced at the tarblerod she wore, the leaves a rich orange and red which clashed in just the right way with her dress.

The old Master of Books sat at a small table in the library, a lantern flickering on the table in front of him and a book spread beneath his nose. Grey hair sprouted out from his head wildly, and his spectacles had slipped, dangling dangerously close to falling onto the table. Wire wrapped around part of the frame holding them together; clearly this would not be the first time they had fallen.

Eris approached him slowly. "Master Billiken?" she asked softly.

He sat up with a shake, his eyes blinking in a furious spasm. The master of books looked down at what he read, pale blue eyes quickly scanning the page, before shutting the book and sliding it off to the side.

Eris glanced at the title and saw that it was some sort of insect guide.

"Ah, just a little research for the Conclave," he said importantly. "They are too busy to sit pouring over books, and I am, of course, always willing to help the king's councilors."

"Of course, Master Billiken." Eris wondered why the Conclave would want Billiken to study insects, but couldn't think of any reason to ask him more without offending him. "I was hoping you could help me with *my* research."

So far, all the books she'd found came up with nothing more than descriptions of the flower varieties found in the Svanth Forest other than the one she wanted. She had spent days looking, flipping page by page, reading all she could about the native flowers but had come up empty. Eris began to wonder if she had been led astray. What if Terran and Nels were wrong? What if the flower was not from Svanth?

It still bothered her that Lira refused to tell her more about her flower. What did she want to keep her from?

"Of course, my lady," Billiken said. "You said you research flowers?"

She nodded. "It is called a teary star. I only know it's found in the Svanth Forest but haven't been able to find anything more about the flower from the books you pulled down for me."

Billiken frowned, pushing his spectacles back up his nose and then tapping his chin. "I cannot say I have heard of that particular flower, though with all of the varieties the mistress of flowers brought to the garden, there are many I have never heard about. Still," he continued, pushing himself up from the table. "If you know the name of the flower and the region, we should be able to find something for you."

He tottered toward the tall shelf with the books on flowers. The ladder Eris had used to climb and look on her own still leaned along the edge of the upper shelf. Billiken glanced at her, a frown etched on his face, but said nothing as he shifted the ladder.

At the top, he pulled several books out and glanced at the cover. "You have searched these, I take it?"

"I have. How did you know?"

He frowned at her again. "They are out of place, my lady. The library has a certain order, otherwise we would lose track of where anything is located with all the books I have collected."

"I'm sorry, Master Billiken. I thought it easier to climb up and look on my own. I know how busy you—"

"Nonsense," he said, but his face softened. "I am always available to help with your search, my lady. I must say that it is quite refreshing having someone else in the library with me. Most of the time—such as with the request from the Conclave—I am simply asked to search for certain books. Often I am asked to read the books as well and provide a report. I could offer the same for you, if you like, my lady."

She shook her head. As frustrating as it had been searching through the few books about flowers from the Svanth Forest, Eris could not deny the fact that she had learned quite a bit. Already, she recognized several of the varieties of flowers found in the garden, even surprising Terran with their names when he tried to point them out to her.

"I don't mind searching through the books on my own. It's finding the right one which has been the challenge. You have quite the talent to be able to know where everything is within the library. Since you had already told me which shelf the books I needed were on, I thought I could find what I needed on my own."

Billiken nodded, his eyes suddenly vibrant. "Ah, well…I will not fault you for your spirit, my lady, but it is not ladylike for you to be climbing the ladder to these shelves. I can just imagine what your mother might say if she heard I let you do such a thing!"

If only he knew how unladylike she had been. Her mother would turn as scarlet as a magi cloak if she knew.

Billiken turned back to his books, pulling a few from the shelf as he went and glancing at the cover before deciding against it and pushing it back. Finally, he climbed down the ladder, hands as empty as when he first climbed up, and shook his head.

"I am sorry, my lady. It appears you have seen all the books I have from the Svanth region. There is one book I would like to find but cannot. A larger text with drawings so carefully made that I should think you would find any flower you needed there, but it remains out of my collection."

"Do you know who has borrowed it?" If she could find out, she could possibly ask to borrow the book to see if there is any reference to the teary star.

But Billiken shook his head. "Possibly Master Nels," he said. "With all the new strains brought into the garden, he has been spent considerable time researching them. I don't recall lending it to him, though. It would be a shame to have misplaced it, really.

That text by Feliran is quite possibly the seminal work on the Svanth region."

Eris shook her head, remembering that Billiken had mentioned the book the first time she visited the library. "Do you have others by Feliran?"

Billiken's eyes brightened, and he bobbed his head, pleased that she had taken interest in his collection. "Several," he said, back straightening. "Feliran was quite prolific. Each is lovingly made with the same attention to detail."

"Might I see one?" If she knew what the style looked like, she might be able to recognize the book.

The master of books shook his head. "Unfortunately, no. Master Nels has borrowed all of them."

"How many are there?"

Billiken counted silently to himself, mouthing words that must have been titles as he considered. "No more than ten, my lady."

Eris's eyes widened. "That many books by one person?"

Billiken nodded. "Feliran is widely considered to be the foremost botany authority. It is quite fortuitous I managed to secure as many as I did. Most are quite difficult to come by, but as we now have our own mistress of flowers, it seemed prudent to have a reference for her to access. I believe there might be one or two other works by Feliran as well, but I have not managed to acquire copies of them. Still, I must say, having nearly the complete set is quite the accomplishment." He shook his head. "I had not considered our Master of Gardens would borrow them all."

It seemed she would have to find Master Nels again.

Eris didn't know where else she would be able to go to learn about the teary star other than Lira, and the mistress of flowers had made it clear she needed to perform her own research.

Maybe the master gardener had the book she sought. That would be the best solution. Then she could do her own research and satisfy Lira's requirement without upsetting Nels too much more. Hopefully he was not still frustrated with her and would let her borrow the books by Feliran.

Eris thanked Billiken and hurried out of the library. As she made her way down the wide stairs and into the garden, something seemed off. It took Eris a moment to notice what it was.

The sky was cloudy and grey. Thunder pealed distantly, rolling slowly toward the palace. Fat drops of rain pelted from the sky. Wind whipped at her long dress, and she had to grip it to keep the hem from flapping in the gusts.

Eris couldn't help but wonder what it meant when storm clouds rolled through in the daytime. How long had it been since they'd had a storm in the daylight?

And how long had it been since Adrick had left the city and headed north?

She hesitated. Why *hadn't* she asked Lira if what Adrick said was true? Or at least confronted her about why she refused to help her understand her flower. If Lira *was* what the magi suspected, Eris wanted to know. Her parents needed to know.

Eris turned away from the garden and swept into the palace, entering the west tower near the library. Tapestries lining both walls were made in the southern style with shapes of muted colors and harsh lines. Lanterns set into the wall gave off a flickering glow as wind blew through open doors down the corridor. Eris could not recall the last time their light was needed in the daylight. Servants flitted about, darting in and out of view, bowing briefly when the saw her but otherwise doing what they could to stay out of her way. Unlike Jasi or even Desia, Eris rarely demanded anything of them.

Reaching the wide central stair, she hurried to the second floor and was outside Lira's door, ready to knock before she stopped. She didn't have any idea what she would tell Lira. How she had overheard a conversation in the garden? How she suspected Lira to be some sort of flower mage? Imaging Lira's expression was enough to make her think twice.

A gust of wind fluttered her dress and sent her hair into her face. Eris decided she had to know.

She knocked.

She didn't expect—or really *want*—Lira to answer the door, fearing her reaction. Still, when the door swung open, a strange sense of relief washed over her.

Until she saw Lira's face.

Usually strong and stern, now it was drawn and frail. Deep wrinkles worked at the corner of her eyes. Her mouth pursed in a taut expression of concentration. The muscles in her cheeks tensed and contorted. Her dark brown hair hung limp around her shoulders, pushed back with a small leather band rather than twisted and bound atop her head as usual. She wore little more than a thin shift of pale yellow fabric.

Lira frowned at Eris when she saw her. It was a sign of the change that had come over her that she didn't pull the door to her quarters closed behind her.

"Have you completed your studies then, Eris Taeresin?" she asked. Her tone had not changed, still sharp and stinging.

Eris shook her head, suddenly wondering how to explain why she had come to find her. "Mistress Lira, there is a storm," she started, realizing how foolish the statement sounded.

Lira's hazel eyes narrowed, and she tilted her head in the strange way that she had. "We have many storms here in Errasn." She spoke slowly, almost deliberate about how she formed the words, her accent making them thick.

Eris blinked. "Of course, Lira, only this is..." She trailed off, unsure how to explain her concern.

Lira watched her, head tipped slightly back. "Rain nurtures the flowers, Eris Taeresin. It is the lifeblood for us all. We should welcome the rain in all its forms, not fear it."

"I understand—"

Lira pursed her lips, pulling her back straighter so that she seemed to loom over Eris. "I believe I can look out a window the same as you." She frowned. "Do I need to report to your mother this behavior? You know how busy she is with the wedding planning. More than that, I believe she is already displeased by your progress. We both had hoped you would be farther along in your studies. Perhaps the promise we thought we saw in you was misguided."

Eris shook her head. This was not going at all how she intended it to go. But what had she intended? Did she confront Lira about what she'd heard? Ask her if she was a flower mage as Adrick claimed? Demand to know if she worked with the north?

"Then why have you come to me? You have an assignment to study your flower. If you are prepared to report, then I am willing to meet, but otherwise I will not have you wasting my time."

"I am not prepared to report," she admitted. "It's just…"

Lira tilted her head toward her. "Just what, Eris Taeresin?"

A heavy peal of thunder shook the palace.

The floor shook beneath her. The walls chattered. Somewhere glass shattered.

Lira's face tightened, and her eyes took on a faraway expression. Her mouth clenched, and she spun, turning away from Eris and hurrying back into her room. In her haste, she neglected to close the door.

"Lira?" Eris asked.

Lira didn't answer. Instead, she hurried to a wide window and looked out.

Eris took a tentative step into the room, watching to see what Lira would do.

The room smelled like the garden. Cut flowers arranged and set in vases almost cluttered the sitting room. A pale wooden chair sat looking toward the largest collection of vases rather than toward the hearth in the corner of the room. A simple desk pushed against one wall, a partially completed arrangement sat near the edge. A small cluster of flowers rested on towels on either side, the shape of the blue petals making them likely a daisy or carnation. Next to the wall at the back of the desk was a stack of books, all bound in dark brown leather.

Eris crept toward the desk, curious. She glanced over the arrangement on the desk and looked at the books. Gold lettering embossed the leather of the topmost book. She could not make out the title easily, but that was not what caught her eye. It was the author she noted. Feliran.

Hadn't Billiken said the master gardener had borrowed the books? Why had Lira taken them from him?

Eris grabbed one without looking at the title and pocketed it.

A sudden gust of wind made Eris turn.

Lira had opened the window and leaned forward. Wind whipped around her head, spinning her hair and fluttering her dress. Cold air filled the room, heavy with the scent of rain. Flashes of lightning streaked from the sky. A few seemed close. Thunder rumbled once, and then again and again in a steady drumbeat.

"Mistress Lira?" she asked again.

Lira ignored her. Rain pelted into the room, soaking the floor and running along the edges of the wall. The flower master's hair was soaked and hung in strings along her face. Another flash of lightning came so close that Lira had to lean away from the window. Her face stretched pale and taut.

Eris realized that she was mumbling something, words so soft she could barely hear. She stepped closer, worried about Lira's sudden strange behavior. Lira seemed oblivious to Eris' presence in the room with her, concerned only for what she witnessed outside the window.

As Eris neared, she saw what Lira was watching.

The window overlooked the garden. She had not realized Lira's rooms could see the garden, but it made sense. Probably Lira had watched her every day and knew how little she managed to get done. Something she should have considered before now.

Eris looked out the window. Through the flickering lightning strikes, fires burned in the garden. There came another blinding strike and another fire bloomed.

Just then, Lira turned as if aware that Eris was next to her. Her eyes grew wide and her face was slack. Her mouth worked soundlessly.

Then she collapsed.

CHAPTER 10

*E*ris hesitated. Whatever happened now was the result of the magi. Somehow, she was certain of that. And if Lira *did* work for Varden or the Kelths, then perhaps she should leave her. Wouldn't it be better if Adrick succeeded and protected the kingdom from whatever she planned?

Lira moaned, ending any debate.

Eris tore out of Lira's room in a run. All around her, the palace shook with thunder. The heavy pounding slowly eased, replaced by a steady rumbling that rattled windows but did nothing more.

She looked around the wide hall. Lanterns flickered from wind blowing through an open door or window somewhere down the hall. A few had blown out, leaving gaps of light along the hall, dark shadows shifting strangely. The air felt heavy and wet.

Finally, she saw a servant poke a head tentatively out of a door. Eris raised her hand, waving.

The servant was a young girl, probably only a year or so older than Eris herself, and dressed in the plain white cotton of the housemaids. Her eyes widened as she saw Eris waving, and for a moment, Eris thought she might scurry away.

"Send help! The Mistress of Flowers is injured." She tried suffusing her voice with all the authority she could, unintentionally channeling Jasi as much as her mother.

The girl nodded and darted off.

Eris turned back toward Lira's room and stepped inside. Lira lay on the ground. Rain still streamed through the open window and splashed on her now-soaked yellow shift. Lightning streaked continuously outside the window and thunder rolled like a constant drumbeat.

"Eris."

Eris hurried over when Lira called her name, all hints of formality in her voice gone. Instead, she sounded weak and tired.

Lira leaned on her side, her head lolling weakly on her neck. In spite of the rain soaking her, she looked like a wilting flower. Wrinkles seemed to have appeared over the last few minutes, lining sunken cheeks and her forehead.

"Lira?" Eris asked. She did not mind the water soaking the hem of her dress as she crouched next to the master of flowers. "What happened? What is this storm?"

Lira stared at her, eyes changing, losing focus. "You knew."

Eris shook her head. "I didn't know anything."

Lira blinked. "You knew about the storm."

Eris considered denying it, but this was her opportunity to learn more. "I overheard Adrick last week."

Lira sighed, took a deep shuddering breath, and sat up. Some of the strength seemed to be returning to her. Already the lines on her face faded as her skin seemed to smooth. "What did you overhear?"

There was another bright streak of lightning, followed by an explosion of thunder and then silence. The rain softened, falling in a gentle patter on the floor.

Eris swallowed. "I...I heard him talking about you," she said carefully. "At least, I think it was you. He referred to you as a flower mage and seemed to think you were building the garden to oppose the Conclave of Magi. That you work on behalf of the north." She watched Lira's face but saw no reaction. "He said he was going to travel to the Svanth Forest to destroy your garden." She said the last in a rush.

To her surprise, Lira smiled.

"Did he? Took him long enough." She swallowed, and her eyes brightened. "He will be lucky to enter the forest, let alone destroy what grows within its boundaries." Lira shook her head, sending droplets of water flying across the room. Outside, the storm faded, dark clouds blowing across the sky. "The Conclave will find the enchantments set along the border of the forest different than any they have ever experienced."

Lira quickly regained her strength. Now she appeared no different than usual, if only wetter. She stayed close to the window, tilting her face to the clearing sky.

"So...you are a flower mage?" Did that mean the rest was true? Could Lira be a traitor, too?

Would her mother believe her? Would anyone?

Lira's eyes flashed with bright energy. "A flower mage?" She said the word disdainfully. "Is that what you think, Eris Taeresin?"

Eris looked around the room, eyes touching on the vases full of flowers to the now blue sky outside the window before looking back at Lira. "I don't know."

"That, I think, is a wise answer."

"Then what is this all about? What happened here?"

Lira turned and looked out the window, inhaling deeply of the cool breeze. "A struggle happened here. Perhaps had they challenged me earlier they might have succeeded, but earlier I was no threat."

"I don't understand. Does my mother know? My father?" Eris edged toward the door, ready to run.

"Your parents know what they are willing to hear," Lira answered. "Your father, in particular, finds the magi useful."

Eris hesitated, determined to get answers. "If you're not a flower mage, then what are you?"

"I am a gardener," Lira finally answered. "Only, my garden was destroyed."

"A gardener? Like Nels?"

Lira smiled slightly and nodded. "Like Nels, but not like Nels."

"But he's the Master Gardener," Eris said.

Lira nodded. "And he serves your mother well."

"Don't you serve my mother as well?"

"I serve," Lira said. Eris noted she didn't say who she served. "That is the purpose of this garden." She glanced out the window and shook her head. Sorrow lined her face. "Was the purpose."

Eris glanced out the small window.

Below her, the garden was abuzz with activity. Gardeners hurried about, pouring water on still smoldering flames. Smoke twirled toward the sky from dozens of small fires. There were several huge black rents in the earth where lightning appeared to have struck the ground, throwing dirt and flowers around, destroying the beauty and colors in the patterns. Eris noted that much of the damage was focused at the center of the patterns laid out in the garden.

For some reason, she ached with what had been lost in the storm.

"Now that the garden is destroyed, will you be weakened?"

Lira looked at her, a strange light in her eyes. "This is not destroyed, Eris Taeresin," she said. "I have seen gardens destroyed, gardens that once were without rival. I watched helplessly as fire and lightning rained down on those gardens and I was unable to intervene. Such beauty lost. So many flowers will never regrow, destroyed forever." Lira sighed, her eyes taking on a faraway look. "Now what few of us remain are dispersed. I alone remain in this realm, and if the magi have their way, even I would not exist."

Lira shook, her eyes snapping back to focus. Her lips pursed as she stared out at the garden. Already Nels had the gardeners organized, destroyed plants uprooted, and the space cleared. Eris could tell it would only be a matter of days before the garden was replanted. Within weeks, the flowers would regrow and blossom, their colors spreading.

Eris wondered what Lira held back from her. "What will you do now?"

Would Lira admit her plans? Did it matter?

Lira turned to her. "Now, Eris Taeresin? Now we return to our studies. You still have not reported to me on your flower. Such curiosity. I admit I'm pleased you're finally showing some interest."

There was the sound of footsteps, and Eris looked over to see her mother sweeping into the room wearing a long pale purple dress and her golden hair ran in curls down her back framing her sun darkened face. Even following a storm, she stood proud and beautiful. Behind her came a white-gowned handmaiden. To her right was a scarlet-robed magi, his hood pulled back and a strange expression twisting his face. Eris thought he was the one who came with the King and Queen from Saffra, but found it difficult to tell.

Worry etched in lines next to the queen's eyes, and she glanced from Eris to Lira. "Lira," she said, looking at Eris. "I received word that you were injured."

Lira tipped her head slightly at her mother's entrance, but Eris noted how she did not take her eyes off the magi. "Doubtful, my lady."

"So you weren't injured?" The queen glared at Eris.

Eris feared Lira would deny what had happened.

"I slipped, my lady," Lira answered. "The rain came on suddenly, and I had my window open to smell the lovely flowers."

Her mother's face changed, an expression of sadness coming to her eyes. "A terrible loss, Lira. Especially before the wedding. I had so hoped to have beautiful arrangements prepared before the ceremony. Now I imagine it will be years before the garden is back to where you had it, and just as the colors were looking so wonderful together!"

Eris noted the soft smile tugging the magi's mouth.

"A loss, indeed, my lady, but your master gardener does wonderful work. I suspect that the garden will be back nearly as it was within a week."

"Truly?"

Lira nodded, tipping her head toward the magi. "The destruction provides an opportunity to try new groupings. I have wondered if a different arrangement might be more pleasing."

Eris debated saying something about Lira. But the look on her mother's face convinced her otherwise.

Her mother smiled at Lira. "You are always so positive, Lira." She moved toward the window, not mindful of the water still pooled on the ground. Her handmaiden hurried behind her, grabbing at the dress and lifting it from the water. "Ah...perhaps you are right. Master Nels has already begun the preparations. I will look forward to what new arrangement you create. We are blessed to have such a wonderful mistress of flowers. The courtyard was ever so drab before you came."

"Not drab, my lady. The flowering elms had a distinct beauty and provided such lovely shade."

Her mother nodded. "I remember. When Hanrik and I used to sit beneath them and simply enjoy the sounds of the courtyard when first courting. A shame that the storm took them from us."

Lira simply tilted her head.

"And fortuitous for us that you arrived when you did. Now we have color and vibrancy in our garden unlike anything else!"

"You flatter me. It is the master gardener who does the work. I simply provide guidance."

Her mother looked at Lira and winked. "You provide more than just guidance."

Eris tensed. Her mother knew.

The queen glanced around the room as if seeing it for the first time. And possibly, Eris realized, she was. She looked at the different arrangements set in vases, some bright with reds and blues, other arrangements more muted, before sweeping toward the arrangement on the desk. There, she gently touched the flower before leaning in and taking a deep breath.

"Wonderful," she sighed. Her mother straightened and looked over at Lira. "A new arrangement?"

Lira tipped her head. "A demonstration."

Her mother smiled. "How are the lessons going?"

Eris noted how she didn't look over at her. She knew her mother was disappointed in her lack of progress and probably thought she didn't take Lira's lessons seriously. And truthfully, until she came across the teary star, she had not. But over the last week or so, she had devoted much of her time to finding out all she could about the flower. It wasn't her fault none of Master Billiken's books had any reference to her flower.

"Your daughters are doing quite well with their lessons. Jasi, in particular, has quite an eye for colors," she said, looking over at the magi. "She will find that useful in the years to come. Especially now that she has agreed to the wedding."

Eris heard the note of disappointment in Lira's voice.

"And this?"

Lira nodded. "An example of her work. She has learned to take flowers, regardless of variety, and place them in such a way the colors are pleasing."

Lira pointed to one of the smaller vases set on a low shelf. Blue lisanthis and yellow corinths circled the striped perisal at the center of the work. Eris couldn't help but notice the colors did not seem to complement each other very well. The striped perisal, in particular, stood out, seeming to clash with the flowing lines of the lisanthis. The corinths seemed tossed in for color, ignoring the way the shape of their petals contrasted the soft curves of the lisanthis.

"A shame her lessons will end soon," her mother said.

Lira smiled. "On the contrary. I intend to continue them after she leaves for Saffra."

Her mother looked up, frowning deeply. "You will leave us?"

"Not leave, but I might take some time to travel. Even now, my garden is nearly complete here, and I imagine Jasi will need assistance establishing her own."

The magi watched Lira with a dark expression. His eyes were unreadable.

Eris wondered what it meant that Lira readied Jasi for her own garden.

"You think Jasi ready to manage a garden?"

Lira nodded, eyes fixed on the magi. "Perhaps not at first. I might need to guide her, but she is quite far along in her studies. A small garden shouldn't be too much for her to manage."

Her mother did not seem to care. "How lovely!" she said, lifting the vase and turning it. "I knew she would have an eye for arrangement."

Lira nodded. "Indeed she does."

"What of the others? Desia and Ferisa continue with their studies?" Her mother looked over at Eris, disappointment clear in her tone.

"They do."

"And how do they do? Desia tells me she enjoys her lessons. With her eye, I should think she is skilled as well."

Eris hid a laugh behind a cough.

Lira watched her as she turned away. "They have much to learn yet. There is more to the arrangement than colors, but in time they will prove adequate, I suspect. I have examples of all their work. Each week they create a new project to demonstrate what they have learned."

Her mother looked at the vases on the low shelf, a slight smile turning the corners of her mouth. "And Ferisa?"

"She does quite well," Lira said. She stepped next to the queen and pulled a tall, thin ceramic vase off one of the low shelves. A collection of lilies and green leaves seemed almost tossed into the vase, but there seemed to be some semblance of pattern to the flowers that Eris could almost see. Of the vases made by her sisters, Ferisa seemed to have the most order though lacked in creativity.

"Ah…she does love lilies."

Lira nodded. "A simple flower but it suits her well."

"When will I see something from Eris?" Her mother looked up and met Eris's eyes.

Eris only shrugged. She could not begin learning the art of arrangement like her sisters until she learned about her flower.

"Eris is on a different schedule," Lira answered.

Her mother's mouth turned in a flat line. "Always on a different schedule, I'm afraid. If she troubles you, Lira, do not be afraid to send her to me for discipline. There are better ways for you to use your time, especially now that the garden has been damaged. She should consider herself lucky to have such an opportunity."

Eris noted her mother did not speak directly to her, preferring to speak through Lira. Were she Jasi or Desia, possibly even Ferisa, she was certain her mother would make a point of speaking to her.

At least she made no mention of her other studies. Either her mother didn't know how she'd neglected them, or the instructors simply didn't report. Eris enjoyed the time away from sitting on the hard chairs with the seamstresses and the lessons with the master of maps on geography. Did her sisters continue those lessons? Since she hadn't been allowed into Lira's classes, she hadn't really asked. Maybe she was the only one ignoring her other studies.

"She has been no trouble, my lady. Do not fear—I will continue to work with her. There is potential there, whether she chooses to see it or not."

Eris suppressed a shiver. What kind of potential did Lira see in her?

"It would be nice if she showed promise in something," her mother remarked, looking at the arrangements made by Eris's sisters.

The magi cleared his throat. "As it appears the flower mistress is quite well..."

Her mother turned toward him and waved her hand. "Yes, yes, Davin. You may leave. I thank you for accompanying me." Dark eyes brushed over Lira as he left. "The King sent him to offer guidance about the storm when the serving girl found me. He seemed quite concerned about your well-being."

"I am sure he was," Lira said.

After the magi left, the queen leaned toward the flowers again and took a deep breath. "Wonderful." Then she turned and swept out of the room, her handmaiden trailing after her.

Eris watched her leave, wishing her mother would have asked her how she was doing, shown a real interest in her other than to compare her to her sisters, but she had not.

"You should be learning about your flower now, Eris Taeresin," Lira said softly after her mother left.

Eris opened her mouth to say something before clamping it shut. Lira had already given her all the answers she needed.

CHAPTER 11

A gray sky hung overhead the next day, the air smelling damp from the rain that had passed over. A gentle breeze blew out of the north, pushing cool air down and through the garden. Eris suddenly wished she'd chosen warmer clothes than dark green pants and a simple woven shirt, but a dress wouldn't do for what she planned. She still laughed at the reaction she'd gotten when she made her way through the palace. Likely the servants thought she'd lost her mind.

Master Nels moved quickly throughout the garden, hurrying from place to place as he went, directing some of his assistants as they replaced flowers in dark beds of earth. Most of the flowers remained surprisingly unharmed, just uprooted when wooden planters had been destroyed. He glanced at her and almost made a point of ignoring her, before remembering propriety and hurrying over.

Eris stood near the center of the garden. Glass from the greenhouse glittered beyond the trees. Rows of beds were set onto the ground with varying degrees of damage. Some were splintered, wood cracked or even singed, spilling dirt onto the ground. Plants were tossed to the side or tilted in the soil. Other planting beds looked salvageable. The plants in these were in better shape, most solidly in place.

She looked around. This seemed a sort of triage area. She hadn't noticed on her way toward the center of the garden the damage around her. The planters in some places were gone, small craters all that remained. Now that she noticed, a hint of charred wood hung on the air, though the wind helped push most of it away. Assistant gardeners moved quickly, carrying the long beds to new locations or cradling damaged plants they brought toward the greenhouse. She didn't see Terran anywhere.

Master Nels swept his hat off his head when he reached her and nodded briefly. "My lady, please don't take this the wrong way, but I can't have you interfering with our work today. With the storm damage and the coming wedding only a week off, you understand that I need to work quickly?"

She understood. He didn't want her bothering Terran. She had expected that reaction, but was determined to spend time in the garden. How else would she learn what Lira intended for it before Adrick returned? And when he returned, she would speak to him, find out the truth about Lira.

"I understand, Master Nels. I simply came to offer my assistance." She held gloved hands up and wiggled her fingers.

A debate raged across his face. Did he accept any help, especially with the time constraints suddenly placed on them, or did her turn away the princess?

"I'm certain your mother would not want you working in the garden, my lady. Such things are simply not proper."

Eris laughed. She could just imagine how her mother would react to knowing she dug her fingers into the dirt, gloves or not. "Mistress Lira wishes me to help," she said. She counted on the fact that Master Nels wouldn't have time to find Lira to verify. And if he did, Eris only faced a minor punishment and could state she needed to learn more about the planting of flowers to understand hers. Surely Lira would agree to that?

Nels' brow furrowed. His eyes flickered from side to side, the amount of work left undone plain on his face. "The mistress wanted you to help?"

Eris nodded.

"But you will need guidance. I can't have you replacing flowers in the wrong bed. There is structure here. Some need more water, others more sunlight. You don't know these things."

"You don't think you could use the extra help?"

Of all the places Eris could offer to help, this was the one thing she thought herself most suited to do. She couldn't help Jasi with wedding planning. Desia seemed too preoccupied with assisting Lira with the floral arrangements. And Ferisa was almost overwhelmingly distraught over the garden. She stayed locked in her room, with the offer to work on the embroidery for the wedding dresses as a way to calm her mind.

"She can work with me."

She turned and saw Terran standing behind her, his hat pulled tight down over his head. The heavy bags under his eyes looked almost like streaks of dirt, leaving her wondering how little sleep he'd gotten overnight. Had they stayed up all night working?

In spite of the dirt, there was something surprisingly handsome about him. He tipped his head and his lopsided smile spread across his face. Eris looked away. She shouldn't feel like that around some gardener.

Master Nels frowned. "I need you focused on the pattern—"

"I know the pattern, Master Nels. She can help with the shade plants along the perimeter. You said those were important to get reestablished first."

Master Nels nodded slowly. "Yes. They take longer to solidify their roots. A disturbance like the one last night can be especially dangerous to them. And the mistress requests they be planted first. Somehow she expects me to increase the shade in the garden to support *more* shade plants." He shook his head. "Perhaps it's a good thing we didn't get the delivery from Baylan. We wouldn't have been able to support that and the dozens of new plants Mistress Lira supplied."

Eris looked from Master Nels to Terran. "You will let me help?" she asked.

"You don't have enough help along the perimeter of the garden," Terran started, "and I don't think I can work quickly enough to get all of them established by the full moon."

Master Nels crushed his hat between his hands and then stuffed it back onto his head. "If you think you won't be slowed."

Terran shook his head.

"But if I see you're taking longer than it should, I'll send her back to the palace. The mistress can find her own way to use her." Nels started away, pausing to bark directions to one of the assistant gardeners working nearby.

Terran grabbed her arm and pulled her down one of the narrow side paths.

"Thanks," she told him as they moved away from the center part of the garden.

Terran looked over and seemed to take in her attire for the first time. He laughed, a deep rich sound. "Did the mistress really assign you to help?"

"You think I'd lie to Master Nels?"

Terran laughed again. "Yes."

Eris looked away to keep from laughing along with him. "So, Lira wants the shade plants taken care of first?"

They had nearly reached one of the outer walls. The damage was not as much here, but still terrible. Eris had to step over and around flowers strewn on the path or piles of dirt and cracked stone from a particularly powerful lightning strike.

"She wants the garden repaired," Terran answered.

"Why do you think the storm struck here?"

Terran looked at her with a knowing expression. "Bad luck, I guess. Master Nels hasn't seen anything like it before."

Eris didn't push but had the sense that Terran knew more than he shared. Did he know about Lira? About what she planned?

He stopped in front of a row of damaged flowerbeds. The flowers had already begun to wilt, their deep violet petals rolling in and sagging. Terran pulled them out of loose soil and held them carefully in his hand. He motioned to Eris. "Hold them carefully by the stem. Try not to touch the roots or the petals while they're out of the soil."

She copied him, gathering the flowers carefully in one hand. When she had nearly a dozen, he pointed her toward a nearby empty bed resting on the ground. It had some damage, the wood frame was singed, leaving the once-white bed now streaked with dark soot. A long crack worked through one end.

"Now we're going to dig a hole wide enough for the roots. Then you set the teraspal in carefully." He demonstrated by digging a hole and then holding one of the flowers in the soil. "Cover the roots carefully. Don't pat it down. Once they're established they aren't so sensitive, but until then, most of these shade plants are pretty delicate."

Eris started working. Digging her fingers into the dirt felt strangely relaxing. She worked carefully, burrowing out craters of soil before resetting the teraspals into place. When she finished the collection in her hands, she looked over at Terran.

"There's plenty more. We'll stick with the teraspals for now. When we're done with those, we can really have fun. You can try not to prick your fingers planting spiny loras."

"Maybe you won't need my help then."

Terran laughed. "Well, since the mistress sent you out here to help, you wouldn't want her to hear how you abandoned your work too soon."

Eris tossed a handful of dirt toward him.

The work went quickly. As they planted the teraspals, Terran would occasionally pause and show her some additional trick—a way to make certain the flowers stood straight, or how far apart they should be, or some tip to heaping the soil to make it harder for pests to burrow in. Eris found herself increasingly impressed with just how much he knew.

She stole a few glances at him as he worked. Terran had broad shoulders and a steady hand as he dug through the dirt, quickly moving plants. He had an interesting way of pursing his lips as he did, almost as if he might whistle.

When he saw her looking, she flushed and turned away.

Eventually, an easy comfort fell between them. Neither found it necessary to fill the silence as they went, content to work. Terran moved with efficient motions, digging and planting, propping the flowers in such a way she could hardly tell they'd ever been disturbed. When they finished with the teraspals, he moved her closer to the wall.

Thorns rimmed not just the stems of the flowers here, but the leaves also caught her gloves. Even the flowers themselves, long reddish needle shaped things, hinted at the danger of the rest of the plant. "I take it these are spiny loras?"

Terran gripped one by the stem and lifted it. These flowers hadn't wilted as much as the teraspals. Stems stood rigid, and the thorns remained firm along the sides. He held them carefully between his fingers. "They are. Odd little flower, if you ask me. Grow best in thicker shade, though Master Nels managed to coax them here near the wall well enough."

Eris hadn't seen them before, though if Master Nels was right, there were over two thousand different flowers in the garden. There seemed no way for her to have seen all of them. The beds of the loras were not as damaged as others. She wondered if the wall protected them or if they simply hadn't been targeted.

She picked up one and held it like Terran demonstrated. "The thorns of the spiny loras grow first. It takes a generation before the flower even emerges." She remembered reading that in one of the books Master Billiken found for her, one on shade flowers.

He nodded. "That's correct. Most of these have been here a few years."

"I thought the garden only recently reached the walls."

"It did. But spiny loras and a few others have been here for a while."

Eris didn't remember any flowers along the wall before the garden stretched this far. "Where were they before?"

"They've been here."

"I haven't seen them."

He shrugged. "The shadows off the wall likely hid them. That's where these really thrive. Now, with these, you need to dig them deep. They're a little hardier than the teraspals because their roots will essentially regrow, but they won't have enough support as they do. So the soil has to support the entire stem."

Terran made a deep hole in the dirt, placed one of the long-stemmed flowers into it, and pushed the soil back around it. When he let go, a spot of blood bloomed on his finger where one of the thorns had bitten.

"Does it hurt?"

He shook his head sheepishly and wiped his hand on his pants. "I've still got a few things to learn. Master Nels wouldn't let them bite him like that."

"I'm not sure anyone can really avoid the thorns on this plant."

Terran grunted. "You haven't seen Master Nels work."

He grabbed another of the spiny loras and carefully placed it into the dirt. This time, he managed to do so without the thorns poking him. Terran moved carefully, his motions slightly exaggerated so Eris could see what he did and could copy. Once she'd demonstrated she could plant the loras without injuring herself, he nodded and simplified his movements.

A steady hammering came from near her, and Eris looked up. One of the palace carpenters worked to repair a nearby flowerbed. As she watched, he tore off the end of one splintered bed and replaced it with a flat unfinished board before moving onto the next damaged bed.

Eris suddenly wondered—even with the gardeners and their assistants working at full tilt, how could they replace all the plants in the beds within a week? Doing so was not just a test of how quickly the gardeners could work, but of how well they could get the beds repaired. Had Lira exaggerated when she'd said they would have the garden back in shape in a week?

"And she wanted more shade plants?" She said the last aloud, remembering what Master Nels had said to Terran.

"Ow!" Terran pulled his hand away from the spiny loras and shook his finger. He scratched his cheek as he looked over. "What was that?"

"Nels said Lira wanted more shade plants?"

Terran shrugged. "She's using the storm as an opportunity to create different arrangements."

Eris frowned. "In the garden."

Terran only shrugged again. "Can't say what the mistress wants. That's between her and Master Nels."

"What do you think of her?" Eris asked suddenly.

Terran worked for a moment before looking up. "The mistress? The same as you, I suspect."

Eris doubted that. She no longer knew what to think of Lira. But she didn't know who to talk to about her fears, either. Her mother wouldn't listen—she supported Lira fully—and she hadn't managed to see her father in the last few days.

"Master Nels doesn't determine the arrangement within the garden?"

"They work together. She suggests ways the flowers might complement each other, but Master Nels knows how to get the flowers to succeed where she suggests. A balance of sorts between the gardener and the keeper."

"Keeper?" She'd heard the term before but couldn't remember where.

Terran tipped his head in a nod. "The mistress."

"Why would she want more shade plants?"

Terran shrugged. "Can't really answer that. I just do what Master Nels asks of me."

Eris frowned at him

Terran laughed softly. "Well, most of the time. When I don't have princesses bothering me."

"I bother you?"

Terran's face flushed. "I didn't mean it like that. Just that I—"

This time, it was Eris's turn to laugh. Terran's flush deepened. He winced and jerked his hand back.

"Let's finish with the spiny loras and get on to something a little less painful?" Eris suggested.

Terran nodded. "Might be best."

"We could leave these for Master Nels."

Terran laughed. "If only I could. He wants nothing to do with spiny loras. Made it clear these were my responsibility."

"Just these?"

He shrugged. "All the shade plants, really. Thought it'd be good if I became more comfortable with them. As I said, they take a different touch than those in full sun."

"You don't seem annoyed by that."

"Should I be? I mean, these have a different type of beauty than those in the rest of the garden. And besides, you're stuck here with me."

"You think I'm stuck?"

Terran laughed, an easy and warm sound. "You said the mistress wanted you to help. And Nels wouldn't let you help without me working with you. So...stuck."

Eris laughed again. As she did, one of the thorns on the loras caught her palm, and she winced. If only there was a way to work with them and not fear the barbs. What was Master Nels' trick?

"Like I said. Stuck."

Eris considered tossing the plant she held at Terran but decided it might hurt the plant. Instead, she pushed it down into the dirt with the thought that it had better not hurt her. Thankfully, it didn't.

CHAPTER 12

*E*ris sat along a long bench near the front of the garden. She held the book she'd taken from Lira's room propped open on her lap, bright sunlight spilling over her, keeping her warm. The wedding was only a day away, and Master Nels wouldn't let her help in the garden any longer. To her surprise, she and Terran had managed to get most of the shade plants replaced over the last few days. She should be feeling proud of what they'd accomplished; instead, she felt uneasy.

She made a point of hiding what she did. She carefully tucked the gloves she wore under her bed each night and rolled the pants so none of the servants coming into her room would question. Each morning she hurried out just as the sun crept over the wall and stayed until most of the light had faded. Terran worked longer, but he refused to let her stay with him. And Eris had to make an appearance, especially as the wedding neared.

Now she sat and flipped through the book, waiting on her sisters. The book had diagrams of hundreds of flowers, some she even recognized. The detail in the book amazed her, but made no mention of the teary star. Instead, it catalogued shade plants. Many were flowers she'd planted alongside Terran, like dearth-swain and taranth, or the meticulously detailed diagrams of the spiny loras. Others she hadn't seen. Eris read each page, finding the details fascinating as she wondered *why* Lira wanted these shade plants.

She sighed and tucked the book into a hidden pocket of her dress. How long had she waited? Long enough to finish the book. She glanced at the garden, now almost back to what it had been before the damage sustained by the storm. Master Nels had skillfully guided his assistant gardeners—and her—in the replanting. Eris imagined Lira watching from her room, overseeing the rebuilding. Did Eris aid in her treachery by working with Terran?

From where she stood, the colors of the garden swirled, drawn into a pattern she thought she should recognize but didn't. It looked different than the way the garden had before the storm, but just as beautiful.

Eris made her way into the palace. Decorations for the wedding ceremony lined walls all around. Servants hurried from place to place. None bothered to do more than glance at her before hurrying on their way.

She rounded a corner leading to the main section of the palace. In the distance, a flash of crimson caught her eye. One of the magi.

Eris hadn't seen Adrick since he'd gone north. After everything that had happened, she wondered how he felt about the garden repair. Would he be angry at her for helping? Would he even know?

"Adrick," she said as he approached, and nodded.

He flicked a dismissive gaze over her. He really only tolerated her father and Jacen. Others in the palace didn't matter as much. "Princess Eris. You look...different."

Eris tensed, worried that he'd seen the dirt staining her hands. She'd been careful to hide it by wearing gloves, but if Adrick saw it so easily, perhaps she'd been careless. "You've been gone for a while."

His eyes narrowed and he frowned. "Yes. Your father sent me north."

Her father. Not the king. "Does that mean Jacen is back?"

Something shifted on his face. His leathery skin flushed with a hint of red. "Jacen will be returning shortly. His men..."

Eris frowned. "What about his men?"

"There was...a skirmish...along the border with Varden. I'm sure you shouldn't worry about it. But I really must be hurrying now. Your father is expecting me for the full report." He started to move past her.

"What kind of skirmish?"

Adrick paused and looked her over. "Princess...it's not really the kind of thing you need to fear. Your father's men—"

"My brother went to the north. I just want to know if he was injured."

Adrick took a quick breath. "Your brother is unharmed. The cavalry, unfortunately...well, it's well I chose to head north."

Eris worried about what he didn't say. What had happened to the men sent with Jacen? Had the Vardens attacked?

Did Lira have anything to do with it?

"There was a storm while you were gone," she started. This was the most she'd ever spoken to Adrick, but she felt this important for him to know.

"So I have heard."

"The garden was damaged."

Adrick pursed his lips. "Not from what I've seen."

Eris looked down, hoping to hide the sudden flush to her cheeks. Did it matter that she helped Terran? Did the work she assisted make it more likely there would be attacks on Errasn?

"Master Nels repaired it quickly."

"He is quite skilled," Adrick said.

He studied her for a moment before starting past her. She had the distinct impression that he saw *through* her. Eris suppressed a shiver.

"Are you certain there won't be an attack at the wedding?" What would happen if Lira tried something to disrupt the ceremony? Would the magi be able to intervene? Would her mother let her?

"The wedding will go on as planned."

She nodded slowly. "And you? What will you do?"

Adrick said nothing, leaving her watching his crimson cloak disappear.

Eris found Jacen outside near the stables. His once bright blue eyes had taken on a haunted sheen. A ragged beard covered his face, but he was otherwise well dressed in his sharp uniform.

"You made it back," she said.

He jumped and turned to face her. "Eris?"

His eyes looked different than she'd seen before. Darker. And where was the smile he usually offered her?

"Adrick said the trip was more dangerous than anticipated."

"Did he?"

Eris found the response odd. "What happened there?"

"Nothing that you'll have to worry about." There seemed a hint of bitterness in his voice.

"Well…I don't really have anything to worry about, do I? I'm just to learn about flowers and stay out of the way until I get married."

She didn't mean to take her frustration out on Jacen, but it came out anyway. With all that had been happening, she felt powerless to do anything. What did it matter that the Vardens seemed to be attacking in the north? What did it matter that Lira might be a traitor, using strange flower magic to work against her father? And what did it matter that Jasi was being sent away? Eris could do nothing about any of it.

"Eris...it's not that."

"Then what is it? Why shouldn't I be allowed to know? What do you think to keep me from?"

Jacen looked as if he might answer, but then clamped his mouth shut. He sighed and ran a hand through his hair. "Just be thankful you weren't born to lead. Some decisions are more difficult than they appear."

She glared at him. "And what is that supposed to mean?"

His eyes took her in and hesitated at the flower pinned to her dress. A smile twisted his face. "It means nothing. Go back to your garden, Eris."

CHAPTER 13

On the day of the wedding, clouds circled in the distance. Eris spent the morning, attending to her sister, holding the arrangement of flowers Jasi had proudly announced she'd created, and prepared to say as little as possible during the entire proceedings.

She stood in place in the great hall. Decorations for the coming feast covered everything, from the tapestries on the wall to the lines of plates already set atop tables waiting for the meal to commence. A raised dais on one end held spots for her family, with one additional spot for the groom. Flowers littered across the table, clearly Lira's touch, though Eris couldn't help but think the petals appeared more wilted than usual. Some of the colors even seemed faded. Arrangements had been set on each table as well, colors and flowers placed in such a way that they complemented each other. Eris found she recognized most of the flowers.

Lira was nowhere to be found. Eris found it odd, but said nothing.

Desia stood on one side of her, waiting for their summons to join the ceremony in the chapel of the Sacred Mother. She looked beautiful with her golden hair curled and pinned atop her head, the clutch of flowers she held different than the others—likely Desia had added her own flourish—and her long white dress flowed away from her elegantly. Ferisa stood on the other side, a soft smile on her pink lips. She held a mixture of lilies and listhanis.

The silence around them grew to be too much. "Soon you'll be next," Eris said to Desia.

Desia didn't look over. "You say that as if it's such a terrible thing."

"You don't think it is? Forced to move from home, married off to someone so they can improve ties to father?" She said nothing else about her private fears. Desia was much like Jasi, willing to do whatever was needed for their father. To Desia, that *was* her role. But Eris needed more.

Desia turned and looked at her. "Honestly, Eris. Maybe it's too bad Ferisa came along. You would have been much happier serving the Sacred Mother."

"She still can," Ferisa said softly.

Desia looked past Eris and shot Ferisa a dark look.

Ferisa didn't look over. "Just because tradition demands the youngest serve, doesn't mean Eris can't as well. The Sacred Mother will take all who wish to serve her."

Desia sighed and looked away. "The only thing I worry about is how to keep you from disappointing Mother."

Eris didn't need her to clarify to know she meant her. "As if Jasi has done so well at that?"

"At least you respect her."

Eris didn't want to argue with Desia, at least not here. "It appears Lira has been preoccupied with the wedding."

Desia followed her gaze and saw the flowers twisted into a lovely arrangement. "Not too preoccupied to teach, Eris. Had you cared to see, you would know she's been spending possibly even more time with us. Jasi in particular."

Eris wondered why Jasi would get extra attention before marrying Prince Petra. Did it have anything to do with the attack in the north? Could Lira hope to influence Jasi even after she left the city?

"If you only pretend interest to get out of your other studies, I'd understand. Lira might not, but we would. But we see how you simply wander through the garden, as if you'd rather be there than anywhere else. You even took to helping the gardeners this week!"

Eris thought that had gone unnoticed. Clearly it hadn't. "I wanted to help. With everything happening for the wedding, I thought I could be of use."

"And you didn't think Jasi could use you?"

"How would I have been any use to Jasi?"

Desia shook her head. Her grip on the flowers tightened, her knuckles turning pale. "After the wedding, she'll be *leaving*. Ferisa and I have been working to help her prepare for her travel, not knowing when she might return."

She hadn't thought about how Jasi might need her. Eris didn't think she could do anything to help her sister, but that didn't mean she shouldn't have tried. Suddenly, she very much felt the time she'd spent in the garden had been wasted, even though she thought Terran had needed her at the time. But what if she was only aiding in what Lira attempted?

"And how does it look for a princess to be digging in the dirt?" Desia went on. "Thankfully, Mother hasn't learned of it, or I'm certain she would be quite displeased. Again."

Ferisa laid a hand on Eris's arm and patted. Eris looked over at her younger sister. She said nothing, but Ferisa's deep blue eyes looked back at her, almost as if trying to provide support.

Eris looked at Ferisa. "I…I'm sorry."

"I'm sure Jasi will forgive you," Ferisa said.

A small door at the end of the room opened, and their father stepped out. Dressed in a regal robe of deep blue and green, the heavy golden ring of office glittering on his finger, he smiled at each of them in turn as he approached.

Adrick followed closely behind. He wore his usual scarlet robe, though more heavily embroidered than usual. The long silver staff he'd carried the day before tapped along the ground as he followed their father. Adrick frowned at Eris.

"I am to lead each of you into the chapel," their father said. His eyes were more drawn than the last time Eris had seen him. The news of the cavalry falling during the border skirmish had hit him hard. He looked back to Adrick and waved his hand, the large gold ring flashing along his middle finger. "You didn't need to follow me here, Adrick."

"Of course, my lord. Just making certain my services are available if needed."

"I think I can manage fine without you for the next thirty minutes. I did fine while you went north, didn't I?"

Adrick tipped his head. "I made certain you had others available."

"You mean the Saffra magi? I wouldn't have trusted him the same as I trust you, Adrick. He serves the King of Saffra while you—"

"I serve the Conclave, no different than Davin, my lord."

Her father turned and frowned at Adrick. "But you represent the realm first. That is why I allow you to advise me."

Adrick's head dipped, revealing the top of his balding leathery head. Deeply tanned skin flushed with a deeper red for a moment. "I do serve the realm. That is why I went north to aid in the... proceedings...but I have never hidden the fact I serve as a representative of the Conclave, my lord."

Her father twisted the dark band on his middle finger, a

marker given to him by Adrick. "And the Conclave serves the realm."

Adrick said nothing, only bowed his head again.

Her father turned to Desia and held out his arm. She took it with a wide smile. They started from the room in a slow walk, Desia's dress swishing across the stone. The massive set of doors leading toward the chapel opened as he approached, and they stepped through, disappearing.

Adrick looked from Ferisa to Eris. For a moment, it seemed as if he wanted to say something, but he changed his mind and turned away, departing through the small door they'd entered from.

Eris waited for her father to return. She would be next, paraded up to stand alongside her sister during the ceremony, asked to kneel before the Sacred Mother and swear to aid in upholding the vows Jasi would say. As if Eris could ensure the vows were upheld. Once Jasi left the capital, she wasn't sure she'd ever see her sister again, except at formal events. After all the times Jasi had tormented her over the years, that should provide some satisfaction. Instead, Eris felt strangely empty. Jasi was moving on, as she was always meant to, starting her new life with her prince in a strange and exotic land. Eris would stay behind, stuck in nothing but sameness.

The great double doors opened, and her father reappeared. He smiled at her, his dark eyes twinkling as he neared. He ran a hand through his black hair and stuck out his arm. "Eris," he said.

She nodded, and he started forward.

They walked slowly, her father giving her the chance to glide as she'd been taught. She held the bouquet of flowers Jasi had chosen for her, bright corinths and dahlias, flowers she would never have chosen for herself.

As they neared the door, he leaned toward her. "After Desia, this will be you."

She looked up at him, afraid to say anything. That was what she feared most.

"It may seem a long way off now, but Jasi waited. Well, we all waited for the right union. Desia, I think, already knows who she prefers. Making that arrangement will not be nearly as difficult. And given the current circumstances, it might provide us a certain level of protection. But I haven't heard from you."

Eris hadn't realized Desia was already planning her arrangement, but of course she was. So like Jasi in that. The sooner Desia married, the sooner the pressure would begin to build on Eris. She was expected to work with her mother and decide on the union. For so long she'd figured she had plenty of time, but maybe she'd been wrong.

"I might choose to serve the Sacred Mother," she said.

Her father chuckled. The doors opened before them. "An honorable choice, and one I'd support, but you don't have the faith needed to serve the Sacred Mother. In that, you're too much like me, I'm afraid."

Eris frowned, but her father was right. She didn't have the faith that serving the Sacred Mother would require. Worse, even her father thought she had nothing else to offer except to marry.

"We'll have to find someone willing to support your individuality, I think. So much like Rochelle." He spoke her name wistfully as he glanced at Eris's eggshell dress. She hadn't been able to help herself and had added a few strips of color along the hem. Standing still they weren't even visible, but her father had noticed.

"You miss her?" They were always close.

He patted her hand. "As much as you, I suspect. Had she only..." He stopped before finishing. "I hope she found what she was looking for. That's all I really want for you. Happiness."

"I won't find happiness marrying some stranger like Jasi."

"Your mother was a stranger to me, once." He sighed. "Already, you are much like Rochelle. Don't follow her in this as well."

Eris didn't need him to explain what he meant. Rochelle had refused to marry, spending her days wandering. Always reading, she'd claimed she was a scholar or a philosopher or…whatever had struck her fancy that day.

"Sometimes you have to put away what you want and do what is needed. That is what your mother did, and it has turned out well. Now Jasi will see if it can happen for her. Soon it will be your turn, Eris."

Her throat seemed to swell as she tried to say something. "I don't want to study with Lira any longer," she finally said.

He looked at her, and a bemused smile crossed his face. "I've heard you don't always agree with her methods."

Eris shook her head. "It's not that. I don't think we know—"

"You won't convince your mother to let you out of your studies, so you might as well stop trying."

Eris swallowed and fell silent. Even her father wouldn't listen.

Her father took her silence as assent and they started into the chapel.

A harpist played near the altar. Desia knelt before the High Priestess who would oversee the ceremony. People from all over the realm filled the benches--some she recognized, others she did not. She made a point of not looking at any faces. Sentries were stationed at the end of each row, either as an honorary guard or as protection. They stared straight ahead, hands on hilts. When Eris reached the altar, her father kissed her on the cheek and released her from his arm. She slid toward Desia and knelt alongside her.

Jacen stood off to the side, dressed in the royal navy and green silks. She hadn't seen much of him since his return from the north, just heard rumors of what had happened. The dark hollows under his eyes were new, and he seemed gaunter than before. His long hair had lost some of its luster. He made a point of not meeting anyone's eyes.

Eris hated how he looked and wondered how much of what

happened was Lira's fault. She'd seen her slip flowers into his satchel before he left. At the time it meant nothing to Eris, just another oddity of the Mistress of Flowers. Now she wondered. Had she *targeted* Jacen?

If only her parents would listen. But bringing it up to her father had only irritated him. And her mother—Eris looked to where the queen stood, flowers woven into her hair—she'd hear nothing against Lira. Especially from Eris.

Eris watched Lira during the first part of the ceremony. A band of flowers circled her neck, each brightly colored. Her lips moved in time with the priestess, as if saying words too soft to hear. To Eris, it seemed the color faded from her flowers as she went on.

Adrick stood near where her father would stand. His face appeared more reddened than usual, and his eyes were tight. He tried to make it look like he watched the ceremony, but Eris couldn't help noticing how he fixed on Lira out of the corner of his eyes.

Eris spent the rest of the ceremony looking from Lira to Adrick. The ceremony itself passed in a blur. Ferisa and Desia kneeling on either side. Jasi entering at one point, her father leading her proudly toward the priestess. Then Petra with his parents flanking him, dressed in a sand-colored wrapping. Another wrapping twisted around his head, almost obscuring his eyes.

When they reached the altar, the priestess went through the motions of the ceremony. Eris lost focus as Jasi and Petra said their vows to each other. And then the ceremony concluded, the priestess leading Jasi and Petra from the chapel to stand under the rising moon to speak their promise to the Sacred Mother.

Finally, Eris stood. Her parents made their way toward the back of the chapel. Adrick followed close behind, leaning on his silver staff. An older man in a flowing, crimson-colored robe stood prepared to follow behind. Completely bald and deeply tanned, he looked even more leathery than Adrick. A deep frown wrinkled his cheeks and black eyes scanned the chapel before settling on Eris and her sisters. Eventually, his gaze drifted to Lira.

Eris wished she understood what was happening between Lira and the magi. Her father sided with Adrick, and her mother clearly supported Lira. But if the magi were right, then Lira aided the north. Varden. And Jacen had barely survived his time in the north.

She suppressed a sigh, wishing she knew more. But knowing more wasn't her place, if she even had one.

CHAPTER 14

The next few days passed in a blur. There was music and feasting and chaos throughout the palace for three days. And then it ended, the people departing, leaving the palace cast in a strange pall as Jasi and the delegation from Saffra departed while Tholen organized an assault on Varden.

"I will miss you," Eris said.

They stood in the garden, looking out over the flowers. Jasi had come to see the garden one more time before leaving Eliara. She stood dressed in a deep red dress, a yellow stone now stuck to her forehead in the style of Saffra. A hint of sadness edged her eyes.

"You won't. You're glad to get rid of me."

"Not really. That leaves only Desia before me."

Jasi turned and looked at her with an amused expression. "Please try to do what Lira asks of you."

Eris didn't answer. Instead, she nodded. How could Eris explain her fear of what Lira intended?

"Mother wants all of us to find happiness. I think seeing you succeed with Lira would bring her much joy."

Though she didn't say it, Eris grasped the unspoken comment. With Jasi leaving. "Will Lira be coming with you?" she asked.

"Not at first," Jasi answered. "The storm affected her more than she lets on. And you know how much damage the garden took. I think she'll need some time to rebuild before she comes for a visit. By then, I should have time to begin my own garden."

Her own garden? A shiver worked through her. Did that mean Lira hoped to push her influence to the south and into Saffra? Would she use Jasi for that? And what of Desia when it was her turn to marry?

"With parisals?"

Jasi didn't take the bait. "I have learned much about flowers from Lira. She even lent me a book on desert flowers which might be useful in Saffra. Quite an impressive book. The detail of the diagrams is nothing like I've ever seen."

A Feliran book, Eris suspected. Much like the shade plants she'd found. But while Eris had to steal the book from Lira to have the chance to read it, Lira simply gave it to Jasi.

"I'm sure your garden will be lovely. I hope Petra appreciates what you have learned."

Jasi's face clouded briefly before clearing. "He finds this garden to be a bit...ostentatious. Perhaps coming from Saffra, it is. That's why I think Lira's suggestion of focusing on desert flowers will be better. I wouldn't want to come with too many changes and have him rebuke me."

Eris looked at her sister and realized Jasi felt even more anxious than she. Jasi was leaving the only home she'd ever known, traveling to a foreign land, and expected to eventually become queen. How scared must she be?

Yet, standing dressed in a gown made of bolder colors than any Jasi would ever choose on her own, Eris couldn't help but think how lovely she looked. Her golden hair caught the sunlight and practically glowed. Her cheeks were painted with just enough rose to give them a pleasing blush. Even the way she stood looked regal. As much as Jasi might fear it, she had been raised for this moment. She would make a perfect queen.

Not like Eris. Ever closer to whatever fate she'd face, she didn't think she was raised for anything like Jasi. Or even Desia. Both of her older sisters carried themselves with dignity she couldn't replicate. And baby Ferisa, already pleasing the Sacred Mother. It was increasingly clear that Eris had no place.

"Jasi," she began, "you will be the perfect Queen of Saffra someday."

Jasi smiled. She leaned toward Eris and gave her a small hug.

CHAPTER 15

erran shook his head as Eris asked the question, not even letting her finish. "No, my lady. I won't let you go to the Svanth Forest. And you shouldn't even be asking, considering all of your father's men are marching north."

"Won't let me?" she asked. It was not the response she had expected. She'd thought she might have to convince him to accompany her—had looked forward to the idea, if she was being honest with herself—and might even have to coax him a little, but adamant refusal? After Jasi had left, she'd decided she couldn't just wait around any longer. She needed to see what Lira hid from her about the flower. She might not have a place, but that didn't mean she couldn't still be useful.

They stood near the edge of the garden. Eris had found him working, hands buried in soil as he continued work on repairing the storm damage. Terran had smiled as she approached, probably thinking she wanted to play their game of finding unusual flowers. At first she'd agreed, uncertain how to present her offer to him. So far today he'd managed to show her three flowers she suspected would have impressed Lira had she brought them to her before finding the teary star. Why hadn't she met Terran before?

The sun was up, high and hot today, but thick clouds pushed in from the west. In the shade along the edge of the garden, cooler air still smelled of the gentle rain they had received last night. Each day since the heavy storm had been the same. The threat of rain hung over the otherwise clear skies during the daytime. At night, the rain came, sometimes fast and heavy, other times soft and gentle. There had not been the same ferocity as during the initial storm, but Eris imagined Lira battling with the Conclave to keep the skies clear, before finally relenting and relaxing at night.

After Jasi left, everything felt off. Desia and Ferisa remained tied up in classes with Lira. Jacen still hadn't returned from escorting Jasi to the borders of Eliara, though she wondered how much of that had to do with him simply taking his time in returning. And she still had not found anything in the library. The book she'd pilfered from Lira's room was mostly an index of shade flowers. She patted a pocket hidden in the folds of her long brown dress where she'd hidden the book. Somehow she would have to return it to Lira.

"My lady," Terran said, having the decency to at least look ashamed. "It would not be proper for me to escort you out of the city. You would need a full guard and the king's permission. And after the wedding, there is no way the king will allow—"

"I should think I would know what I need, Terran," she said, jabbing him in the chest with her finger.

He took a step away, holding his hands out in front of him and shaking his head. "You know I can't do this, Eris," he whispered. Even now, he struggled with saying her name aloud, as if doing so would get him into trouble.

"Why not, Terran? You told me you came from the northlands. Lanerth, I believe?"

Terran nodded carefully. "Lanerth is not the Svanth Forest."

Eris smiled. Finally the studies her parents forced on her would have some use. "Lanerth is on the western edge of the Svanth. I would imagine anyone raised in Lanerth would have familiarity with the forest. At the least, he would be able to lead me to the forest, but he probably knows how to navigate the woods as well."

Terran closed his eyes, a pained expression turning his mouth. He shook his head and wiped his hands roughly on his sleeves. "You don't need a guide to reach the forest, Eris. You could follow the Kingsroad."

"The Kingsroad does not lead into the forest."

Terran sighed, opening his eyes to look at her with an expression that seemed to beg her to do anything else. "The Svanth is not safe for you. There are things there—"

"You think I cannot manage in the forest?" she asked angrily. That might be worse than simply refusing to accompany her.

Terran shook his head and then grabbed her sleeve as he ducked behind one of the larger planters. Eris glanced back. Master Nels checked on a bed of camogines, pulling their long narrow petals out to examine them before letting the petals roll back into place. Nels saw them standing near the planter and frowned.

Did it anger Nels how she bothered Terran? For an assistant gardener, he was quite knowledgeable and seemed to truly enjoy what he did, especially sharing what he learned. Most times, Eris enjoyed how Terran worked as they talked, especially with as much as he'd already shown her. He made a point of talking her through what he did as he checked the soil for dampness, looked for pests on the flowers or stalks, or simply shuffled arrangements around. Lately, there had been a lot of simply moving flowers as Lira's new arrangement took shape.

"I know you can manage." Terran leaned toward the nearest bed of flowers. Confident hands parted the stalks, prying them so he could see down to the soil where he squinted, fingers working in the dirt. He pulled up a pinch of soil and sighed. "There are things other than plants in the forest. Animals who call it home. They are not always welcoming of intruders."

Eris laughed, and Terran looked over, offended. "My father's men hunt near the Svanth. I have seen what they bring back. Boars and deer mostly."

Terran spun the long narrow flowerbed away from the others, setting it in the middle of the path. "There's a significant difference between hunting in the Svanth and hunting near it, my lady," he said, dipping his finger into the soil of the next bed. He seemed satisfied with what he saw and left the box alone. "The boars and deer your father's men capture have usually fled from something else."

She laughed again. "My aunt used to tell me tales like that when I was younger. Stories of ancient and ferocious creatures at the heart of the old growth trees, places men weren't allowed to visit for fear of what might befall them." She didn't think about her Aunt Rochelle often—doing so was difficult since her death—but had loved listening to her spin tales of magical places and strange creatures. Even then Eris knew they were too impossible to exist.

"Your aunt sounds wise."

Eris shrugged. That wasn't the word others usually used to describe Rochelle.

They walked along the outer wall and neared where she'd first found the teary star. Every time they came close to this part of the garden, she paused and looked up, hoping that the bed might have returned to the garden and she might find the vine draping down, the strange braided tendrils twisting together as it worked its way out of the wooden box. Each time she felt disappointed to see nothing more than the spicy-scented hopis vine. Today was no different than any other.

With the heavy rains, the vines had flourished. Long, thin creepers clung to the stone as they grew wildly along the wall.

Small buds of green and yellow, little more than the size of the nail on her small finger, popped where the vines branched. Nearer the base of the box, a few buds were thicker and almost threatened to flower.

Terran continued to work, looking at the plants and then checking the soil before moving to the next one. Eris watched him, curious what he did.

"My mother always said my aunt was troubled," she said. Thinking of her aunt brought memories of a different time, before Lira had come and built her gardens and separated her from her sisters.

Terran looked over at her.

"I look much like her, I have been told. I suppose that means I'm troubled as well."

"You're not troubled, but I can't decide if you *are* trouble. Especially if you think I'm going to take you to the forest."

Eris smiled at the gentle teasing. Perhaps the idea of leaving the city and heading to the forest had been a bit rash, especially if staying meant she might have more time with Terran.

She shook the thought away. She couldn't have such thoughts, not with what her father had planned for her. Like Jasi, she would be used for political gain, regardless of what she might want.

"What are you doing?" she asked, after he had pinched another clump of dirt and held it up to his face. He sniffed it before shaking his head and taking the bed and setting it out on the path with a grunt. "And can I help with any of it?"

"Since the wedding, the last few storms carried new critters to the garden. Master Nels has us looking over the plants each day for them. There is a particularly nasty red-bodied beetle that can chew through a plant in a day."

Eris looked at the plant he had set aside, remembering the book she'd seen Master Billiken reading. Was this what the Conclave was after now—trying to destroy it from within? But she didn't see any beetles on the plant. "Are they on this?"

Terran shook his head. "I haven't seen any of the beetles today. But I'm also checking for armyworms. They like to crawl on the roots and will destroy the flowers that way. Never had much a problem with them until recently."

She looked at the dahlias before standing again and sighing. Terran continued working, careful to keep moving around the edge of the garden, his fingers separating and probing quickly as he went. Every so often he would shift one of the beds out of its place and set it onto the path.

"What will you do with these?" She nodded to the bed he'd set on the path.

Terran looked up from where he hunched over a yellow tulis. "Have to comb through the soil for other worms. The worms get destroyed. Most of the plants will be reset." He stood up, a look of victory on his face. A small red insect pinched between his fingers. As she watched, he squished it with a distasteful expression on his face before wiping his hands on his pants. "Found one."

Taking Terran with her might serve another purpose, she realized. What did she care if the gardens were weakened, especially if Lira worked against her father? "Clearly this is important work, Terran. You would rather do this than help me travel to the Svanth Forest?"

He looked hurt. "It *is* important work. In a garden this size, without the gardeners, these pests would consume the flowers. Master Nels thinks they are extra aggressive this season. Hasn't explained why."

She crossed her arms over her chest. Terran started to reach toward her but caught himself, instead wiping his hands on his pants again. As a gardener, he had no right to touch the princess and should not dare do so. Of course, she should not be talking to him so freely either. Eris probably overstepped the bounds of decency by spending so much time in the garden with him. The way she spoke to him probably placed him in a difficult position. Asking him to lead her to the forest put him at even more risk.

Suddenly, she felt terrible even asking. She *was* trouble.

Terran smiled at her with his lopsided grin, and Eris felt herself relax a little. "Give me a chance to see if I can help you with what you need to know. I have a stack of books I haven't even looked at yet."

Eris studied the hopis where they reached the top of the palace wall as she nodded. Maybe she wouldn't have to travel out of the city. Honestly, she wouldn't even know how to begin arranging travel for a trip to the forest. Even following the Kingsroad, she'd likely get lost. She could ask Jacen, but her brother would just as likely tell her parents what she planned as help her.

A relieved look crossed Terran's face. "I'll look through my collection and bring you what might work." He swallowed, stopping as he reached for her again. "Don't worry—we'll find something in those books. As many as Master Nels has stacked there for me to study, it would be impossible *not* to find anything. Promise not to do anything...rash...before I have a chance to look though?"

He seemed relieved when she nodded.

Nels appeared near one of the flowerbeds, and Terran gave her a nervous grin before hurrying away toward the nearest flowerbeds where he continued combing through the plants and pinching the soil. Eris watched him until he disappeared along the path and then turned away.

Nels studied her for a while, but Eris only looked at the wall, staring at the ledges set into the wall as she wished she could find the flower again here. Even though Terran planned to look, she didn't expect him to find anything useful unless he found Feliran's book. So far, books had failed her.

More than that, the thought of escaping the palace and making her way to the forest excited her. Just thinking of it gave her a thrill. Unlike Jacen, she and her sisters were confined within the palace and its walls. And Jasi. Even Jasi now got to have an adventure as she traveled south to Saffra. As nervous as she'd been before leaving, Eris saw the excitement she felt as well.

She could ask her father's permission to travel to the forest, but he would send her with a handful of men. And while they might all be determined to protect her honor, they would likely do little more than prevent her from entering the forest to explore.

But Terran promised to look for her. She needed to give him the chance to search his books and see if he came up with anything useful. If he didn't, she would have to travel to the forest on her own. And then she would somehow convince Terran to accompany her.

CHAPTER 16

"*Y*ou didn't waste any time returning."

Eris looked up at Jacen as he made his way toward her. He wore flowing black pants and his shirt hung open. A chain symbolizing the Sacred Mother hung across his chest. Haunted blue eyes which hadn't been the same since returning from the north flashed at her as she approached. A dark smile pulled at his lips.

"You miss me, sister?"

He paused as he approached, looking over the garden with an expression of curiosity. He wiped an arm across his face, smearing the sweat dripping from his brow. Were she to do the same, she'd have to fear her mother admonishing her. Jacen...as the crown prince, they left him alone. He never caused enough trouble for their parents to pay him much mind anyway.

Eris wondered whether he would keep the garden when he assumed the throne. Likely not. Jacen had no fondness for the flowers, though whoever he chose for his bride might disagree.

"You went with Jasi?" She knew it hurt Jacen not being allowed to go north with Tholen.

"You know I did. With the attack…" He shook his head. "Father wanted an honor guard to escort them through our lands."

"How far did you ride?"

Jacen shrugged. "What does it tell you that I'm back barely two days later?"

"Why didn't you see them to the edge of the realm?"

He shrugged again and coughed. "The King's magi felt it unnecessary."

Eris frowned at that. "The magi sent you away?"

The dark smile on his face widened as he started walking, looking nothing like the Jacen she used to know. Eris made a point of keeping up and walking alongside him. "I think he feared my intention with the beautiful Princess Shanis."

"And what intention is that?"

Jacen winked but didn't say anything.

"So where are you going now?" she asked. Jacen had returned late last night and now already headed toward the stables again. The short sword hanging from his belt and the bow slung over his shoulder told her he didn't intend to return quickly.

"I'll be leaving for the north tomorrow. I thought today I would hunt."

"You're going by yourself?"

Jacen stopped and looked her over. His eyes flashed with anger that slowly faded. "I think I have proven I can handle a bow. Do I need to demonstrate for you?"

They entered the stables. The air smelled of dung and hay, and she sneezed.

Jacen looked at her with amusement flashing in his eyes. "This isn't the best place for a proper princess," he suggested.

This time, she did punch him. "I've never been a proper princess."

Jacen grabbed her arm as she hit him, squeezing more than necessary. "Careful. Too much of that behavior, and father will marry you off to the Lord of Hops. I hear since his wife died, he's looking to take on another bride."

"Father would never do that," she said, jerking her hand back.

Jacen shrugged. "Jasi helps bind the south. I suspect Desia will be used for the north. That leaves you, little sister. Not much left. The Isle of Hops would keep old Arag from pestering father too much and keep the shipping lanes clear."

Horror spread over Eris at the idea. Jacen could be right. He'd actually spent the necessary time studying politics and geography. And who else would want the third daughter?

"Don't worry. Arag is pretty old. He might even die before you'd get married. And I'm not so sure his daughter wants the competition for his seat."

Jacen reached the stall for his tall roan stallion. The horse flicked its tail as Jacen stepped into the stall and turned its ears toward Eris. Jacen patted its strawberry sides for a moment, murmuring something soothing under his breath meant only for the horse. Then he turned and started saddling the horse, waiving off the stable master running over to help. He cinched straps tight and patted the horse again.

"You haven't said where you're going."

"Doesn't matter, does it?" Jacen said.

She narrowed her eyes. "Why doesn't it matter?"

Jacen clasped the reins and walked the horse from the stables. He paused at the open door, looking around at the palace spreading out before him. "Best you get back to your lessons, don't you think?"

"Let me come with you."

Jacen chuckled as he swung up into the saddle. "You know I can't do that."

"Why?"

He looked down at her. "It's not proper."

"Riding with my brother isn't proper?" she asked. She tried channeling the same tone Jasi always managed when admonishing Jacen but didn't think she succeeded.

"By yourself? Or did you think to bring your handmaidens with us?"

"When have you seen me dragging handmaidens anywhere?"

He said nothing.

"Besides, since the wedding, everything just feels…off," she started. "I need to get away from the palace, even if it's for the day."

Jacen seemed to consider for a moment before nodding. "Just for short ride. But you're not going dressed like that."

She looked down at her dress. Strips of white met bright orange and reds, stitched together so it looked like petals on a flower. She wore it hoping to annoy Lira, but hadn't even seen the mistress of flowers in the last day. Instead, she simply wandered the garden.

"Fine. Then you'll wait for me."

Jacen frowned before finally nodding.

"Why are we going north?" she asked. "If Varden is out there—"

"Varden won't attack in our lands. And we won't get close enough to make it matter."

"But with what happened to you—"

Eris sat on a short grey mare, nothing like the powerful horse Jacen rode. He refused to listen when she'd argued she could ride a larger horse, trying to convince him this mare would slow them down, but he ignored her pleas.

"If you planned on asking so many questions, I would have left you back at the palace."

"You don't want to talk at all?"

He looked over at her with a feigned threat. "Too many questions and maybe I'll ride you to Hops myself."

They had ridden for nearly an hour. Jacen looked comfortable in the saddle, riding slightly ahead, careful to look back every so often to make certain Eris was still with him. The sun rose toward its zenith, burning down and making her hot in spite of her thin riding dress. In her haste to change, she'd forgotten to take off the heavy slip she'd worn under her other dress. Jacen had only laughed when she rejoined him in the stables.

"What else is to the north?" she asked after a while.

They made their way mostly west, slowly veering slightly north. The ground rolled around them, nothing but green hills scattered with the occasional copse of towering trees.

"You get the plains. Try not to go there if you don't have to."

"Why?"

Jacen laughed. "Grasses up over your head with sharp blades that can practically peel the flesh from you. It's like they want to lap at your blood. Blasted grass. Can't convince Father we should just burn the field down. Probably good soil their farmers could use, but he said Aunt Rochelle always liked it so he won't."

Eris shivered at the thought of burning a field of grass. Doing so reminded her too much of what she'd heard the magi talking about doing. But grasses like Jacen described weren't any type of garden, no more than the short green grasses flowing over these hills were. And she remembered seeing similar grasses growing at the palace. Needlegrass. The gardeners working around it all wore long sleeves and gloves. Eris thought them silly until she'd come too close one time and scored the fabric of her dress. Even in gloves, she suspected the gardeners weren't entirely safe.

"Do you ever hunt around the forest?" She thought of Terran and how he'd described the forest; the anxiety he seemed to have about her riding to the Svanth on her own.

"Which forest?"

"Well...isn't the Svanth north of the plains?"

Jacen laughed. The sound disappeared into the gusting wind. "The Svanth is pretty far north. Not sure we're going to make it there in just one day." He paused and turned to look at her. "Not sure that's the kind of ride you'd be looking for anyway. You'd have to sleep out in the open and risk the rains."

She spurred her horse a little faster to catch him. "You think I'm so delicate I couldn't handle it?"

"I think all my sisters are too delicate. No offense, Eris, but you spend your days wandering through the garden, looking at pretty flowers, and making arrangements. At your age, I spent my day learning the sword and battle formations and political alliances and..." He shook his head. "Just different. Not bad or good, just how the Sacred Mother made us."

Eris couldn't help but think his calling her delicate was some kind of insult, as much as Jacen might not have intended it to be. "I could have learned the sword," she muttered.

Jacen just laughed.

"Besides, there's value in what I've learned."

He looked over, the smile spreading across his face again. "Oh? And I need to know the names of this flower?" he said, pointing toward a pale yellow corinth. "Or that one?" He pointed to a cluster of tulis.

Eris was surprised to see any growing here. "And knowing how to slaughter a boar is such a great skill?"

"You can eat the boar."

Jacen made a point of letting his horse trample the tulis as he passed, ignoring Eris glaring at him as he did.

They rode in silence for a while. Eris hated that he was probably right. Knowing how to fight and hunt and work within political alliances was probably more valuable than what she'd learned. She might be able to see how the gardeners placed certain arrangements, could name more flowers than she could count, but she couldn't feed anyone with that knowledge. She couldn't protect her family like Jacen could.

They stopped near a copse of trees. A thin stream burbled through, and they both took a drink. Jacen pulled thick strips of jerky out of his pocket and filled a waterskin she hadn't seen him carrying.

Eris took a bite and chewed it slowly. She sat with her back resting against the tree, the horse's reins held loosely in her hand, and sighed. Jacen's words troubled her. With as little as she'd focused on her studies, even Jasi had more use than her. Not just being the oldest daughter, but she'd gained the skills needed to serve as queen. One day, she would rule Saffra alongside Petra. Desia might marry into some northern lord, helping her father solidify an alliance. What would Eris do?

"What happened while you were gone?"

Jacen blinked as he took a deep breath. His eyes went flat. "Whole company was attacked. Most men were lost." He shook his head. "A few...Tholen, me, Dens...made it away." He closed his eyes. "Didn't even see the attackers coming."

"Where were you?" She wondered how close to Varden they might have been.

"No more than a day's ride to the border. Getting ready to turn back. Had Adrick not arrived..."

He didn't finish. Eris could tell from his expression that he didn't want to say anything more.

"I'm sorry, Jacen."

He nodded, his jaw tensing as he did, and his eyes turned a hard blue. "Me too." He looked over at her, and something in his eyes softened. "After what happened, maybe Father won't push you anywhere you don't want to go. Jasi got to choose, didn't she?"

Eris sniffed. "I don't think Saffra was what Jasi had in mind."

"Why not? How is Saffra any worse than a Varden lord?"

Eris shook her head. "We haven't fought the north for as long as I've been alive."

"Until now." Anger heated his words, and his face flushed.

"Why do you think they suddenly attacked?" She wondered how much of it had to do with Lira. When she got back to Eliara, she vowed to convince her father to look into what she'd learned.

Jacen's eyes narrowed. "Have you ever traveled there?" He stood over her, leaning close. "Have you seen the way they look at us? The way they view the kingdom? The hatred so many of the northerners feel for us? Do you really think marrying Jasi off to one of the northern kings would change that?"

"Marrying Desia will?"

Jacen sagged. "No. That's why I've been trying to tell Father not to make those arrangements. Thankfully, Adrick helped steer Jasi toward a southern alignment."

"And will that help? Will it keep you safe the next time?"

Jacen closed his eyes and shook his head. "I don't know—"

He never had the chance to finish.

Something struck him on the side of the head, and he sagged forward, blood dribbling down his temple. Eris looked up, heart pounding, but didn't see what hit him.

Then she was struck.

A blurred shape moved around the tree as blackness overcame her.

CHAPTER 17

*E*ris awoke with a pounding headache.

She lay on her side on nothing more than a hard dirt path. Someone had removed most of her outer clothing, leaving her clad only in her thin shift. Cold air blew over her. The heavy scent of earth filled her nostrils, mixed with a sharp sulfury stink. Her mouth tasted of blood, and her tongue throbbed.

Darkness surrounded her. She heard crackling flames somewhere behind her which provided just a hint of light, but nothing else.

She shivered...or tried to. Her hands were trapped behind her, bound together. Eris could not even move them except to flex her fingers. Anytime she tried shifting, pain shot through her shoulders. Even her legs were tied. From what she could tell, they were bound to her arms as well.

What had happened?

Her mind was foggy, and she struggled to remember. She had been sitting near the tree talking to Jacen.

Jacen. What happened to him?

Eris heard a rough voice behind her. "I think she's awake."

"Doesn't matter now."

"Might be easier with her awake."

One of the voices grunted. "Or not. Unconscious can't cause problems."

The other laughed. "She's just a princess. You think she can cause problems?"

"Only if we're caught." The other coughed quietly. "Go drag her over to the fire. Probably should feed her. But don't touch her—we have to keep her alive for now."

Eris froze, waiting for one of her captors to come over, wondering who would have abducted her before the answer came to her. Northmen. Varden.

She smelled him first. There was the heavy scent of smoke edged with a hint of char. Beneath the smoke was something else, a bitter odor, that of sulfur. It grew stronger. Eris knew of flowers that smelled the same, flowers she had always avoided because the stink would linger on her hands. She could think of nothing else like it.

Only when he loomed behind her did she hear him. His footsteps were light and soft, barely making a sound as he crouched behind her. Instead of lifting her, he grabbed her bindings and simply pulled her along the ground. Her shoulder and back dug into soft ground as she was pulled along. Dirt and mud bounced into her mouth.

"Fighting won't do you any good," he said.

Eris considered saying something but thought better of it. All she had to do was stay alive. Someone would notice her missing and report to her father. How long before her father's men came looking for her?

How long had she already been gone?

With one final heave, her captor dragged her up to a hard rock and leaned her against it. She couldn't see anything, but at least the firelight gave off enough light she might have a chance. Now she wanted to know who had captured her. And why.

"You made a mistake," she said.

"Quiet," one of the men said.

Eris shifted , trying to adjust so she could see her captors but couldn't. "If you're after ransom, you chose the wrong daughter." But if they had Jacen too, it wouldn't matter.

She heard coarse laughter.

"She is fierce. Surprising, considering the others."

"You saw what happened."

The other grunted. "I saw. But that's not possible with her. Not from a princess."

"I thought they were all scattered."

"They were. All but *her*. Saw her when he came for the wedding. That's why we were summoned."

One of the men grunted but neither said anything more.

Eris lay where she was, resting her back against the rock. For a while, she tried to slide her hands together, thinking if she was given enough time and slack, she might be able to free her wrists. Then she could work on her feet. The ropes bound her too tightly. Any movement seemed to do little other than send pain shooting up her shoulders and across her back.

She pressed her hands against the rock, hoping it might have a sharp edge that she could use to saw through the ropes, but found nothing useful to tear at her bindings.

Eris was trapped and at the mercy of her captors.

She chose to stay motionless and silent. After a while, one of the men shoved a piece of hard bread between her lips. Eris spat it out, unwilling to risk whatever poison these men might have for her. Or worse. Her Aunt Rochelle had told stories of men using poison to get their victims to say something they would never otherwise say and do things they would never otherwise do.

"Eat," the man said, shoving it against her closed lips. "You won't get much more than this."

She shook her head as she spat out what remained in her mouth. She tasted dry crumbs and pushed them from her mouth with her tongue.

"Let her starve," the other man said. He had a deeper voice and a heavy northern accent.

"We only need her for a while longer anyway. Besides, we've got the other one, too."

They had Jacen. Her father would send men for him, but how long before they knew they were missing?

"Only if your plan works. If not..."

"Not my plan."

"His plan then. It still needs to work."

"If not, then we leave her. Either way, it won't matter."

"When my father's men find me—" she started, but one of the men cut her off.

"By the time your father sends men who can find you, it will be too late."

"Too late for what?" she asked, trying to twist her neck. All she managed to do was wrench her back, leaving her feeling worse than before.

"For you. Them. Everyone."

A calloused hand struck her face painfully, and she fell into unconsciousness.

Eris shivered.

She was slung over a horse, arms trailing behind her and tied snugly with rope. Her legs were bound the same, leaving her unable to move as they clopped slowly along the cobbled road. The Kingsroad. Her father's pet project, extending his reach and a promise of protection far across the realm, was visible beneath the horse.

The air had grown cooler and damp. The sky remained a murky grey that really hadn't changed since first light this morning. She felt naked and exposed wearing nothing more than the thin shift. If not for the burning at her wrists and ankles from the rope, she would feel even colder.

She heard her captors but still had not seen them.

By now, she suspected they had put something in the water they forced down her throat. Eris had tried not to drink, but the longer she went, the thirstier she became. As much as she didn't want to swallow their tainted water, she knew some of it dripped down her throat and into her stomach. She hated herself for wanting to swallow it.

They rarely spoke. Other than learning they had no intention of ransoming her off, she did not know what they wanted from her.

Her body ached all over from the way they had her tied. Face-down across the horse, she had to twist her head to keep the stink of its hide out of her nostrils. They moved at a plodding pace and each step jarred her. The sky was too grey and overcast to get a sense of direction, but from the way the air had cooled, she suspected they moved north.

The legs of three other horses moved in and out of view. A captor to each horse. She knew of two—those she'd heard the first night—but didn't yet know if there was another on the third horse. If she could only move...

Eris continued to look for any way to free herself from her binding. So far, there had been none. Her captors were nothing if not careful. Instead, she had to be content with the possibility of learning the reason for her capture.

After a while, they slowed. One of the men slipped a dark sack over her head, just a small hole cut into it for her to breathe through, and smacked her on the backside. She tensed, fresh fear racing through her as she wondered if they might abuse her. If they didn't want ransom, they might have a different use for her in mind. Lands to the far west used women like that, places she'd heard about in stories.

She had to suppress a bitter laugh at the thought. Again, one of her sisters would have been a better choice.

Instead, she wondered what Terran would think of her missing. Would he worry about her or would he simply be happy the princess was gone? But there wasn't anything Terran could do. He was nothing more than a gardener, albeit one with deep brown eyes and soft hands for someone who spent so much time digging in the dirt.

"I think she's fully awake."

"Must be. She tensed when I squeezed her ass."

Eris felt her face go warm. She recognized the voice as the man who'd dragged her toward the fire the night before and then forced bread into her mouth. He had a cruel tone, deep and harsh, each word tearing at her like sharp thorns through her mind.

The other man grunted out a laugh. "She needs to remain whole or else she might be useless to us." His voice was softer but just as hoarse, as if too tired to carry far.

"You should worry about your own. Besides, you don't know what she needs to do."

"No. And neither do you, but she'll be little use to us if she's mute."

There was a dark laugh. "I'd leave her mouth alone."

The other man shuffled toward them. Eris held a sliver of hope that they would fight and she could somehow escape. She had no idea what she would do afterwards. But first she needed to get her bindings free.

"After. Then you can play with what's left. Until then, we leave her whole. When they meet us, we'll know what she is to do."

"I'm not certain this one will be of any other use."

"Give it time. If they're right, the demonstration will not take long."

Eris heard a frustrated grunt, and the man stepped away from her.

"You think either of them will make a difference? After everything we've already tried?" This from the deep-voiced man.

"I don't know." He sounded uncertain. "I saw what happened with the last envoy. Only *he* returned."

"I saw as well," he said in a grunt. "That's why I think we might be better off ditching them here."

So Jacen was still with her. But what did they want with both of them?

She suddenly wished she hadn't pushed him to bring her along. If this was only a kidnapping to ransom Jacen, she wouldn't matter.

"I don't dare cross him. Not after what I've seen him do. And we won't be the ones sent to counter the spells this time. Once it is done, the reward for us will be great. Finally, we can work unencumbered. Undo some of these blasted changes the flower bitches made which block our access to the source."

The man nearest her laughed. His hand brushed her leg and rested atop her thigh. Eris held her breath, forcing herself not to react, knowing there was nothing she could do if he wanted to harm her. Or touch her with his rough and familiar way.

She needed to work her hands free. Somehow she had to find a way to at least get that far. And she needed to find out who else had been captured.

"What will happen to the flower mage?"

In spite of herself, Eris tensed as she realized they meant Lira. Was this not about Jacen? Did her abduction have something to do with the Mistress of Flowers?

"If this succeeds, she will be weakened. The last of her gardens will be destroyed. Then we can do whatever we please to her. And the rest of this land."

"And then?" the other asked.

"Then the Conclave can finally work unencumbered." He laughed. "Choose who sits on the throne. Burn these damn grasses away…"

The words hung in the air. Securing the throne. The Conclave.

The *magi* had abducted her?

It made no sense…unless Lira protected the palace, not the magi.

Did her father know?

She thought of the way he trusted Adrick, the way Adrick seemed concerned about helping ensure the safety of Errasn. But what if he wasn't concerned about the kingdom? Could Adrick really have been working against him all this time?

Eris felt like she'd been kicked in the stomach.

All this time she'd thought Lira had been working against the kingdom, but it had been the magi. What hurt the most was how she could have done something…could have stopped them by just telling her father what she'd overheard. Maybe Jacen wouldn't have been hurt, changed by what he'd seen from happy boy she'd known growing up.

She swallowed a lump in her throat. Even knowing her father wouldn't have believed her made it no better. Had it been Jasi or Jacen, he would have believed.

Why did the Sacred Mother have to make her so different?

"We practically have the throne as it is," the nearest man said. He slid forward, running his rough hand down her leg and squeezed her calf painfully. He made a satisfied breath, and she tensed again. "Fighting makes it better," he whispered. He had leaned close, and his voice was hot and moist and fetid.

"The king only thinks he learns the secrets of the Conclave. What he learns only binds him closer. Had it not been for the flower mage, he would have been fully bound by now. None of this would have been necessary." He grunted. "Soon, it won't matter. The Conclave will be fully reborn, and we can finally have these lands."

The man touching her leg laughed. "You speak as if we matter."

"You think that this won't bring you the power you seek?"

The man's hand shifted, sliding up toward her inner thigh. Eris squeezed her legs together and tried to kick, but it did nothing but send pain shooting through her arms. The man laughed.

"That's not the reason I sought the Conclave." Eris felt certain of the northern accent now.

"No?" The other man stepped closer, the sounds of his boots along the hard stone muted in the grey day. "I said leave her," he hissed.

The man grunted as he pulled away, the rough presence of his hand finally leaving her leg.

"Were he here, you would not dare touch her until this is completed."

The other man laughed, deep and derisively. She imagined he had a cruel face and dark eyes. From the way he touched her, she sensed he was muscular. None of the magi she had seen would be described as muscular. That meant someone she had never seen before.

"But he's not. Instead, I'm stuck with you."

"Be glad you are. Anyone else would have little tolerance for these games you think to play."

"If these two don't work, there are two more we can grab."

"You think it so easy? Once it's known they are gone, there will be no getting closer to the others."

Eris felt a flash of pain and fear. Two captors and two remaining.

Eris knew who the others would be. Desia and Ferisa.

At least Jasi was safe.

CHAPTER 18

They rode slowly onward. At some point, they veered off The Kingsroad and tall grasses slashed at Eris's face. Hot blood welled to the surface and ran down her cheeks from tiny slices. For some reason, she thought of how angry her mother would have been to see her like that. Not captured and bound, but injured and bleeding while wearing only her thin white shift, the knife-like grass leaving her disfigured as blood soaked into her underclothes. Even captured, her mother would expect her to be dressed properly.

All the time she had spent in the gardens wasn't the reason Eris recognized the grass. The name of it drifted to the surface of her mind from the conversation she'd had with Jacen as he'd described his desire to burn the field down. With newfound appreciation, she decided it was aptly named.

When her captor noticed she was bleeding, he laughed. She still hadn't seen his face, only flashes of pale, scarred cheeks. The other man stayed away from her, as if content his point had been made. More than once as they rode, a hand crept along her leg or thigh.

She couldn't help but clench her thighs. It did little other than encourage him.

Eris still hadn't heard anything more about Jacen. She assumed he'd been captured along with her, but the magi hadn't mentioned him. Still, if Jacen were captured, their father would send men looking. More than anything, the thought gave her hope.

And her father—and Lira—needed to know what had happened. Eris owed Lira an apology...and an explanation.

But even if Lira knew, what was one woman—regardless of whether she possessed some sort of flower magic—against the Conclave? What was the kingdom?

More than that, she wanted to see Terran, to hear his reassuring voice as he worked, explaining what he did.

If she didn't escape, she might never see him again.

The horses slowed as they moved through the grasses, as if intentionally tormenting her. The farther they rode, the thicker the grasses became, soon rising up over her head, the long needles ripping along her cheeks and arms, tearing her thin shift apart. She imagined she was bloodied and red, but couldn't see anything but the horse's brown hide and flashes of grey from the sky.

Her head pounded from being slung over the horse. Wouldn't it have been simpler to strap her into the saddle? And what had happed to Jacen's and her horses?

The slowed pace left her wondering if they neared the destination. The captors mentioned another several times. Someone they feared. Someone of great power.

She shivered, wondering if it were Adrick.

What would she say to him if she saw him?

After a while, they veered off into trees. Time had lost meaning, and Eris had no idea how long the needlegrass tore at her before finally thinning. Now, wide bases of large trunks were just visible. Undergrowth thinned, the long sharp grasses becoming sparser the closer they came to the trees. A few thorny, flowering shrubs cropped up. Eris didn't recognize the flowers. The air became more damp and earthy, and she breathed it in, trying to ignore the stink of the horse.

Then they stopped.

She held her breath, hopeful they would pull her from the back of the horse and at least lay her on the ground. Even loosening the bindings a little would provide welcome relief. Her shoulders and thighs throbbed. Wrists and ankles burned where the rope rubbed.

Already cool, the temperature dropped again when they reached the shade under the trees. The change reminded her of the palace garden when she neared the wall, of shade and the work she'd put in helping Terran replant the flowers. As much work as it might have been, she'd enjoyed the time, mostly because she had been able to spend it with him.

Her body ached from shivering, and her mouth was dry. The skin of her arms and face from where the needlegrass slashed stung and itched painfully. With nothing else to focus on, the sensation was terrible and maddening.

A soft moan came from near her.

Everything else left her mind, all her own pain, the agony of the bindings on her wrists and ankles, the itching across her skin, the throbbing in her head, all vanished in a strange and sudden protective urge.

"Jacen?" she whispered. He needed to know she was there with him.

There was another soft moan, this time clearly pained. Eris shifted her head, trying and failing to see where he was. The sound came from where the horse's flank blocked her view.

"It's Eris."

She didn't even know if he could hear her. What would happen if her captors learned she tried to speak? After last night, she feared the sudden violence which had knocked her out.

"Eris?"

Her name was whispered and soft.

"I'm here," she said.

"Quiet!"

The man smacked her hard on her back, adding new fire to her injuries. Pain jolted through her shoulders and legs as she spasmed against the bindings. The rope dug into her flesh, and she bit back a scream.

His hand rested again on her thigh, and he squeezed it, massaging her with a repulsive familiarity. "She's a fiery one."

Eris heard footsteps.

"They will be here soon."

"Good. And then I can have this one. They can keep the other for themselves."

"They need them both. We don't know which of them will be successful."

The other man laughed. In the forest, the sound was muted and didn't carry, but he left her alone, relaxing his grip on her thigh as he disappeared.

She didn't hear the other man approach. "You would be wise to remain silent. This will go better for you."

It took Eris a moment to realize he spoke to her. "I'm dead anyway." Her head pounded and thoughts seemed to move slowly.

The magi laughed. Not nearly as deep or rough, the sound was still chilling. "Yes," he admitted. "But you can choose how you leave this world."

In answer, she tried to kick, knowing it was useless.

The magi laughed again, softer and more bitterly. "He's right. You do have fire. Too bad that will not serve you where you must go."

"And where is that?" Her heart hammered. Anger surged through her; anger at being captured, anger at being taunted as she was, anger at the way the other magi thought to touch her—a way that she should only be touched by a man who cared about her.

The rage boiling through her was almost enough to let her tear through her ropes. She kicked again, not caring about the way the ropes pulled on her flesh, ripping through her arms.

A soft whimper came from nearby but nothing else. How badly had they hurt Jacen?

The magi grunted. He stepped closer. She could see his feet. He wore black leather boots and dark pants. There was no sign of the scarlet cloak, as if they sought to hide their presence. She smelled something bitter and fetid, a heavy perfume hung above it all.

"You will go where we cannot."

"Just me?"

"Either of you. It matters not, at least not to me."

"I'm sure Adrick has a plan," she said.

He chuckled. "It's not Adrick you should fear."

Eris tensed. Who else other than Adrick? "Why us?"

The magi laughed and didn't answer. She heard him walk away, the sound of his boots stepping through the underbrush softly moving away from her.

Eris didn't know how long they waited in the trees. Even if it weren't a cloudy grey day, moving out of the grasses and into the heavy tree cover made it difficult to determine how much daylight remained. Minutes or hours could have passed; Eris lost track, able to focus only on the pain working through her and fear for Jacen.

After a while she heard something new, a rustling mixed with heavy hoofbeats across the ground that carried dully into the trees.

"You have them?"

Eris didn't recognize the voice.

"We have them." This from the magi who had not touched her. His voice was harsh but hushed.

"Good."

Footsteps crunched across the ground toward her.

She felt him first. It was like a raw energy rubbing against exposed skin. After the pain of the needlegrass tearing her, this seemed a thousand times worse. Then he leaned close. Unlike the others, he wore his scarlet robe. As he leaned down, she smelled the hot sulfuric scent again. A bald head drifted toward her.

Was it Adrick?

He grabbed her face in a tight grip and turned it to look at him. Surprise bloomed in her when she saw the face. Not Adrick, but one she'd seen before at the wedding.

The High Seat of the Conclave.

Dark eyes narrowed and anger lit across his face. "Which one is this?"

One of the other magi shuffled over. "Does it matter? They all take lessons from her."

The High Seat stood. Energy seemed to crackle from him. "It matters."

He leaned and grabbed her face again. His fingers burned where they touched. "Which one are you?" His voice sounded like a hiss of steam.

Eris coughed and shook her head, but he didn't let go. "Eris. I'm Eris."

The High Seat squeezed her face for a moment and then released. "As I feared. This one is useless to us."

Eris tried to spit at him but had no moisture in her mouth.

One of the magi laughed. "I can find plenty of use for her if you don't want her."

Thunder cracked overhead. "You think too small. Always too small. We need the flower mage's students."

"And Eris Taeresin is widely known to be the least useful of the sisters."

This came from a voice she recognized. It took a moment to remember why. The magi advisor for the King of Saffra, the one she'd overheard speaking to Adrick in the garden, the one who'd come when Lira had fallen during the storm. But if he were here...

"At least we have the other."

"We might need more than one. We do not know how her protections work."

"Why not send them both? Does it matter which one we grabbed?"

Thunder cracked again. "Perhaps I will send you with them when they enter the forest. Trust me when I tell you I have seen firsthand the effect of the enchantments worked on the forest. Though she is only one flower mage, she is skilled. Many have died because of her protections."

Eris twisted in her bindings until she saw a hem of the crimson cloak the High Seat wore. "My father will find out what you have done."

The air sizzled with energy as the High Seat closed in on her. Heat flared across her skin, leaving her feeling ragged and raw.

"I would not count on your father managing anything at this moment," he whispered.

Eris shivered. What did that mean? Had Adrick done something to him? "Why? Why are you doing this?"

"The answer is more than you can understand."

"Lira will stop you. I've seen what she can do, seen how her magic keeps the city clear from your storms. I saw Adrick when he returned from the Svanth Forest. He failed to destroy her garden there," Eris said. Everything made more sense now. The way the magi had acted around Lira. The way Adrick seemed weakened after returning from the north with Jacen. Yet...this was the High Seat of the magi. Could he overpower Lira? Especially if she didn't know what they planned?

The High Seat moved closer as she spoke. The corners of his mouth tugged and his forehead twitched.

She didn't know why she pushed him. "Lira was too strong. And the attack on the palace garden failed. Whatever you plan now will fail! She will—"

Davin knelt in front of her, and his harsh laugh finally cut her off. "I am counting on what the flower mage will do. Either she remains to protect her garden or she comes for you both." His smile deepened. "Yes—I know how you have been left to wander the garden, not allowed to enter the class with your sisters. You should thank me. Soon the flower mage will be weakened beyond what even she can manage to easily repair." He laughed. "I see from your face you know it is true. Too bad you will not be there to see her fall. I wonder if it might not bring you a certain satisfaction, especially given how she has kept you out of lessons with your sisters?"

He watched her, his eyes narrowed and hard. "It must hurt being held out like that, set apart. As if you don't belong. Eris, always so different." He grabbed her face in a rough grip so much like the High Seat and squeezed. "She even looks different than her sisters. None of the lovely grace of the queen. No trace of the fair skin or golden hair. Even her eyes look different. The king claims you take after his side of the family, but I hear even he has doubts. Had I more time, I think it might have been fun to play with those doubts, help him wonder about where you might have acquired your looks. Perhaps your mother wasn't always faithful?" he suggested. "Your father is often away, and there are just so many men in the palace who could satisfy her needs..."

"Enough!" Eris yelled. Anger surged through her, and she kicked again against the ropes holding her arms and legs. Blood dripped down her arm, and she cried out.

Davin released her face. "Interesting," he said. He leaned forward and met her eyes. She stared back at him defiantly. She knew it was hopeless, but somehow she would escape and alert Lira. "Too bad it has come to this. I sense a deep anger in you. You have been wasted with that flower mage. With all the darkness, nothing can grow as the flower mage would intend. But I know how such rage can be useful. I think the Conclave could help you find a different outlet. Then you might see being different is not all that bad. Perhaps we still can take you with us to Saffra. You would like that, no?"

She pulled her face away from him. "And end up looking like you?"

Davin smiled and patted her cheek. "Such is the price of power. Do not worry. Soon you will see."

He stood and walked away from her, leaving her sagging back against the horse, pain shooting through her body, her skin burning and raw, and her mind reeling as if she had been violated.

"When do we begin?" someone asked.

"Nightfall. We begin our preparations at dusk. They will enter the Svanth at nightfall. That is when her power will be weakest, and we have the greatest chance at finally destroying her garden."

CHAPTER 19

"You're late," the High Seat said. His voice filled with fire and anger.

"There were...complications."

Eris recognized the voice. *Adrick.*

She had been holding out hope that Adrick didn't know about what the High Seat and Davin attempted, but his arrival told her he did. What did it mean that he came? What had happened with her family?

"This must happen tonight. She is weakened, but will not remain that way for long."

"What of the others in the north? Can she bind with them?"

"It does not work the same. And they are...distracted." This from Davin.

"How?"

Someone laughed, a harsh and violent sound. "Have you not heard?" Adrick asked. "Varden readies for war. I had thought to encourage it sooner, but the king could not be so easily swayed. His son, though...well, we have seen what happened there.

Between the Kelths attacking from the east and what we will soon encourage…these lands will burn."

Eris realized what Adrick was saying. The north had *not* attacked, but what had happened with Jacen? What did he mean about her brother?

"Tie them to the tree while we prepare," the High Seat said.

The other two dragged her toward a tree and bound her quickly to it before cutting loose her arms and legs. Eris stretched. Finally released from the ropes binding her for so long, their absence came as an agonizing relief. She rubbed a hand against her wrist, carefully shifting the remaining ropes so they didn't rub against cracked and bleeding skin. Any thought of escape was dashed by the fact Davin stood watching her.

Night had fallen fully. Darkness stretched around her. Eris shivered against the cold. Her body felt numb, as if all the pain she'd accumulated during her capture finally reached the point where she no longer felt anything.

Eris huddled against the base of a towering oak. Though she had never traveled much beyond the palace, she knew with certainty the tree marked the edge of the Svanth Forest. That she had been brought here, especially considering how she had tried to convince Terran to travel with her to the forest, seemed a cruel twist of fate. Now she didn't care if she found anything about the teary star. All she wanted was to escape, return to Eliara, and warn Lira.

The magi stood circling around a fire. All wore scarlet cloaks as they hovered in front of the slowly building flames. Hoods were pulled over their faces as they performed their magic. Smoke swirled around them, twisting into their cloaks and disappearing. Energy built around them, crackling the air and pressing in on Eris' senses.

She marveled that she could feel it. How much power must they be working for *her* to be aware of it?

She glanced over and saw a dark outline against a nearby tree. Jacen. At first, she feared he was seriously injured, but saw his chest rise and fall steadily.

His head sagged forward, golden hair hanging lank and over his eyes. He didn't turn to look at her. They must have treated him worse than they'd treated her, or else he'd fought more. Bruises worked along the skin of his thigh and shallow slashes crisscrossed his arms. Eris had similar injuries from the ride through the needlegrass.

"Jacen!" she hissed.

He didn't move. His breathing seemed to quicken.

"Jacen! I know you can hear me. I need you to wake up."

He seemed to breathe a little faster. Finally, his head twisted slightly. Hair hung lankily, blocking his eyes.

What had they done to him?

Behind them, the magi chanted softly. Energy in the air slowly built around them. It pressed on her uncomfortably and made it hard for her to breathe.

"Jacen!" Eris said, louder.

She knew the words would carry but didn't care. Something had happened to him that kept him from being able to speak or even move. She strained against the ropes. If only they would give, if even a little...

Eris closed her eyes, imaging the way the ropes flexed around the tree. If only the tree were not so wide. Lira could probably make the tree lengthen, as if taking a deep breath, just enough to relax the pressure on the ropes so she could free herself.

She sighed, pushing against the ropes in frustration.

Surprisingly, they gave.

Eris stifled the gasp poised on her lips and pushed on the ropes again. There was just enough slack that she could untangle her hands. The rope crusted where it had dug into her skin and stained with blood. She was glad to be rid of it. Even her legs were loosened and she unwound the rope from her legs.

Once freed, Eris stood there against the tree. Had they seen her get free?

Eris dared a glance back. The magi focused on their ritual, tendrils of smoke snaking around their bodies and up arms that pointed at the sky. Lightning crackled overhead, sending streaks of light shooting. With hoods of scarlet cloaks over their head, none of the magi seemed to pay her any mind.

For a moment, she could not look away.

Eris had never seen the magi working their spells—she had only heard of the strange magic they worked. Her father was known to watch. Some even said he participated, learning the magic of the magi. Now she knew it was little more than a ruse for the Conclave to gain power.

The voices of the magi chanting around the fire mixed together into something different and twisted. The sound was rough and coarse, almost as if they screamed at the lightning they called.

Above it all, Eris felt power.

It was a constant pressure on her senses, a twisted and raw sensation, like an exposed wound. The pressure felt so powerful it made it difficult for her to take a deep breath.

She had felt this before, though had thought at that time it was little more than the heat and moisture in the air. She recognized it from when the Conclave attacked the garden, when Lira had collapsed, how her breathing had suddenly eased when the skies began to clear.

No longer daring to waste her freedom, Eris slid around the tree until she was out of sight of the magi. Across from her, Jacen hung against his bindings, head bowed. She looked around the ground, hoping to find anything that might work to cut him free; she did not think she would have time enough to untie the ropes before the magi realized what was happening. Her hands felt too numb, her arms and wrists too sore, to make that happen.

A dried strand of needlegrass was the only thing she saw. With as sharp as the blade was, she hoped it would be enough.

Picking it carefully, she hurried toward Jacen. Eris rested her hand on him, lightly brushing the hair off his head. And then gasped.

Not Jacen. Jasi.

Eris froze. How would Jasi be here? Her hair had been cut, left shorter and ragged. Standing this close, now Eris saw only a thin shift covering her. Old bruises marred her face.

What had they done to her? And what had happened to Jacen?

As the chanting and energy built behind her, she knew those were questions for later. There was a definite sense of something building—the power in the air, the energy, the *pressure* on her—all seemed to crescendo. Whatever they were working, she suspected she had little time before it was complete. And then they would return.

Eris prayed that the needlegrass was stiff enough to cut through the ropes.

She worked quickly. Finally, the rope released. Jasi fell forward.

Eris struggled to catch her, barely holding her up. Were Jasi to fall, she wouldn't be strong enough to lift her or drag her from the clearing.

"Jasi! You will have to walk." Her breath came ragged and heavy.

Jasi barely registered that she had spoken, but she seemed to bear her own weight. Eris took it as a sign and pulled her by the hand, dragging her around the tree and out of sight of the magi.

The energy on her was nearly unbearable. What would happen when it was released? The magi would recognize they were gone. Then they would come looking for them.

She refused to think what would happen if they found her.

Looking past the line of trees, she considered heading back onto the plains. She could reach the Kingsroad and follow the road back to the palace. But the magi had horses and would ride faster. The chances of recapture were great if she chose that way.

The alternative meant entering the Svanth.

As much as she had thought she wanted to travel to the forest to find her flower, the idea that she now *needed* to enter the forest sent anxiety coursing through her. Even Terran, who had grown up around the forest, warned against entering its boundaries unnecessarily. But if she didn't, neither of them would survive.

Eris turned toward the trees.

Tall oaks and elms loomed overhead. Darkness surged beneath their branches.

"This is the only way, Jasi," she whispered as she pulled her toward the trees.

Eris ducked from tree to tree, hiding as best she could as she moved. Soon, even the light of the fire diminished and faded, leaving her in near darkness. Lightning flickered overhead from the spell the magi called, giving just enough light for her to not lose her footing. Jasi was a different matter, stumbling alongside her, but she managed to remain upright and standing.

Eris could barely breathe. Her body felt like it was compressed, as if a band squeezed on her chest, keeping her from taking a full breath.

And then, in an explosion of light and thunder, the sense lifted.

Lightning rained down on the forest, streaking in blue-white toward the trees around them, and deeper, toward the heart.

Eris cringed, thinking she'd chosen the wrong direction. The plains might be more open, but whatever the magi hoped to destroy was here, in the forest.

The lightning ended high above the trees, fizzling out before even reaching the tender leaves on the highest branches.

Lira's magic.

Blinding lightning slashed down in continuous streaks. Each time, it crept ever closer to the treetops. How long before the forest could no longer hold the lightning at bay? How long before the magi managed to penetrate the forest? Then, like the palace garden, it would burn.

She turned, pulling Jasi with her. They could suffer through the needlegrass and hide from the magi as long as they needed to reach safety. That way made more sense anyway.

The sudden roar of anger stopped her.

"How did they escape?" Even through the trees, she recognized the rage in the High Seat's voice. "Who tied them?"

The question was punctuated by another blinding streak of lightning. This one struck along the edge of the forest, crashing into the trees where they had been tied. Light bloomed, surging up as if striking something deflecting the bolt of lightning.

"Innash tied them, Great One!" one of the magi screamed.

Eris wondered if the High Seat had turned the attack upon the magi. She would not mind if they destroyed each other.

"Find them! Take the horses and search. They cannot have gotten far!"

"But the spell…"

"We will maintain it until you return with them."

"Even without the princesses, we can still damage the flower mage. Let us turn our attention to the forest."

Eris realized the suggestion came from Davin.

"You think the five of us alone can accomplish what an entire emissary failed to achieve? A full thirteen?" The High Seat asked. "No—the girls are the key to this plan. Find them before they get too far."

Eris froze, daring to wait and see which way the magi chased.

One of the horses started toward the trees on plodding hooves. There came a harsh neighing that ended abruptly. Then the horses started away again, this time out into the grasses.

Lightning strikes began anew.

This time, they struck the outskirts of the forest. At first failing to reach the trees, but after a few bright blasts, the topmost branches were struck. Fire bloomed where lightning touched, scorching the sky. Now, with each strike, lightning reached the trees.

Soon, the outer edge of the forest burned.

Now Eris had no choice but to move deeper into the forest, away from the magi, away from the growing flames. Would the field of needlegrass burn as Jacen had wished?

She stumbled forward, moving toward the near blackness. They passed through something cold which made her skin tingle, and Jasi jumped.

"What was that?" she moaned.

Eris shivered, clutching her sister's arm tightly. "We have entered the Svanth Forest," she answered as she dragged her forward.

CHAPTER 20

A heavy chill settled over them as they moved deeper into the forest.

Had there not been light from lightning streaking down in rhythmic succession, the blackness around them would have felt oppressive. Faded images burned into Eris' eyes following each blast and she used them to keep from stumbling over the knobby roots and ever-thickening undergrowth. The texture of the trees changed as they plunged deeper, the trunks becoming thicker and the upper most branches higher. Soon, they did not have to duck to avoid any reaching branches.

Jasi remained silent but at least managed to keep moving. Other than her single question, she had not managed to put together anything more than a soft gasp at the sound of a particularly strong blast of concussive thunder. Eris decided to worry about her mental state later, when—and if—they were safe.

They still hadn't reached a point of safety. Though the magi were now behind them, trapped by Lira's magic outside the forest, they weren't safe. Whatever they planned, whatever dark magic they worked, would not be easily stopped. Eris needed to move them deeper into the forest.

"This is the wrong way."

Eris jerked to a stop at the suddenness of Jasi's words. She looked over. In the flashes of light from the lightning, some of the energy had returned to her eyes. No longer blindly unfocused, she still looked around with a wild energy.

"They can't enter the forest," Eris said.

"Why?"

Eris shrugged, wrapping her arms around her for warmth. The night air continued to grow cooler, but she knew better than to wish for fire. For some reason, she suspected it would only draw the magi to them. She had seen the way the smoke wrapped itself around the magi, almost caressing them, the flames not managing to hurt them even though their cloaks practically rested atop the fire.

"I don't know. Something Lira did. She has a garden here."

That woke Jasi more than anything. She looked around. A strange cry echoed deep within the trees, and she jumped. "Here? How can a garden grow within the forest?"

If they found the garden, they would have even more protection from the magi. Lira's protection, whatever it was worth. But Eris had no idea where to look. She shook her head, wishing she had found the book from Feliran about the flowers of the Svanth. Then she might understand how such a garden was possible.

"I don't know, but there is power here. I feel it."

With the words, Eris knew it was true. As she felt the oppressive magic the magi worked, she felt the welcoming power of the forest. This was different, softer, more delicate, and...comfortable. Eris felt no sense of threat from the power around her. If only Lira were here to use the power to protect them.

"I don't feel anything," Jasi replied.

Eris glanced over at her sister. Her clothing was torn and tattered. All sense of grace and dignity gone from her stance. Her hair was a tangled mess. After everything she had been through, she was not surprised Jasi felt nothing.

"Is there anything Lira taught you that might be useful?"

"Lira taught us about colors and arrangements. How can any of that help?"

Eris frowned. "That can't be all she taught you." How many months had she wandered the gardens searching for her flower while they worked with Lira? During that time, they must have learned something useful, some bit of magic which might offer them protection while they hid in the forest. "She's a flower mage. The gardens are her source of power. And the magi think she has one hidden in the forest."

"A flower mage?" Jasi repeated. The confused expression returned to her face, leaving her eyes looking clouded. "That can't be true."

"You didn't know?" How was it after all the months that Jasi had worked with Lira she still didn't know about her magic? Eris figured Jasi especially would know; she had chosen her flower almost immediately, had been working with Lira for months, all while Eris still wandered the garden, searching for her flower.

And now she'd reached the Svanth Forest with the teary star tantalizingly close, but all she wanted was to get home, to get Jasi home safely—away from the magi in Saffra—and make sure her father and Lira knew what the magi intended.

"Lira is one of them?" Jasi asked, turning back toward where they had left the magi. A loud explosion of thunder punctuated her question. Lightning streaked from the sky, crashing almost to the treetops near them. The air hissed and sizzled.

"Not one of them. All they care about is destruction. They seem to have been plotting against Father for years. They want the throne for the Conclave."

"But not Lira?"

Eris shook her head. Apparently, she didn't know anything about Lira. "Her garden works against them. I think it prevents their magic from influencing father."

"How have you learned so much?"

"I haven't learned anything. No one has been willing to teach me," Eris said bitterly. "I've seen what happened, overheard the magi. First in the garden, and then once we were captured."

"Why did they want us?"

Eris shook her head. "They didn't want me. They wanted Lira's students." She realized that was the intent of the magi. "I think there's something you know they intended to use against her."

Jasi turned and took her hands. They felt cold and damp and had little strength remaining. "I'm glad it was you. You're the only one who would have been strong enough to get us free."

The compliment surprised her. How hard must it have been for Jasi to say?

"How did you do it?" Jasi asked.

"Do what?"

A blinding blast of light struck the tree line. It dipped past the tops of the trees. Fire bloomed briefly before fading. Whatever the magi were doing seemed to be working.

Eris grabbed Jasi's arm and started them forward, deeper into the forest. If the magi managed to get past Lira's defenses—whatever they were—maybe the heart of the forest would be safest.

"Get free. The magi had bound us tightly. I could barely breathe I was tied so tightly. I heard the spell they used to bind us."

Eris considered explaining to Jasi it wasn't the bindings making it hard for her to breathe; rather, it was the magic of the magi. She wondered if being this close to the focus of Lira's energy made them more sensitive to it.

"I don't know how I managed to get free." She hadn't given it much thought. She remembered pushing against the ropes without managing to get them to give...and then wishing the tree would somehow stretch. "That was probably Lira, too," she decided aloud. Another protection.

"We need to return to the palace, Eris. Father needs to know what has happened before he sends his men after us. They need to know about...about the other things."

Other things?

Eris faltered. "What did they do to you?"

Some of the usual strength came back to Jasi's eyes. "They took me while I slept. I don't know if Petra knew what they intended. I..."

"Jacen was with me. Father will send men looking for him."

Jasi nodded. "Not just him. For you, too."

Eris didn't argue but doubted it was true. How often had days gone by before anyone came looking for her? She had assignments and teachers, but most were like Lira and had given up on her long ago. No one in the palace would notice her missing.

"We need to return. But I don't think the Kingsroad is the safest way to get there. If the Conclave and Adrick were willing to abduct us, I fear what they'll do to prevent us from reporting what happened to father."

The voice of the magi who'd abducted her, the one who'd touched her with a dark longing she felt through his fingertips, came to mind. She shivered. He would be more than pleased to keep her from returning to the palace. Already he had promised what he would do, if given the chance.

"If not the Kingsroad, then how do you expect us to make it back to the palace? Across the Verilain Plains? Take the Sofil River? Circle around to the north and climb through the mountains?"

Eris shivered when she mentioned the plains. The prospect of moving through the long needlegrass again frightened her almost as much as facing the magi. "Not through the plains. And not through the river."

"You can't intend us to cross through the forest!"

Eris looked around. Lightning surged overhead, but the farther they walked, the less they heard the thunder crashing. The lightning gave enough light to mark their way.

A question came to mind that almost made her turn back. What happened when the light faded? There were other things to fear than the magi. Even Terran had been nervous about entering the forest. What were they—two princesses unarmed and unaccustomed to the woods—in the face of that?

"I don't think we have any other choice," she said.

Jasi's eyes went wide, and she pulled against Eris's grip. Eris held firm, unwilling to let her sister go crashing away from her. Now freed from the magi, she wasn't going to let her sister wander off for the forest to claim. They were better off together. Safer, if anything.

Besides, she hated to admit she just might need Jasi's knowledge.

Those months she had spent wandering the garden, mindlessly searching and failing for the flower Lira determined she needed, Jasi and her sisters had been allowed to work with Lira, to learn from the Mistress of Flowers. There was much they might have learned, much more than colors and arrangements. Perhaps Jasi didn't even know she could access some of the same power Lira accessed. What if Jasi was already on the way to becoming a flower mage and didn't know it?

Jasi fell silent and allowed Eris to lead her deeper into the trees.

Eris had no clear path in mind. She moved where it seemed the trees were willing to let her move, following the outline of the undergrowth, staying far enough away that it didn't rip at hers or Jasi's dress. After a while, even the light from the lightning wasn't enough to clearly make out their way, and Eris had to rely on gradations of shadow, sliding her feet carefully along the forest floor. She imagined the trees guiding her, steering her where they and Lira wanted them to travel. She prayed it was toward safety.

After travelling for what seemed like hours, a thunderous roar split the night, and the sky erupted in light. Blue-white lightning surged from the sky far behind them, visible even as deep as they were in the forest in a constant wave of fire crashing down from the night sky. An oppressive sense of heat followed, and the constricted feeling to her breathing returned.

Jasi cowered close by, and Eris held her arm in an attempt to comfort her. Other than the sound of the thunder, the forest remained silent around them.

She struggled to breathe. Her chest felt heavy. She swallowed against her dry throat, tasting the earthy flavor of the forest around her. The pressure of the lightning built behind her ears and in her chest.

Jasi shivered, and Eris looked over at her. For the first time in her life, Jasi looked back with an uncertain expression, as if resigned to her fate. Jasi did not expect them to live.

Eris closed her eyes. What could they do against the magi?

If only Lira were with them. Someone else other than just the two of them.

Why did she wish it would be Terran?

But they were alone. They would just have to manage on their own. Somehow.

Another blast of thunder came, this time closer. Jasi jumped again, and Eris shivered. If only the protections of the forest held. *Keep us safe*, she wished silently.

The forest seemed to sigh. A soft breeze picked up beneath the trees, pushing through and out of the forest. Rain began pattering down on the treetops but did not penetrate through to the deepest layers, leaving them dry. The lightning bursting around them slowed.

As they pressed onward, deeper into the forest, their way seemed easier. The space between the tangled undergrowth opened around them, letting them move more easily. The arching roots seemed less prominent the deeper they went, so they weren't forced to climb over or move around them. Moonlight began trickling in through the canopy, and an almost glowing light reached the forest floor. A few flowering plants—none she recognized—bloomed along their path. Eris wondered if they neared Lira's garden, before deciding Lira would have more than just a few plants.

Jasi held tightly to her arm but had slowed her steps. Soon, Eris was dragged her along, trying to get her to keep up. Behind them, the lightning continued but diminished. Either the magi were weakening or simply giving up. Eris cared not which, just wanting to get the two of them to safety.

"We have to stop," Jasi said. Her voice sounded weak and thready, the strain of hurrying through the forest almost too much for her to manage. "We have gone so far. I don't think we should keep moving into the forest."

"We need to go on, Jasi. We need to get deeper into the forest."

The trees themselves seemed to guide their way. She suspected that was Lira's doing; that the flower master reached across the distance to help them made her feel less alone, less frightened of what had happened.

Jasi pulled against her. "I'm *scared* to go any farther."

Eris looked at her. It wasn't the forest Eris feared; it was what would happen if the magi caught them. The farther they went into the forest, the safer she felt.

"We have to keep moving, Jasi. If we stop..." She didn't want to say what she thought would happen if they stopped moving.

Jasi wrenched her arm free. "I'm tired, Eris. We should find a place to rest. In the morning we can start making our way back out, back toward Eliara. We'll tell Father what happened. Everything will be fine then."

Eris looked from Jasi to the forest around them. Nothing would be fine, not with the magi attacking. What did it matter if they warned their father? Could anything he did actually matter against the magi? Could Lira really help against so much strength?

But Jasi...she'd been through so much. Eris couldn't push her any harder. "We can rest. You're right. We need to get you back to the palace."

Eris was not as exhausted as she expected after running from the magi. Part of her felt invigorated; the damp earth and the mixture of scents in the forest seemed to clear her head. She felt as if she could press on for another few hours. By then, they might be able to reach the heart of the forest.

Would she find the teary star then?

For some reason, it nagged at her.

"Eris."

Jasi sounded near exhaustion. But where had she gone? Had Eris kept walking after Jasi stopped?

Eris turned, looking around the forest.

Her heart started fluttering. Had she managed to help her sister to escape the magi only to lose her within the Svanth Forest?

"Jasi!" she called.

She didn't answer.

Eris looked around. Trees seemed to lean toward her, large roots leaning out of the ground as if trying to keep her from turning around. The path she had been following had disappeared, fading back into tangled undergrowth. Even the moonlight slipping through the canopy faded, leaving shadows stretching around her.

"Jasi!" she called again.

Faintly, she heard, "Eris?"

She turned toward the sound of her sister's voice and pushed through the branches blocking her way. Eris had to step over tall roots and moved slowly as she did. "Jasi! I'm coming for you!"

Her voice faded quickly into the forest.

Jasi did not call back.

For the first time since entering the Svanth Forest, Eris felt afraid.

CHAPTER 21

*E*ris stumbled forward. Fatigue finally caught up with her leaving her drained and weakened. The lightning crashing into the treetops had faded and stopped some time ago. Thunder still rolled distantly, but even that became little more than a soft roar she barely heard above the breeze blowing through the trees.

She still had not found Jasi.

Several times she thought she heard her sister, but each time she finally managed to reach where the sound seemed to originate, she found nothing. Eris pushed onward, not willing to rest. Now that she had managed to get them away from the magi, she would *not* lose her sister in the forest.

She kept calling out, yelling for Jasi as she went. Occasionally, she heard her sister yell back, but her voice grew weaker. Eventually, sleep or distance would keep Jasi from answering.

The forest pushed against her. Where it had seemed to guide her, now it seemed determined to trap her where she was, to keep her separate from wherever Jasi had gone. If only her sister would stay in the same place; Eris thought she could manage to find her were she willing to just wait.

Or maybe it was Eris who made it harder. Should she sit and wait, or—better yet—move back into the deeper parts of the forest as she searched?

With the thought, the trees seemed to relax, and the underbrush which had begun scratching at her legs and snaring her feet almost backed away, as if willing to give her space to move. Eris decided what she saw was simply the effect of her tired mind.

She continued to call out for her sister, but moved in the direction the forest allowed, following the moonlit path through the trees as she went. A few times, she thought she saw motion and spun, but nothing was there. After a while, she no longer even heard Jasi answering.

The trees in this part of the forest stretched so high she could not even make out their tops. Somehow, moonlight still made its way through the branches to light her way. The small thorned bushes and scrub trees around them thinned, leaving her with an increasing sense of openness. Patches of vines worked up a few of the trunks, and Eris was surprised she recognized some of them by the pale white flowers. She had seen them in one of the books she had read, though could not remember what they were called.

Eris paused. A small clearing opened around her, rimmed by the immense trees. Not oak or elm like those on the outskirts of the forest, these were different, older—almost ancient—and seemed to have an aura of power and age to them. She wondered if she had finally reached the heart of the forest.

She looked from tree to tree, making her way around the clearing. If this was the heart of the forest, would she find the teary star flowers?

Exhaustion finally won. She sat on the soft forest floor and wrapped her arms around herself to keep warm. The ground was slightly damp and smelled of earthy decay; it was a pleasant scent but mixed with it was something else, something…familiar. As she was pulled into a comfortable sleep, she realized it was the same scent her flower had.

She had finally found the teary star.

She breathed it in, opening her mouth and nearly tasting it on her tongue.

Then dreams claimed her, dreams unlike anything she had ever experienced before.

Eris opened her eyes and saw all around her young saplings. They were planted in staggered lines, and she sensed a pattern to the way they set into the ground but did not quite recognize what it was. Most were thin, barely any thicker than her forearm. A few scattered closest to the middle were so small they did not even reach her knees. Dark green leaves already flourished on the trees, leaves that were different on each of the trees, some rounded, others oblong, a few spiky. Even though the trunks seemed similar, the leaves were the only way to tell the trees apart.

The sky overhead was clear and cloudless. A warm sun shone down. A gentle breeze gusted around her, tousling her light hair. Something did not seem quite right, though she could not place what it was.

"You think these trees will grow here? The soil is soft and sandy."

Eris turned and saw a man looking at her, brown eyes carrying a warmth and familiarity. Something about his face was familiar as well. Perhaps it was the tilt to his jaw or the way he wore his long hair pulled back in a tail behind his head, or the lopsided smile he made when looking at her. A dark green jacket covered a muscular frame. He stood away from her and looked around at the trees.

"There is solid black earth beneath the sand," she answered. The words were not her own, but she said them anyway. "The roots will stretch and tap into what is stored deep in the earth."

"There are other places you could have planted your forest, mistress."

She smiled at the man, somehow knowing that he was Therin, one of the great gardeners. His hands had planted most of these trees, and his care had ensured they would grow, their long branches stretching toward the sun. The land had failed them for many years, the soil fighting their gardens, forcing the Gardens of Elaysia north and east, never to the west, never across this patch of land where nothing seemed to grow. Even their most hardy plants, flowers and vines that required so little to sustain them, withered and died in the soil here.

This had been her plan, something none of the others felt would work, a folly to even try...yet already in her mind she could see what the trees would become, how the forest would spread from what she first started, how the earth welcomed the presence of the trees, already drawing roots deep, past the sand and clay and into the hearty black earth deep below. The life surging through the land was fledgling but grew stronger with each passing day and with each gentle rain. Even the heavy storms did not seem to unsettle the trees as she had feared.

It would be her greatest arrangement.

"There are," she agreed. Therin did not see what she saw, the future she traced through the roots that would grow. Other arrangements would not have the power she needed. "This place is strong. There is something here deep beneath the earth I sense... something I cannot fully explain." Her eyes took in Therin. His smile never changed. "Perhaps because I was born along the edge of this land I can see its potential where others see only brush. Life can exist here, even flourish."

"Such things have been tried before, mistress," Therin said.

She nodded. She remembered, had participated in several of the plantings and knew the failings as a deep hurt. Chosen specifically for the climate, the flowers still failed. Each season they withered more, slowly disappearing until they rejoined the brush of the desolate plain. It was almost as if nothing was destined to grow here.

Yet she knew better, she felt it, deep within her marrow. "These trees will grow strong. Already I see their potential. The land around them will change, bringing more life, more growth, but here, even the smallest will thrive and grow powerful." She spoke with the conviction of one who could read even the smallest root system and could see what came.

Therin sighed, and it was like a breath of wind. "It is not the trees that you wish to plant, is it mistress?"

She smiled. Always so bright, Therin saw what she hid in her heart from the others. The forest would be strong and unlike any other, but it was what she could grow within the forest she sought. A shame she would not live long enough to see it.

"Cannot the trees be enough?" she asked in answer. "Cannot we enjoy the shade they will create? The strong trunks that will one day tower over this patch of land, land that has for so long resisted growth? Why must we worry about what else there is?"

Therin's smile faded. "It is my duty to worry, mistress. We have tried planting here many times because we recognize the power buried deep beneath the surface, but these," he said, hand sweeping over to the trees, "will outlast any of us. How can you be certain that what you have started will always be used as you intended?"

"You think the gardeners will disappear?" she asked Therin.

His face remained somber. "Like these trees, we weren't always here. I do not possess your gifts—few do—and cannot see what will happen even next season. What we have done here will last many seasons and outlive even the youngest of us."

"Then why did you help?" she asked.

"It is not my role to question. I am simply a gardener."

She smiled and stepped past one small sapling, its nascent

trunk barely wider than her finger, and rested a hand on one of his broad shoulders. "Therin," she began.

He smiled.

"You have always been more than just a gardener. All of this," she said, motioning toward the vast stretches of early growth, "is because of your skill. Do not fear what will become of it next. With enough seasons, I will be better able to read the roots, perhaps even guide them."

Ever stoic, such a statement still elicited a soft gasp from Therin. "Mistress, such a thing is not possible."

"Not with what we have traditionally grown. Our gardens have been too transient, chosen for their ability to focus the power of the sun. What will grow here will be different. Their roots thicker —deeper—and more permanent. With time, I sense I can influence the shape of what will come, what growth will exist here."

"Are you certain that is wise? Such influence is not meant for mortals."

"Do you think *they* will step from the shadows long enough to influence the growth? To them, we are but fleeting lives." She shook her head. "I think such influence is simply the next step in *our* growth as we learn to harness the powers granted to us."

Eris shifted in her sleep, blinking. Distantly, she recognized how strange the dream felt but also how clear it was—how so very real—as if living someone else's life.

The soft bed of the forest floor pulled her back down into deeper sleep, and she did not resist.

The forest had matured around her. Trees stretched overhead, not like they would one day at the heart, but respectable growth had been achieved. Beneath the trees there was the start of some-thing else, of faint undergrowth living in the shadows along the tree. Small vines already wrapped themselves around several of the trunks, snaking their way toward the sky, using the trees as scaf-folding. Soft spikes grew along their length. And rather than choking off the tree, they kept burrowing animals and insects from reaching the bark. Working together, they were much stronger.

"You let the vines climb this season."

She turned. The man standing behind her was older, streaks of grey now in his hair, but the same keen intelligence shone in his eyes, and the same off kilter smile pulled at his lips, though less than it once had. His dark green jacket hung over a frame no less muscular than ever. Older, but still vibrant. She had missed him.

"You have returned."

Therin looked at the trees and walked toward the nearest, where the vine had completely encircled the trunk as it wound toward the sunlight. "This is a single season?" he asked.

She nodded. "For so many seasons I struggled to keep the vines from growing, not wanting to let them squeeze the life from the trunks before they had a chance to grow strong."

"Did you know what would happen?"

She shook her head. "I did not."

He lightly brushed his hand along the vine and winced, pulling his hand back quickly. "Barbed. And sharp. Are you certain letting it grow into the bark is wise?"

She shrugged, sliding across the damp soil. Old leaves and other forest detritus squished beneath her woven slippers. Her pale violet dress swished around her ankles as she walked, letting some of the cool forest air caress her skin. Reaching out, she ran her hand along the vine, sliding it carefully along the barbs, having already learned how to touch them so she would not feel their bite. Therin watched her with a curious expression.

"They grow together," she answered. "Possibly they have always meant to grow together, though I do not know what would have happened to the sapling had I allowed the vine to cling when it first established here."

"Did you plant the vines?" Therin asked.

She sensed that was the heart of the reason he came. There were many who never visited her trees but still passed judgment upon her arrangement. She did not know where the vines came from and did not know what they were; they had simply appeared one season, working from the base of the trunks and climbing toward the top branches. For many seasons she had fought against them, pruning and taming the vines, keeping them from what she had felt was certain destruction. Her hands still held many scars.

Only these trees, only the Svanth trees growing in the center of the forest, at the heart of her arrangement, grew the vines. The rest were left alone. When she recognized this, she began to wonder at the reason.

Finally, this season, she dared to let them grow.

"You know I did not, Therin. With all the time I have spent among the trees, where would I have acquired them?"

"Others grow increasingly uncertain about your arrangement."

"Do their gardens not flourish?" she asked, her voice weary.

"They flourish," Therin admitted.

"Then there is no reason for uncertainty. These trees are *my* garden. They may lack in the colors found among the great gardens, but there is more to the arrangement than color." Even as she said it, she knew it untrue. There were many colors found beneath the trees, shades of greens and browns not found in other gardens that mixed with the shadows and blackness. Given enough time, other colors would grow, colors from flowers which preferred the shadows.

"This has changed you," Therin commented.

She rested her hand on the vine and turned toward him. Beneath her palm, she felt the tiny barbs as they pushed against her skin, trying and failing to puncture her. She pushed back, resisting the effect of the barbs, and felt them soften.

"You think so?"

He stepped over to her and rested a hand on hers, careful to keep from touching the vine. Much like any gardener, Therin smelled of the earth itself. Other odors mingled, giving him a distinct smell, different than any other gardener she had ever met. Had he chosen to, he could have remained with her among the trees.

"I did not say such change was bad. Only that you have changed."

She sighed and moved her hand from under his, sliding along the vine. The barbs pulled back, careful so as not to catch her skin as she brushed along the length. Therin jerked his hand away so he didn't touch the vine either. Husks of captured insects whisked away, their once hard carapaces now disintegrated and dry. The vine captured the tiny creatures, the barbs latching onto their sensitive flesh to keep them from crawling any further. She had yet to learn whether the vine itself fed on them or merely captured them.

"Change is inevitable. With enough seasons, we all change, guided by what we have learned and seen, so that one day we might awaken and not recognize the person we once were."

Therin captured her hand and squeezed. "Is that how it is for you?" he asked. "Do you no longer recognize who you once were, the feelings you once felt?"

Her heart ached with the question. Had she only stayed within the Gardens of Elaysia rather than leaving, determined to make this forest, this arrangement work, she might have been a very different person. As it was, she knew Therin would not feel for her how he once did.

"I still recognize her," she whispered.

Her breath caught, and she closed her eyes and took in a deep breath. Smelling the air around her, air that was hers, a force of her creation, she sighed, pushing away the longing she felt. She could not change what had come before, and there had been no way to mingle the two lives, both of which she had read along the roots. That the choice had been hers did not change how much it hurt.

Therin remained still, standing near the trunk of the growing tree that would one day be one of the great Svanth trees at the heart of this forest. For a moment, she thought he might come to her, might take her hand, pull her toward him and embrace as they once had done, making love under the canopy of the forest, but the moment passed.

"The others are uncomfortable with your influence."

She smiled. Of course they were uncomfortable. It was one thing to read the possibilities among the roots; it was another to influence their growth. "I do not do so often."

"But still you do it."

She tilted her head. She would not deny what she had done. These trees would one day be massive, their root systems complex. A gentle touch was required to guide them in such a way the roots were arranged so power might be drawn. Such influence had never before been attempted, had never been thought possible, and perhaps it had not been possible before she moved her garden and selected these trees to be her arrangement. What was possible here was different than what would be possible with the growth of small flowers whose lives were limited. These trees would live for centuries, outlive her even were she able to hold onto life beyond what was expected of her kind.

"What do you see here, mistress?"

He had not called her that for years.

To her surprise, he had come up behind her, standing so close that she felt the heat of his body. So close they could almost touch. She turned and looked into deep brown eyes that looked back at her with fondness which age and time had not completely erased.

"I see potential. Beyond that, even my ability to read the roots fades and becomes hazy. It is the potential that is needed, for one day, when our gardens have all disappeared, this forest will survive, and with it, the memories of what is possible twisted and twined in the roots."

His eyes tilted into a frown that did not reach his lips. "You have woven a story into the roots?"

He did not question whether it was possible—as far as they both knew, it should not have been. And he did not ask what story she weaved. It was not the gardener's role to question the arrangement, only to aid in its growth.

"I have. For one who knows how to look, our story can be revealed not by reading the trees or the shape of the branches. Those will change with each passing season, the small buds of new growth changing its telling so that it is no longer reliable, but in the deepest part of the trees, in the way the roots twist and dive beneath the surface of the earth."

Therin smiled and leaned so close she smelled the hint of mint on his breath. "Few will be able to manage such a reading, mistress. Even among those who live today at the height of the garden's power, there are not more than a handful who would be able to read what you say will be told by the trees."

"That is how it should be," she answered. "Such knowledge can be dangerous."

"Much like the influence you exert over the growth?"

She laughed, feeling like she had not in many years and wishing suddenly Therin would stay with her among the trees rather than return to the gardens. She knew he would not.

Eris stirred, rolling over. Distantly, she was aware that she was dreaming, but the detail to the dreams drew her back. She blinked again.

The trees were taller, stretching high overhead, their thick canopy blocking the sunlight in the heart of the forest. Vines that had simply twisted around the trunks of the Svanth trees now wrapped around them entirely, completely obscuring the soft bark beneath and leaving the trunk looking grizzled and aged. She did not have to run her hand across the vines to know how sharp the barbs had become. The vines and the Svanth trees had become one, working together as they grew tall and powerful in the heart of her forest.

Flowers blossomed along the vines, petals made of many different colors. She stepped close, and it was clear the vines were braided from many different tendrils forming the thicker vine, as if a rope had been woven and wrapped around the tree.

In her dream, Eris stirred momentarily before settling back into it.

Here, her guidance was nearly complete. Years had passed since she'd first started changing the direction of the growth, helping the roots delve deeper into the soil, twisting and coiling into the arrangement she intended to leave. Now, with her own time nearly spent, she felt a sense of peace over what she had done.

"I wish you would have been here to see this," she said aloud.

She turned to a small patch that lay free of growth on the floor and knelt before it. The dark green dress she wore swept leaves and fallen twigs along with her, brushing them over the ground. This close to the earth, she smelled the heavy scent of dirt and decay, the natural smells of the forest.

An aged and wrinkled hand stretched out and stroked the soil. He had returned to her at last, spending only his final days with her, but they were enough. Enough to show them both that neither had changed so much since their first meeting so many years before. Now, at the end, she would once again lie next to him, sleep forever in the welcoming blanket of the earth.

For the last time, she delved into the depths of the roots and traced patterns so familiar to her. The history of the trees was traced there, so easy for her to read since she had been there from the beginning. She hoped the history was clear for whoever came next.

Not just the history of the forest had been written in the roots, but the story of her people, the story of their gardens, the secret to accessing the power locked within each sun-kissed flower, a lesson in arrangements only a few would ever read.

She sighed, hoping she had done enough.

Even now, the others faded, the great Gardens of Elaysia not what they once had been. Even Therin saw it, coming to her in his last days. Neither had to speak of it to know what the other thought. Someday, the gardens would be no more. She saw a future when destruction ripped the gardens from the land, leaving them barren and weakened.

Only the trees would live on.

She lay down upon the ground, lying in the spot next to where the ground had taken Therin. In his last moments, the forest had claimed him, welcoming him beneath its now fertile soil. Soil that once had been sand and clay was now so much more. Her head rested on the ground, a pile of fallen and dried leaves her pillow.

A few rattling breaths escaped her lips.

Light barely filtered through the leaves of the canopy, but overhead the sun shone. In spite of what the others thought, much sunlight still reached through the topmost branches. Few knew how many wondrous flowers flourished even in the shadows of the forest, flowers which blossomed in nearly as many colors as found in the great gardens.

She took another sighing breath. She smelled the blossoms as they bloomed on the vines along the Svanth trees, a mixture of pungent and sweet, and their petals, like small stars, blinked on in the night. A single tear drifted down her cheek and dropped to the earth.

Flowers bloomed in full as the earth pulled her beneath it like a warm blanket.

She sighed out her last breath, pleased with the arrangement she had made.

CHAPTER 22

*E*ris flickered her eyes open. Sunlight streamed through the branches arching high overhead, just as it had in her dream. The forest even smelled the same, the mixture of fragrances both sweet and pungent, so similar to the flower she'd found growing along the palace wall. It seemed so long ago since she had found that flower. Could it really only have been weeks? Certainly no more than a month, but it seemed a lifetime. And now, after everything she had been through, all the struggles she had trying to learn all she could about the flower, she simply *dreamed* the story of the flower?

She sat up with a start. Had she just dreamed the origin of the Svanth Forest? Could it really have been as she saw in her dreams?

Was that the secret to the teary star?

The memory of the dream felt so vivid. She had felt as if she had been the flower mage, remembering her thoughts and sorrows, the pang of sadness when Therin first left to return to the great gardens, the joy she felt when he returned tempered by the knowledge he would not stay, the comfortable way the ground claimed her when she finally laid down to rest alongside him...

Eris shook away the memories. A dream—a creation of the forest—and no more than that.

Still, the dreams were powerful and had felt so *real*.

Brushing a layer of leaves off, Eris stood. She was not as cold as she had been the night before, the sunlight or the leaves warming her. The thin shift she wore, now torn and tattered and stained with crimson streaks from her ride through the needlegrass, was covered with spots of earth and bits of leaves. Eris smoothed her hands along her dress, wiping the remnants free. A few clung to her hair, and she wiped those away as well.

She moved around the clearing, staring at the ground. Though leaves covered this area, nothing else grew, as if the forest preserved this part of it in memorial to the long dead flower mage.

Eris traced a finger in the dirt, remembering how the woman had done the same. Distantly, she recalled how the flower mage delved into the roots, reading them, guiding them to tell their story—her story—so others coming after might share in the knowledge she had gained.

Tentatively, Eris pushed out with her awareness and probed through the ground as she had in her dream. Eris did not know what she was doing. She only mimicked what she remembered so vividly.

A sense of awareness grew around her and stretched out, almost filling the forest around her. Were she to focus, she could sense each tree living within the forest and would know where each of the flowers blossomed under the shadow of the canopy. She could even count the passing of animals through the forest.

And then, there, deep beneath the surface, she felt the thick tangle of roots. A story began to unfold in her mind, a story resembling what she dreamt, a tale of the arranger and the gardener who'd helped her plant these trees, a story that played out just as she had dreamed, but one filled with more sorrow, more a sense of longing and loss than even the arranger had ever admitted, wishing she had been able to share her creation with another—with Therin particularly.

She saw massive gardens where certain colors and combinations of flowers and plants lent great power. Some combinations Eris recognized, having seen similar formations in the garden at the palace, but now she understood how those arrangements could be improved upon, ways in which the colors could be shifted to harness more of the power of the sun. Different plants would augment the others in ways which allowed even more power to be drawn from the soil, even soil as weak and thready as found within the palace. Eris knew where plants could be placed to trap the biting insects, keep their destructive teeth away from the tender buds, and where even now the gardens failed against the force of the magi…

Eris gasped, pulling away.

The force of the vision nearly overwhelmed her. The power of this place, power even now she somehow knew was not utilized to its fullest potential, a potential the arranger recognized so long ago when she first placed these trees into the soil with Therin's help, filled her.

She understood why the magi feared this place. Enough power grew here to destroy the Conclave, to render even their magic futile.

But how? How did she know this? Was it the forest…or something else?

She dared not consider any other alternative—within her was potential to access the stories held within the roots. Could that be why Lira seemed determined to keep her out of the classes with her sisters?

Did she fear Eris?

No…Lira feared nothing. Not even the magi when she'd been

attacked. So she wouldn't fear Eris. More likely, the forest pushed its ancient presence onto her.

She wiped her hands on her shift, clearing the dirt from them, and stood. Towering trees circled the small clearing, and she regarded them with renewed interest. In her dreams, the trees grew from tiny saplings to the enormous size now around her, the trunks wound with the strange vines, the blossoms bursting into color as she lay upon the ground, taking her last breath...

Eris shook her head, trying to keep her mind clear of the strange pull of the forest. Everything seemed determined to pull her back down, to overwhelm her with these visions and memories that were not her own.

And yet, she recognized the vines growing around them. Not from her dreams—at least not entirely—but from the braided vine from the planter at the edge of the palace garden, the vine she had never been able to find again, the teary star which she had named as her own, a flower Lira seemed not to recognize.

Leaning close, she peered at the vine but kept a cautious distance. Her dreams reminded her of the sharp barbs present along the vine which helped it cling to the tree. Eris circled around the trunk, looking for flowers, but there were none. Not even a tiny bud.

She sighed. Even in the heart of the forest, she hadn't managed to find the flower.

All around the clearing, other trees were the same. Svanth trees, she knew, certain that part of her dream was accurate. Trees she remembered as tiny saplings, grown to a massive size from trunks once barely more than the width of her finger.

Eris had found the heart of the forest, had found where her flower grew, had even managed to learn about the flower—even if it was through dreams.

Only there were no flowers.

The flower no longer mattered. Not if she wasn't able to leave the forest and return home to warn her father and Lira, to find Jacen. The magi had said nothing of what happened to him, and Eris knew she needed to reach him—to reach Jasi—but to do it, she needed to leave the forest.

How long had she lain here? It seemed a single night but she didn't really know. So much life had been lived to be viewed in just one dream.

And if more than just one night had passed, had she lost her sister entirely?

She remembered the forest pulling her toward the heart, the way the trees and the underbrush parted as it pulled her along. But in the process, it separated her from Jasi. Could Jasi have survived the night in the forest?

If only there was some way to find her.

Maybe there was.

If what she sensed was real, could she use the forest itself to help her find Jasi?

Eris stood in the center of the clearing and touched a finger to the soil, kneeling in a position similar to what the arranger had done on her last night in the forest. With the connection to the earth, she pushed into the awareness of the forest as she had in her dreams. Eris did not know why she did, or even if what she sensed was real or simply her imagination.

The awareness of everything threatened to overwhelm her with its sheer enormity. Eris closed her eyes, as if to push back the onslaught of sudden understanding.

She felt the trees most strongly. They were like a rigid fortress, like walls of the palace, meant to protect and guide the forest itself. Past the Svanth trees, she felt smaller oaks and elms, each towering and sturdy in their own right, but nothing like the majestic power of the Svanth trees.

Within the trees came the thready sense of dense undergrowth, that of thorny bushes whose names suddenly cropped into her mind as if she had seen them before: tendersithe, jasline, spiky hawthorne. And maybe she had in the shade book by Feliran that she'd borrowed from Lira. All grew solidly and comfortable under the trees, preferring the shade than the full sun. Those with thorns helped protect the more delicate plants and kept intruders from pressing too deeply into the woods, a different barrier than the trees created.

Then there were the flowers. Eris felt them. Countless species flashed through her mind, flowers of all shapes and colors, some she recognized from her time studying in the library with Master Billiken, others she had never seen or heard of before. In her mind, she even smelled their different perfumes, as if she leaned over them and inhaled, mimicking what she had seen Lira do so many times before. Their scents filled her nose, clung to her tongue, so lifelike she was certain they were real rather than visions in her mind. Vipeslar and taranth, both with potentially deadly toxin flowing through their stems. The spiny loras and sicklethorn, growing with bold reds and blues that stood out in the forest, but their own defenses kept them safe. A flower called the dearthswain, colored with such a dark purple as to almost be black, which created a sticky secretion to trap the insects trying to crawl upon it...

Beyond the flowers, she felt other life, shapes and forces less permanent, moving relatively freely throughout the forest. Small shapes, like the squirrels and rats which pulled the seeds falling from the trees to new places, allowing the forest to grow and flourish, no longer confined by the arrangement made so long ago. Their chatter filled her mind, continuous and busy. Larger shapes, those of wolves and tree lions who prowled, hunting the smaller creatures, were scattered. The wolves rested, preferring to hunt at night. The large tree lions, jumping from branch to branch as they hunted, rested in between their hunts, hiding in the branches high above, not mindful of her presence.

Eris felt even larger shapes, creatures she saw in her mind but had no name for, things that feared neither the wolf or the lion, and minded not that she had entered their realm, a place they considered theirs alone. Still, she sensed were they to find her, they would kill her and eat her with no more concern than were she a wolf or a possum. They were the creatures Terran had warned her about.

Other creatures roamed, though they wandered along the periphery of the forest, less a part of it than simple intruders upon it. The trees worked to push out these intruders, holding out those that did not belong.

Eris sighed and shifted her focus away until she found another shape, something she recognized in her mind. This shape felt small and delicate compared to what surrounded her.

Jasi.

She lay resting against a massive oak out in the forest not too far from her. Eris could tell she breathed steadily and regularly, and knew she slept. Somewhere overhead, one of the stealthy tree lions crept toward, drawn by her strange scent and the fact that she did not move.

Eris started forward, begging the trees to protect Jasi.

With the thought, she sensed a shifting of branches, as if one of the shrubs extended arms to cradle her sister—a spiky hawthorne, she noted. Somehow she knew the tree lion would not try to penetrate that barrier, preferring an easier kill, or simply content in knowing that eventually its prey would have to emerge and then it could pounce.

Eris thanked the forest and felt a sigh of wind in response.

She shivered.

How much of this was imagined?

Had she been gone so long her mind now played tricks on her, creating thoughts and images that simply could not be to keep her company and to keep her sane?

The idea terrified her. Now she truly *was* becoming like her Aunt Rochelle.

Eris ran in the direction she felt Jasi. The forest opened a pathway for her, and she hurried along it, not worrying about her safety. The entire time, she felt Jasi sleeping, knew when she came close. Her connection to the forest told her there was nothing in the trees for her to fear. Even the tree lion seemed to have crept away, sensing her coming and preferring an easier target.

When she reached the spot where the hawthorne cradled around Jasi, the spiky bush pulled away, as if freely releasing Jasi.

Her sister rested just where Eris had seen her in her mind.

How could this be real?

She pushed away the question and leaned forward, resting a hand on her sister's head, brushing a strand of hair away.

Jasi stirred and blinked her eyes open. "Eris? Are we home?"

Eris shook her head. "No. Still in the Svanth Forest."

Jasi mouthed the words back to her, eyes going wide. "We got separated. I thought you were lost. I tried to call for you—I tried until my voice was hoarse—but when I didn't hear anything, I think I gave up and went to sleep." She choked back a sob as she looked at Eris. "How did you find me?"

Eris didn't know how to answer the question. Now that she'd found Jasi, whatever connection she made with the forest seemed to have faded, leaving her with little sense of what happened around her. For some reason, the absence felt like a physical loss. Part of her longed for its return.

But it was still there, distantly. That sense of so much more. Of the trees and the flowers and the plants and life around her. Were she to delve into the depths of the roots, pull from them the stories the arranger had long ago left and she was able to read, first through her dreams and then through whatever power of the forest made it so she was able to delve deeper, she would know that power.

On the edge of her senses, she recognized another shape. Not one of the usual forest creatures, this was something—someone—who did not belong.

Through the remaining tenuous connection she managed to maintain to the forest, she felt them moving through the trees, slipping past the barriers the trees and the undergrowth worked to maintain, climbing over towering roots and skirting skillfully away from the reaching sharp thorns and spikes. Eris felt the person pause every so often, as if searching for something, before moving on, steadily deeper into the forest as if tracking. She shivered.

Whoever it was making his way through the trees, was coming right toward them.

CHAPTER 23

*E*ris grabbed Jasi's hand. "We should go."

Jasi stood slowly and brushed the edge of her tattered dress free. "You didn't answer."

Eris shook her head, shaking away the annoyance she felt at her sister. "Like you, I fell asleep. I think the capture and everything with it simply exhausted me. I don't know how long I slept." She swallowed, trying to ignore the sense of the forest around her. "When I awoke, I started toward where I thought I'd heard you last. When I got here...I came across you."

She took Jasi by the hand and pulled her to her feet. Then she dragged her through the trees, just as she had the night before. She needed to get her sister back to the palace, before the magi made it back, but it meant they would have to move through the forest as quickly as possible.

A path stretched in front of her, a narrow gap in the brush.

Eris pushed forward along the path. The sense of the forest continued to fade, but she felt the presence of whoever else was out there, still moving toward them.

What if it was one of the other creatures she sensed when standing in the heart of the forest?

Or worse—one of the magi?

She had thought Lira prevented the magi from entering the forest, but what if she was wrong? If Adrick chased them using some dark spell, Eris couldn't do anything to get them to safety. After what she'd seen of their power, the protection of the trees would not be enough to keep them safe.

If the magi were capable of throwing lightning and thunder at the forest in continuous waves, what was she against that onslaught?

Jasi looked over at her, a strange light in her eyes. "What happened to you last night?"

Last night...at least it had only been one night and not any longer. That answered one of her concerns. "When we were separated, I kept shouting out for you," Eris said. She remembered how she had called Jasi's name, pushing through the forest but never quite able to reach her. "Many times I thought I found you, but each time you were gone. Eventually, I couldn't go on any longer and fell asleep."

"Good thing you found me as easily as you did."

"Not easily," she said.

The connection to the forest had been real enough to help her find Jasi. Farther from the heart of the forest, the sense faded, but the knowledge about trees and flowers and creatures that wasn't her own had been real enough.

They rushed through the underbrush. Thorns which tore at Jasi's dress turned away from Eris. The path was only wide enough to go single file, and Eris pushed her in front, letting Jasi go first.

"Why are you hurrying?" Jasi asked.

Eris realized she was moving as quickly as possible, practically running through the forest. The narrow path widened as they reached smaller trees, and Eris moved alongside Jasi again. Soon they'd reach the edge of the forest. She didn't question how she knew. Then only the stretch of the plains separated them from the palace and their home.

If they were fast enough, they might even get there before the magi.

"I'm sorry. I told you Jacen was with me. I think he's hurt somewhere. We need to get you home, tell Father to send his men after Jacen. Warn Lira."

Jasi smiled bitterly. "Just me?"

Eris turned and looked at her sister. She wanted to get home as well. Mostly for the sense of safety, to be free of whatever the magi intended. Hopefully Lira could cast out the Conclave, but what if it was too late?

And now she had questions for Lira. After sleeping beneath the Svanth Forest, a night living dreams that seemed so real, a life not her own, she wanted answers. Did Lira know about the teary star? What did it mean that she viewed the dreams?

And why did she seem able to sense everything in the forest?

Then there was the growing desire to see Terran. Had he worried about her? Had he cared that she was gone? Returning home was the only way to know.

"I want to go home," she said softly.

Jasi looked at her with an expression of concern she had never shown while they were in the palace. Once back, Eris wondered if the old Jasi would return or if this ordeal had changed her.

"Maybe Lira will let you join her lessons soon."

Eris only shook her head. After everything, that was where Jasi's mind went.

The path twisted and turned, guiding them through the forest. Something about the direction didn't feel quite right. With most of the sun hidden by the dense canopy, Eris had no real sense of direction. The connection to the forest faded to nearly nothing. Even the earthy odor changed, that sense of ancient age dissipating the farther they went. Now the air carried with it an almost fruity scent mixed with the tart tang of cut greenery, either of grass or leaves. With each gust of wind, she could almost taste it.

Eris still felt someone behind them, twisting and turning with every movement they made. And gaining on them.

"Do you think the magi are still out there?" Jasi asked suddenly.

Eris almost jumped. The thought mirrored the fear she had, the quiet worry that whoever was out there was one of the magi. "I hope not."

"They need to know," Jasi said.

Eris looked over and arched a brow.

"They need to know what the Conclave intends. What they did to me...to us. And Lira needs to know about the magi attack."

"I suspect Lira already knows about the attack." How could she have not felt what happened last night?

"And Father?" Jasi said. "Will he know? Would Lira tell him about the attack? What it means? Would he believe his advisor would betray him?" Her voice had regained some of her usual strength, almost as if leaving the denser part of the forest brought Jasi out of whatever shell she had been in.

Strangely, Eris felt the opposite. Leaving the deeper part of the forest left her with a strange longing to return. Within the heart of the forest, she knew there were more stories for her to delve and read, more lessons the roots of the great trees could share, had she only the time.

"I don't know." Eris looked back over her shoulders, eyes searching through the trees, almost able to see through the shadows to the deeper part of the forest.

"Mother knows?"

Eris turned back. "Knows what?"

Jasi sniffed, annoyed. "Knows that Lira is a flower mage," she said. "Honestly, Eris, even out here you seem so distracted. It's almost as if you don't want to return."

"Mother knows about Lira." She thought of the way they shared a look when Lira had fallen during the attack on the garden. But if her mother knew, then why had their father not banished Adrick? "So does Father, I think. Neither of them know about what the Conclave plans. Had the attack last night been successful, I don't know what would have happened at home."

"You don't think it was successful?"

Eris frowned. The forest had seemed unharmed when she'd sensed it earlier. Would she not have felt more had there been some sort of injury? The magi thought to destroy Lira's hidden garden, the one she'd started within the forest. Had they?

As she considered, she *felt* where the garden was located, could turn and walk straight to it were she to want to, and knew it was not damaged. The garden was massive, larger even than the one growing within the confines of the palace walls. Flowers of such varieties grew within Lira's garden, flowers whose names suddenly flashed into her mind before fading. It was a garden of great power.

That was what the magi had been after. And had failed.

"No. It wasn't successful." Whatever else had happened last night, at least the magi failed.

She thought about why the Conclave had abducted them. What purpose could they have in bringing them to the forest? What could Eris and Jasi have done that the magi had been unable to accomplish?

But she knew that as well. Lira had planted her garden with a particular arrangement, one that conferred great power and kept everyone else away. Even the usual forest life left the garden alone.

Only...it would not keep out everyone. The keepers, much like they could enter the forest, could enter the garden easily. And then, whatever magic Lira's garden lent would be able to be broken.

Could she and Jasi have managed to break the enchantments?

Would their time working with Lira really have made a difference? That was what Adrick had counted on, Eris was certain.

Her fading connection to the forest didn't provide the answer.

"Eris!"

She turned, startled, and looked at Jasi with a concerned expression.

"Have you not heard anything I've said?" Jasi asked.

Eris shook her head. Focused as she had been on trying to understand the forest, she hadn't paid any attention to Jasi as she hurried forward.

"I'm sorry, Jasi. I'm focused on getting us out of the forest."

"Do you even know where you're going? I can't see anything through the trees—how do you know we're going in the right direction? For all you know, we're winding in circles."

Eris glanced back at Jasi and saw the worry etched into the lines of her cheeks. There was a determined set of her jaw and she walked with a little more confidence in her step. "I can tell."

She didn't elaborate. How to explain that she simply *knew* where she was going? How to explain that the glimpse given to her by the heart of the forest had been enough for her to know which paths would be easiest to travel, which would take them on the most direct route back toward the city and their home? Jasi would not understand.

Jasi stopped, obviously deciding she'd had enough of Eris telling her where they were going. "Well, I don't recognize any of these flowers," she said. "And Lira made it clear the first thing to do when exploring new areas was to examine the flowers for ones you know." She turned toward a clump of yellow thistlesprites and leaned in as she inhaled. "I have never seen these before. Some sort of daisy...or possibly a lily?" she went on, speaking mostly to herself. "Their stems are too long to be calyips or anosems. Both have yellow varietals," she said without looking up, using a voice that seemed to try to mimic Lira.

"They are thistlesprites," Eris said.

Her sense of the person behind her had faded to little more than a gentle awareness. How much longer did they have before they were caught? Could they reach the borders of the forest? The needlegrass would slow them there, perhaps provide enough cover to keep them safe. And they weren't far from the edge of the forest. The faster they moved, she hoped they would be able to outrun whoever was behind them. That hope faded along with her awareness and connection to the forest.

"An unusual shape to the petals," Jasi went on. "Long and narrow. Some flecks of blue or black along them. They would look lovely when paired with perisals," she decided.

Eris shook her head. Perisals were all wrong for thistlesprites; the combination would deprive the potential held within both of the flowers. Even the colors together would not complement, the perisals overpowering the softer thistlesprites. "They are thistlesprites," she said again as she grabbed Jasi's arm and pulled.

Jasi pulled back. "Thistlesprites?" Her mouth seemed to struggle to say the name, almost as if the word was distasteful to her. "What are you talking about, Eris?"

"The flower," she said, reaching toward Jasi again.

Her sister pulled away and leaned again toward the flower. "Honestly, if you don't know what they are, you should not make up a name," she admonished. "Lira taught us you should describe what you see, compare it to what you know, and then use that to look for its possible origin."

"I know what it is. It's a thistlesprite."

Jasi turned to look at her. Her usual sense of arrogance had returned, any hint of compassion and tenderness toward her sister now as faded as the sense Eris had of the forest. "How would you know that?"

Eris didn't explain the forest told her. Even to her, the idea seemed unbelievable, more like a dream than anything real. So instead, she answered, "I read about them. I came across them when I was looking through one of the books Master Billiken gave me to research my flower."

Jasi stood and huffed. "You could have said so sooner."

"I tried," Eris said. "We should keep moving. I fear there might be someone else out in the forest after us." It was time Jasi at least knew that. Let her feel the same sense of urgency Eris felt.

"Is that something else you read about in one of the books?"

"No. I have sensed someone tracking us for a while. They grow closer." She didn't tell Jasi *how* she felt it, deciding to hold that back. Besides, it wasn't as if Jasi would believe her anyway.

Her words had the wrong effect. Jasi lost some of her composure, practically wilting in front of her. "It's the magi, isn't it? We aren't going to make it back to the palace. They will catch us out here in the forest and drag me back with them!" She looked at Eris with haunted eyes.

What had happened to her?

Eris slapped her sister across the face. She had meant to be gentle, but the force came off more than intended. Jasi's head jerked back from the strength of the blow. "Not one of the magi," she said. "At least, I don't think so. But we shouldn't dawdle here looking at flowers. We should be moving forward and trying to reach the boundaries of the forest."

Jasi had a lost expression for a moment before she steadied herself and glared at Eris. "We will not be any safer on the edge of the forest than we are within the trees. If someone tracks us, they'll simply follow us out."

Jasi was right. There was only one way to ensure that one of them made it back to the palace to report to Lira and their parents.

"I'll draw them off. You need to hurry back toward the Kingsroad. Stay low and hidden and get back to the city. Tell Lira what happened first and then go to Father. He needs to know about Jacen. We were about a half-day's ride west of the city."

Jasi was shaking her head. "No...we stay together. We'll both make it back to the palace."

How was it Jasi suddenly seemed to care about her? Had she always or was it simply from the effect of their capture? "If it's one of the magi—"

"You said it was not!"

"If it is," Eris repeated, "then we need to separate. If they catch us together, there's not much we can do. Last night you saw what they were capable of doing just as much as I did. Do you think we would have a chance against that?"

Jasi shook her head.

"And it *has* to be me," Eris continued. She hated saying it aloud, fearing it might be true. "After Jacen, you're next in line. If any should stay behind and risk capture—" she took a deep breath and swallowed "—and death, it has to be me."

Jasi took her hand and squeezed. "Promise me you will stay safe!"

Eris nodded. "Just get to the palace. Then we will both have a chance to be safe. Go that way," she said, pointing toward a long straight path. "It will lead you toward the Verilain Plains. Continue west, and you will reach the Kingsroad."

It was a measure of Jasi's agitation that she didn't even question how Eris knew.

Jasi squeezed again. "Eris—"

Eris swallowed. "I know. Just make it back to Eliara. Whatever else happens, you need to inform Father."

Jasi nodded and started to turn before hesitating and spinning back and pulling Eris into a strong embrace. When she turned away, tears stained her cheeks.

CHAPTER 24

*E*ris waited after Jasi disappeared, determined to draw the attention of whoever tracked them. Making a point to disturb the branches of the underbrush, she turned back toward the center of the forest. Whatever else was there, it was her best way of avoiding capture, especially if the trees would cooperate with her as they seemed to have done earlier.

Darkness quickly enveloped her as she moved away from the smaller elm and spruce ringing the outer edge of the forest. When a few oaks appeared sprinkled within, she knew she was getting closer. The air took on more of an earthen scent, that of decaying leaves and dirt and less of the lightly perfumed fragrance of the flowers along the perimeter. Strangely, she welcomed the change.

There was another subtler change as she moved. The awareness of the forest around her began to return.

She began sensing when the next towering oak would appear, where the small streams cut through the forest for her to take a drink, where she might find edible berries. Fatigue still had not set in; she moved easily through the forest, no sense of tiredness taking her as it should, almost as if the forest itself lent her energy.

Eris was aware of when the person following her paused at the point where Jasi had gone off on her own. She waited with her breath held as the person seemed to consider, recognizing the two of them split off. The forest itself seemed to hold its breath, everything silent around her. Eris hoped they turned back into the trees to follow her. If it *was* the magi after them, they still needed one of them to work whatever spell they intended.

Then the person started forward, as if out of the forest.

Eris felt her heart skip. Jasi would not be safe.

She slumped against a nearby tree, wishing there was something she could do, some way she could draw the person tracking them back into the forest and after her rather than Jasi.

A few moments passed, and then she realized that the tracker had turned back. Had they paused at the few bushes she had intentionally brushed against, hoping they would see her charging through the forest?

Whatever it was, they circled around, moving into the trees.

Eris felt a mixture of relief and fear. Relief that Jasi would be safe—at least as safe as Eris could help to make her. Scared that she was alone with whoever tracked her, moving through the forest with nearly the ease she managed. And she suspected the forest itself aided her.

She considered continuing deeper into the forest before deciding against it. That would do nothing other than delay whatever was going to happen. Besides, she suspected she could maneuver to see whoever tracked her before they saw her. Especially given the awareness the forest granted.

Eris moved to a part of the forest which offered shelter but still allowed her to look out through the brush. And then she waited.

She didn't know how long she stood waiting. Minutes. Hours?

The sky slowly changed, growing darker. Soon she would be

facing her second night under the trees. If nothing happened, she would be forced to remain awake and vigilant throughout the night, fearing whatever and whoever was out there.

If only the forest would protect her.

Eris swallowed. She had hoped the trees would sense her need and respond. Earlier, it seemed as if the forest itself aided her, creating a path for her to follow, pulling the bush around Jasi to keep the tree lion away, and helping her to sense someone following them.

Now it didn't answer.

The sense of the person drawing closer was strong. They moved confidently, easily following her trail. Part of her hoped the forest would obscure her passing, protect her from whatever was after her, but that didn't seem to be possible. A few birds calling in the trees nearby fell silent as the person passed, taking up their song again once they felt safe. Squirrels chattered overhead, and Eris pretended she could almost make out what they were saying. The air was still.

And then, through the trees and the brush, a dark shape slowly emerged from the surrounding trees.

Eris froze, hoping the trees gave enough cover that the person tracking her couldn't see her. What would they do when they realized her tracks stopped?

Flashes of darker green came through the trees. The person paused, turning, and she noted the long bow slung over their back, quiver of arrows alongside it. A short sword hung from their waist.

No sign of the crimson cloak. Not one of the magi.

Then who?

Eris suddenly felt quite foolish. Had she really thought she'd able to hold off the person following her? She was unarmed and underprepared, with only the fickle forest to help. The forest seemed content to share its awareness with her, but not more than that.

Leaning back against the tree, she tried to control her breathing, feeling very tired. If she could, she thought she would climb the tree next to her and simply lay down upon one of the branches. Of course, then she would have to contend with the tree lions. Perhaps when she slept, she wouldn't care.

The branches snapped, and Eris jerked back.

A hand reached through the trees and grabbed at her wrist, clamping down with a firm grip. She jerked back but could not break free.

Then she was pulled from behind the cover hiding her.

She screamed. The sound seemed deadened in the forest. Even the birds nearby seemed not to notice.

With a sudden realization, Eris knew she would die within the trees.

CHAPTER 25

"Careful!" a voice hissed.

Eris's eyes snapped open, recognizing the voice.

Brown eyes she'd once thought soft flicked from side to side, suddenly much harder than she remembered. The dark green jacket he wore fit much better than the one she'd seen on him in the palace gardens, and she could not help but notice how well he filled it out. His long hair was swept back and tied behind his head. There was no sign of the hat he and master Nels always wore in the garden.

"Terran?" There had been little need for her to speak since she'd left Jasi, and his name came out as little more than a croak. How had he found her?

"My lady," he said. "Finally, I've reached you. You need to be careful in this forest. There are things here that do not care for the intrusion of man."

Without thinking, Eris felt for the large dark creatures she had first sensed when she made her connection with the forest, but she found them moving far off, deeper in the forest.

Still, whatever the creatures were, they had little regard for her life. From what she sensed, they would be just as content to attack her as any other creature wandering the forest. Meat was meat.

"I'm not a man," she said.

She immediately wished she hadn't. After everything she'd been through, seeing Terran lifted her spirits. How could she feel so strongly for this gardener and his lopsided smile? But he was the only person to come after her.

"What are you doing here? How did you find me?" She stood in front of him, hands on her hips, not minding her scandalous dress as she stood in front of him.

He frowned, meeting her eyes and not looking at her clothing. "I should ask you the same thing." He shook his head, his brown hair swishing over his shoulder. "When you didn't come to the garden for the last few days, I realized you must have been foolish enough to try reaching the Svanth on your own." He hesitated when Eris glared at him before pressing on. "I warned you how dangerous this forest can be, but you came anyway! I had to tell Master Nels that my mother was ill so he would let me leave…"

"You came to rescue me?" Eris couldn't help how pleased she felt that he'd come for her. She tried to suppress the flush she knew came to her cheeks. But why had Terran come to help?

She took a step away from him, back toward the protective cover of the trees and the tall brush around it.

Terran's eyes softened, taking on some of the look that she remembered, the warmth and the expression almost like affection. "It may seem harsh, but I can't overstate the need for caution within the forest."

"You are here," she argued.

Terran nodded. "Against my better judgment. Had I not needed to reach you, I would not have entered."

"The forest means me no harm."

Terran's eyes narrowed. "Perhaps not the forest, but there are other things who live within its boundaries that do not care who you are. Trust me, my lady, we need to get you back to the palace."

Eris took a step back. While slung over the side of the horse after being abducted by the magi, she would have given anything to be rescued; she would have gone willingly with Terran then. But she had escaped—had helped Jasi escape—and she did not want to have Terran thinking that she was some poor girl who needed rescuing.

"Please, my lady...Eris." He said her name with some difficulty. "We must return to the palace. Something is amiss. Your brother has gone missing. If that weren't bad enough, another storm swept through Eliara in the last few days, nearly uprooting the majority of the garden."

Eris swallowed. If a storm had gone through, that meant Lira might not have the strength to fight off the magi. Were her parents already at risk?

"Master Nels is quite beside himself to keep everything in order. Had it not been for the steadying hand of the mistress of flowers..."

"I didn't seek the Svanth on my own," Eris said. She took another step back and toward the trees. She felt them behind her like a soothing hand, a steadying sensation on her back that granted her a sense of strength and confidence.

Terran frowned. "What do you mean? How else would you have gotten here?"

"Not just me. Jasi, too. That's who I was with." She swallowed, wishing she knew where Jasi had gone, but she'd traveled beyond where Eris could sense. "We were abducted, Terran. I went riding with Jacen when they found me. I don't know what happened to him, but the Conclave brought Jasi to the forest. They needed us for some dark magic."

"Abducted?" Now it was Terran's turn to look confused. "But she was just married. She should be halfway to Saffra by now."

"There is some plot against Lira. They needed one of her students to make it work."

"You're one of her students," Terran reminded.

Eris shook her head. "Not like Jasi. I still haven't even been allowed to join the lessons with my sisters." After seeing what Jasi had learned, she was no longer certain she wanted to be a part of the lessons. Eris thought the combinations and colors that Jasi thought lovely were harsh and unimaginative. Perhaps she had been better off not studying with her sisters.

"You think the Conclave would attack the Mistress of Flowers?" Terran asked. The tone of his question was off, almost as if he knew the answer without asking.

Eris had reached the edge of the trees again and felt comfortable rough bark against her back. "She is not just the Mistress of Flowers. She's a flower mage."

Even that incompletely described Lira.

Terran had been inching toward her as they talked, but he suddenly froze in place. "When did you first learn?"

First learn? Eris felt her eyes go wide and she was rooted in place. "You know?"

Terran nodded. "Of course I know. She's the one who asked me to come to Eliara."

"Why?" After seeing how easily he moved through the forest, Eris thought that she understood, but she needed Terran to say.

"I am a gardener."

As he said it, a staggering flash of knowledge resonated within her. Not just a gardener as she had always thought, but a *gardener* like those from her dream. Like Therin from her dreams who helped cultivate the forest, guiding those first plants.

"A gardener," she repeated.

Was Master Nels a gardener as well? He had been in Eliara long before Lira, had worked for her grandfather in the years before her father took the throne. But that didn't mean he *couldn't* be a gardener.

"That is how you were able to move so easily through the forest," she realized. The forest had not minded his presence. "That is how you were able to track me."

Terran gazed at her with a strange look on his face. "You were not easy to find. This place has much power. Makes tracking difficult, especially for certain..." He trailed off, the strange expression not leaving his face. "For untold years, the gardeners have worked near the Svanth Forest, some few daring to work within the trees themselves, a connection to it nearly in our blood. My father was a gardener and his father before him. Once, they worked in the great Gardens of Elaysia, helping the Keepers, building places of beauty and power. They are all gone now, scattered, their gardens destroyed. Only the forest remains."

As he spoke, Eris felt through her connection with the trees the story that Terran told, could almost trace back his ancestors and see them in her mind. Had she dared, she could have delved into the roots and read the story written there and would have known everything with certainty.

"I can see from your face that you know all this," Terran said. "Care to tell me how?"

"Know all what?"

"The history of the forest. The history of the gardens. Did the mistress teach you?"

"She never tried to teach me anything."

Terran stepped closer, the strange expression leaving as a warmth spread across his face. "You believe that? All that time you spent walking through the garden, and you learned nothing?"

"She didn't try to teach me anything!" Eris didn't know why she argued with Terran, but the familiar frustration resurfaced, worse since Terran seemed to think Lira had tried to teach her something, rather than simply pushing her away, ignoring her while she focused instead on her sisters. She was used to feeling that way with her sisters, but from Terran? "Not like my sisters. They were allowed to have lessons from her, time spent teaching them how the colors worked together, which flowers paired well. Everything I learned, I did on my own!"

To her surprise, Terran laughed. "You don't think you learned any of that?"

Eris frowned. "Not like them."

"My father tells me of a time when there were enormous gardens to wander. Keepers used to wander, to simply take in the combination of flowers, the arrangements attempted, to see what was possible." He sighed. "The gardens are lost, but the mistress tried to recreate some of that in the palace."

"What are you talking about?"

"What do you think you were doing when you wandered the garden? Why do you think she asked me to work with you?"

"Lira asked you to work with me?" she asked.

"Each gardener pairs with a keeper. They work together."

"But I'm not a keeper," she said.

Terran nodded. "Not yet, but I think she saw that you have the potential. At least, I believe it's you." He shrugged. "She asked me to help attend to the garden in the palace, sending word that a keeper trained there. Since Elaysia fell, I never expected to pair to a keeper. No surviving gardener did." He looked at her, intensity bright in his eyes. "My father never did. My grandfather was the last. And the stories he told…" He sighed again. "I was comfortable in Helash, had started to make a life, but when a keeper summons…I had to come."

"You're mistaken. It wasn't me Lira intended." She didn't say it, but likely Jasi. That was why the forest had protected her. That was why Lira planned to go with Jasi to Saffra, to help her establish her garden there.

But if it had been Jasi, why hadn't Lira sent Terran with her?

"When she first asked me to come to the palace, I wasn't sure. The ability of the keeper is rare, usually passed down through bloodlines."

"My parents aren't keepers."

Terran shrugged. "The mistress was convinced of the talent."

"And you?"

He shrugged. "I wasn't sure. I watched all of you," he admitted. "Your sisters claimed a flower quickly. Such a thing is unusual in a keeper. Then I saw how the flowers of the garden seemed to turn toward you. A sign, but just one of many. When you came to me asking to come to the forest, I thought maybe the mistress was right, but it wasn't until I tried tracking you through the forest itself that I really knew."

"Knew what?"

"You have the gift. Keepers have the ability to harness the sun's power using combinations of flowers, but you can do more than that, can't you?" He studied her a moment, and she almost blushed from the intensity in his eyes. "You hear the trees."

She opened her mouth to protest, but closed it again. What he said was true. She didn't know how it was possible—or what it might mean for her—but there was no denying that she was aware of the forest around her. And more than that—everything within the forest as well.

"You'll have questions," Terran said. "As I did when my father explained why it was that everything I planted sprang to life. Or how it was I knew just when something needed to be watered or fed. With the loss of the gardens, there hadn't been much need for the gardeners, not as there once was. We need to get you back to the palace so that you can find the mistress and get your answers."

Eris couldn't even argue with what Terran said. Now that he mentioned it, the flowers of the garden *did* seem to turn to her as she passed. She'd thought it a trick from the way the sun shone, but maybe it was more.

There certainly was something real about her strange connection to the forest—whatever that was—about how she was able to delve into the roots. With enough time, she could read the story written there, gain an understanding of everything around her.

She thought about telling all this to Terran, but instead, she said, "I understand my flower now."

Terran narrowed his eyes, tilting his head. "And?"

"I will show you."

She started into the forest without waiting for him. With her connection to the forest, she sensed where she was going and quickly led him to the heart of the forest. She knew he followed.

The trees around her changed. At first the change was subtle. Without her connection, she wasn't sure she would've recognized it. Flowers thinned before eventually disappearing, as if teary stars preferred to be the only flower present in this part of the forest. The heavy canopy blocked most of the light. A soft breeze fluttered the upper branches that did not reach where she stood with Terran.

Stopping before one of the towering Svanth trees, she pointed at the bark. "Here."

Terran looked at the tree. "There aren't any flowers here."

"Not now," Eris said. She ran her hand just over the surface of the blue grey vines. Tiny barbs withdrew before piercing her skin. Beneath the tough hide of the vine, she sensed the early buds beginning. "But soon. They only blossom every seven years."

"The tree itself flowers?" Terran asked, reaching toward the tree.

Eris caught his hand. He let her take his warm and calloused hand away. Terran leaned toward the vine and stared closely at it, a smile coming to his face. He didn't ask how she managed to touch it.

"Not the tree. A vine grows along the tree, protecting it. It's the vine that flowers."

Terran walked around the tree, his smile spreading. "These are Svanth trees, the namesake of this place."

Eris nodded. Her dreams had told her that much.

"Svanth trees grow massive nuts which fall only in the spring." He looked over at her. "You know, many have tried growing Svanth outside the heart of the forest, but have failed? This is the one tree the gardeners have never managed to grow."

Eris thought she understood, remembering the tender bark of the tree from her dream and the nervous acceptance of letting the vine grow. She remembered how Therin did not think the trees would survive, especially not after the vines were allowed to prosper. Instead, they both survived, one helping the other. "The Svanth trees are delicate. The vines strengthen them. Then they both prosper."

Terran looked from her to the tree. "I never knew that there was more to the Svanth trees. I am not sure how many do. Where did you learn that?"

Eris considered how to answer. Would explaining the connection seem too strange to Terran? Would explaining dreams that had felt so real, almost as if she had lived them herself?

But Terran had come for her. The only one who cared that she'd gone missing.

"A dream," she said. "As we ran from the magi, Jasi and I were separated. I ended up here, in the heart of the forest, where I fell asleep and dreamt of the forest, from its very beginning to when it reached its current enormous size. When I woke, the dream stayed with me."

Terran watched her for a moment and then looked around at the trees. "This place is powerful. Few can reach the heart of the forest without its permission. You were granted a great gift, my lady."

Eris remembered how the forest seemed determined to pull

her and her sister apart, the way it guided her toward the center, and wondered. Was this a gift or something else?

"When I became aware of you, I sent Jasi back to the palace."

"I saw that one of you had continued on. The tracks led out of the forest and toward the Verilain Plains. The other tracks moved back into the forest. I almost followed the other set of tracks."

Eris nodded. "I know."

Terran's mouth tightened. "But I sensed the trees wanted me to follow the other set of prints. When I saw you, I knew why."

"You think I am meant to be a flower mage—a keeper —like Lira?"

He nodded. "I think that's what you are meant to be."

What she was meant to be. Eris had no idea what she was meant to do. Her father expected her to marry and carry on the bloodline. That was never what she'd wanted. But this?

Eris shook her head. She could not be like Lira, could not sit and arrange flowers each day, could not agonize over how the arrangements fit together even if such arrangements gave her power over the magi.

"I don't think I can do what Lira does."

Terran stepped up to her. His presence changed both in how he was physically next to her and through her connection to the forest. He smelled earthy, much like the forest itself. This time, he took her hand and squeezed, and pulled her close.

She looked up at him, and he smiled at her with his lopsided grin. His deep brown eyes seemed the color of fall leaves and almost swallowed her. Eris shivered.

"You may not make the same types of arrangements as she makes, but the gift is no different. Each keeper chooses their own garden. Each chooses the flower that suits them best, which helps start their garden as they work with the gardeners."

"My flower doesn't belong in any garden." Much like her, she realized.

Terran smiled and pulled her closer. The heat of his body pressed on her.

"Are you certain? Look around you. Look at this life. There was purpose to these plantings. That purpose is what grants this place its power. There is more than one type of garden, Eris."

Terran was right. She had felt the power building in her dream even if she wasn't entirely sure what she had felt. The keeper of her dreams had known, had placed her garden—this forest—in such a way as to guide the story she wanted to tell.

"Does Lira know?"

Terran didn't move away. "Probably. Undoubtedly she recognized the flower. Choosing a flower like the teary star names you a certain type of keeper, different than one who chooses a flower that prefers full sunlight."

Different. Always different. But what did it mean?

"What happens now?" she asked.

Terran sighed. "Were this a different time, a time when the great gardens still existed, you would be offered the opportunity to learn from all of the great keepers. Now, with the gardens destroyed, the keepers scattered, you must choose whether you wish to learn from the mistress."

"And if I don't?" Lira had not seemed willing to share much with her, especially if she suspected what Eris was capable of becoming. Holding that information back from her was bothersome.

Terran looked upset by the possibility. He shook his head. "I don't know what will happen then. Perhaps your ability will wilt and fade. Perhaps it will come out regardless of what you choose. I don't know."

Eris wondered whether Lira even knew.

"I have known few keepers, the Mistress of Flowers being the only one. My grandfather told me of a time when there were dozens of keepers, each paired with a gardener, and each with a wondrous garden. The Gardens of Elaysia. Its beauty was said to be unrivaled. The power of the gardens nearly limitless."

In her mind, she saw the gardens as they once were. With more time, she suspected she could delve into the roots of the forest and know the story written there. How much could she learn by simply exploring what the forest's keeper had written within the roots?

"What happened to the gardens?" she asked.

Terran shook his head. "I don't know. My grandfather was one of the last gardeners of that time, and he will not speak of it. My father knows something of it, but he will not tell me much. All that I know is the gardens were destroyed, and the gardeners, along with the keepers, disappeared from this land."

Eris wondered how long ago the gardens had been destroyed. Did the Conclave have a hand in that, too? Had Lira been one of the great keepers in the Gardens of Elaysia?

Things began to fall into place. Lira saying her garden had been destroyed. The magi describing the difficulty in destroying the gardens. Their fear of Lira. But why? What did it mean?

She had so many questions. Most the forest couldn't answer. That left Lira.

"We should return to the palace. Jasi might need help."

"We should hurry. If we're lucky, we will find your sister along the way."

Terran took the lead, guiding them from the forest. Eris noted that he led them on the most direct path. The forest seemed to help, creating an opening in the undergrowth that didn't catch or pull at them.

Darkness had fallen as they walked. The air was still and heavy with the scent of a coming rain. The forest seemed relaxed, as if in anticipation.

They moved quickly, leaving the Svanth trees behind; soon

only elms and oaks surrounded them, not stretching nearly as high into the sky.

When Eris saw a flash of light she hesitated.

Then came thunder.

"The magi."

Terran looked back at her. A sudden blast of light lit his face. Worry lines etched there. "Are you certain?" he asked.

She nodded. The memory of the attack from the night before was still vivid in her mind. Already she sensed the forest tensing, as if forming a defense against the magic the magi summoned.

Thunder began to roll in steady rumbles, but distantly and not as if targeted toward the forest. Lightning streaked again, flashing brilliant. Eris felt the energy building, but it was nothing like the night before, nothing like the near suffocating pressure that made it hard for her to breathe.

This was not an attack on the forest, she realized. This was something different, out toward the Verilain Plains.

With a jolt of fear, she understood.

Jasi.

CHAPTER 26

*E*ris streaked through the trees, not mindful of whether Terran followed. All she cared about was whether Jasi was well. She needed the forest to cooperate, to grant her free passage as she ran. The forest seemed to accede to her needs, opening a path.

Thankfully, the path ran straight and true, cutting through the trees. The thorny undergrowth pushed aside, letting her hurry toward the thunder and explosions.

She didn't bother lifting what remained of her thin shift as she went, not worried about whether it was soiled. The tattered white remains would have to be discarded entirely if she ever managed to return to the palace.

Instead, she was filled with fear for Jasi. The attack was upon her sister. Who else would the magi attack outside the forest?

Trees blurred past her, little more than dark shadows looming. Occasionally, she heard Terran call her name, but it was a distant sound, far behind her. Sooner than should have been possible, she reached the edge of the forest and passed beyond the trees.

The Verilain Plains. Eris rushed straight toward where the lightning struck. Thunder still rolled, almost a constant presence. Did they attack Lira, or had she defended the palace?

Tall needlegrass sliced at her as she ran. Were she anything like Lira, it would just leave her alone rather than tearing at her arms and legs while she ran in the darkness.

Why couldn't the grass simply bend away from her?

And then it did.

Eris almost stumbled. Faintly, she was aware of a connection to the grasses along the plain. She felt it sway in the breeze. Now that the grasses understood what she wanted, they parted, leaving a narrow path for her to slip through.

She ran.

Other than the occasional flickers of lightning lighting the heavy clouds overhead, the night was dark. She felt her way across the plains. No longer did the bright blasts streak from the sky. Only the soft rumble let her know the magi were active somewhere nearby.

Eris paused. The air crackled with energy. Her breathing grew heavy, tight, and she didn't know if it was from her running or the magic the magi performed.

Could the grasses upon the plain aid her as the forest had? Eris touched the ground, ran a finger through the hard dirt as she made a connection, creating what she had seen in her dream the night before. Then she delved.

Eris could not explain how she knew what to do. Perhaps sleeping and dreaming at the heart of the forest had unlocked something inside her. Perhaps she had always known, just had to try. Perhaps she simply imagined whatever it was she did. All were possibilities.

What she felt as she touched the plains was weak, the connection different than what she felt with the trees. A vast expanse opened around her, like a light touch on her mind which carried none of the depth or weight of the forest. The information was different as well, almost muted.

Somewhere ahead of her was life.

The grasses could not make the same distinction as the forest, almost as if unable to tell one form from another. All she sensed was that life existed. More than that, she felt life moving, disturbing the stalks of grass, bending and trampling as they pushed across the plain, the grasses fighting...fighting...fighting... tearing at the life pressing upon it...before falling...falling... crushed to the ground.

Eris broke the connection. The sense was strange and unique. She had no idea why she should be able to sense what the grasses told her.

Again, she ran.

Now she knew where to go. Eris had the advantage; the grasses did not work to slow her, parting, splitting wide in a narrow path so she could move through them unobstructed.

The longer she ran, the more she felt the pressure of the magic against her. Eris grew increasingly certain of what she felt. Fatigue did not bother her as it should. She had run for what felt like hours but didn't feel its effects. Once she dared to glance back and saw the distant outline of the forest. How had she moved so quickly?

Finally, the energy upon her was nearly unbearable.

She slowed to a walk to take deeper breaths. Eris imagined there was some way to counteract the effect of the magi's magic, but she did not know it.

The sense became severe enough that she finally stopped.

Only then did she see the light.

Flames bobbed in the distance, torches or lanterns carried to light the night. Eris counted at least four. The magi.

She crept forward slowly, listening for the sounds around her. The distant light helped her see the grasses spread apart for her, slowly now that she walked. Even without the light she felt what the grasses did.

Ducking low, Eris moved as close as she dared. The tall needle-grass would protect her. Hide her. It seemed strange to be thankful for its presence after she had cursed it when they went through it before, but without the tall grasses, she would be exposed for the magi to see.

She felt it as Terran rejoined her. He said nothing as he crouched next to her. Part of Eris was surprised that he was not winded, that he'd managed to keep up. Were gardeners granted certain abilities?

"What are you doing?" He pitched his voice so it sounded no louder than the soft breeze blowing through the plains.

Terran's large hand rested on her arm. The warmth of his skin sent heat through her as he touched her bared skin. She tilted her head toward the flames. "I need to see if they have taken Jasi."

Terran blinked slowly and then nodded. His deep brown eyes were wide. He didn't argue with her.

Eris crept forward, moving low. The grasses bent away from her just enough so that they weren't tearing at her flesh, just enough to grant passage across the plains.

Terran stayed close, sliding along the ground behind her, nearly silent. Were it not for her connection to the grasses and the sense it granted her, she doubted she would know he was there.

"Strange that she would come out here."

Eris froze. One of the magi spoke and sounded as if he was next to her. His voice was coarse and deep.

"There is much strange about this one," another commented.

Eris recognized the voice as coming from Davin. She stayed low, hoping the grasses would continue to protect her, wrap her in their disguise.

"She has a reason for being here. We must learn what it is."

"How will we keep her secured?"

"She can do nothing against the irons. There are limits to her magic." This from the High Seat, and he spat the last.

With sudden realization, she understood. Not Jasi.

They had Lira.

"Fortunate she is here. Once the last garden is destroyed, there will be no more interference. The Conclave can claim the throne."

"Had you not allowed her to fester, we wouldn't have had to work so hard at this," Davin told Adrick.

"I did what was needed. We've lost nothing. And when Tholen reaches the border, he'll find the attack much stronger than expected. We will soon have the throne here."

"We do already," Davin said.

"Not yet."

"Near enough," the High Seat said.

Eris crept backward, moving carefully, making no more sound than the grasses in the breeze. When she was far enough away, she turned to Terran. "They have Lira."

"How?"

She shook her head. After all the attacks the magi had tried, why had they now been able to capture Lira? What changed? Had she come for her best student, knowing Jasi was in trouble? But if she had, where was her sister?

"I don't know. I don't think they have Jasi."

"If Lira is here, then nothing protects the palace," Terran said. "The attacks will grow stronger. I don't think the palace can withstand the force of the attacks long without her."

"It is not the palace gardens they seek to destroy. It's the reason they abducted Jasi and I in the first place. The magi seek to destroy the forest."

"Then you have to stop them," Terran said.

She shook her head. "Not me. We need to free Lira. She can stop them."

Terran took her hand, looking deeply into her eyes. The distant light of the flames made his deep brown eyes dance. "Lira can only do so much. Like all keepers, she is connected to the forest, can use the vast power stored within the trees and all that grows within its boundaries, but to truly save the forest, we must find the keeper."

She could tell from the way he said it there was a difference. "Are there others?"

Terran pulled her back, moving away from the dancing firelight. A soft breeze kicked up, blowing back toward the forest, as if even the wind wanted to keep their conversation private and prevent the magi from hearing.

"I know little of the keepers other than what my father has shared. The mistress would not share such information with me as I was not her gardener. Each garden is unique. Most keepers begin their own gardens, but some bond to existing gardens, take over its care, work to grow the power trapped in the garden, enhance it. With a garden as old as the forest, there have been other keepers through the years."

"How do you know that it isn't Lira?"

Terran shook his head. "Her flowers grow in the sun. The keeper of the forest prefers the shade. I think Lira can use the forest, but she is not its keeper."

Eris looked up and saw the distant smear of darkness on the horizon where the trees began. The forest stretched out on either side of her, running for hundreds of miles, a massive length of darkness in the night. There was much history within the forest, much power. Even with whatever skills she had, she felt that about the forest. Could the magi really manage to destroy it all?

"How?" she asked, looking back to Terran.

Before he spoke, there was a distant peal of thunder. A blast of lightning came streaking from the sky, striking the ground behind them. They were thrown from their feet, tossed forward and into sharp grasses that slashed at her as she landed.

Thunder rolled again.

The magi knew they were here.

CHAPTER 27

*E*ris jumped to her feet. Lightning flashed in the sky around them, illuminating the night. Another strike might be more than they could take. No longer did the grasses provide protection. It was as if the energy of the storm had flattened the tall needlegrass, laying it on its side, leaving she and Terran exposed.

The air stunk of char and smoke mixed with the scent of broken earth. She tasted it on her tongue. Massive chunks had been rent from the ground, tossed into the air and thrown about, some striking Eris and drawing blood. Her ears rang from the blast; the air now carried an odd muted sound. Her body ached from where she'd collided with the ground. Thankfully, she could stand.

Glancing behind her, she looked for signs of the magi. Lanterns moved through the grasses distantly. How had she moved so far away so fast? Had the explosion really thrown them that far?

"Terran?" she whispered. Her voice sounded strange and soft. She feared raising her it too much, not wanting to draw any more attention to them, already knowing it was too late. If the magi had struck, they knew where they were.

"Here."

She found him lying nearly twenty feet away. The ground around him cushioned his blow, but the sharp grasses had slashed at his jacket, tearing the fabric. His hands and face trickled blood where the blades had attacked, making him look as if he had just survived some great battle.

"Can you stand?" she asked. Moving seemed to make her hearing seem better, the ringing fading slowly.

"I think—" he started. "Eris!"

She felt the surge of energy just as he said her name, instinctively knowing what was coming. Thunder followed, the explosion loud in her ears, shaking her. Her breathing became heavy. In that instant, she knew lightning came straight for them.

Without thinking, she raised one hand to the sky while touching the other to the ground. The earth thrummed against her hand, matching the residual ringing in her ears. She pulled on the energy she felt and pushed back against the sky.

Sharp blades of the grass squeezed in her fist and she closed her eyes, waiting for certain death. Lightning crashed down as a shock running through her body.

And then the energy fizzled around her, exploding in a blue light visible through closed eyelids.

Eris opened her eyes. The grasses near where she knelt had been singed and pressed flat in a circle around her. Otherwise, there was no other sign of damage.

Terran looked up at her. "That last one came straight for me."

"What happened?"

He frowned. "You don't know?"

Eris shook her head. She had acted on instinct, something compelling her to draw through the power of the ground.

"You pushed the lightning away." Terran shoved himself off the ground with a grunt. Once on his feet, he tottered slightly as if he might fall. "Still wonder whether you can be a keeper?"

Without thinking about what she had been doing, Eris had managed to use the power of the plains, to call upon the stored energy to protect them. How could she doubt what she was? Whatever had happened in the forest had forged a connection in her, letting her draw on the power of the trees. Whether it was the dream or the stored memories buried in the roots of the forest, she could not deny it.

Somehow she could access the power just as Lira did.

"We need to get moving," she said. Now was not the time to question what she was, what she could do. They needed to get away from the magi. And then they could try to free Lira.

Terran took a step and nearly collapsed. He winced, grabbing his leg. "My ankle."

Both knew they didn't have time to waste. Already, the storm regained strength. Wind whipped around them and thunder rumbled. Rain spitting from the clouds stung her face.

There would be another attack soon. Or worse, the magi would reach them. Eris didn't think her fledgling knowledge would be of much use then.

She knelt next to Terran and pulled up the leg of his pants. He wore heavy boots, but the leather was cracked and wet, staining through to his pants. Not just wet, she realized, noting the stickiness. Blood.

Working carefully, she removed his boot and sock. Terran bit back a soft cry as she pulled the boot from his foot. Terran's ankle was bent at an awkward angle. A piece of bone stuck out, piercing the skin. Blood dribbled from the wound. Eris knew what this type of injury meant. She had seen some of her father's men come home with broken bones of this type. Most lost the limb.

"How bad?" Terran asked.

She shook her head. "Broken."

Thunder rolled again, distant but moving closer, the loud explosions shaking her each time. Lightning flickered in the sky, but no additional streaks shot toward them. Would she be able to deflect another blast? She had no idea what she'd done to stop the first. Touching the ground had pulled energy through her. If they could reach the protection of the trees, she suspected they would be safe. But with his ankle as it was, she doubted they would reach the trees before the magi reached them.

Terran bent around her and looked down at his foot. He let out a soft slow breath and closed his eyes. Through the pain on his face, she saw flickering emotions. Finally, he opened his eyes. "Leave me here. Get to the forest. You'll be safe there."

She shook her head. "No, Terran, we will both reach the forest."

Thunder punctuated her words. Terran glanced up at the sky, but somehow Eris knew they weren't attacked—at least not yet. The last time energy built before the strike. She would know when the magi struck.

"You need to reach safety. Find a way to rescue the mistress. She will know what to do."

"It's not just about Lira."

"What then?"

Eris didn't know. The magi wanted to destroy the forest, but it was more than that. Power. "The Conclave plans to take the throne."

They needed to free Lira to ensure her family was protected. Without Lira, they would be helpless against the Conclave.

"That's why you must leave me here. It doesn't matter if they capture me. I can't help the magi penetrate the protections of the forest. But you can. As a keeper—even untrained as you are—"

Terran stopped himself. "You must have great potential to be able to protect us as you have, but if the magi capture you and discover what you can do..." He shook his head. "You'll be as helpless as Lira. Probably more so. You're right. You need to find a way to free her. She's the only one who will know how to stop the magi."

"I can't just leave you here," Eris said. If only there was something to splint his leg, hold it steady so that he could stand and try to walk, but out on the plain there was nothing but the painful needlegrass.

She looked over toward the forest. The dark edge of the trees seemed both tantalizingly close and far away at the same time. Even uninjured, she didn't think they could reach the trees in time.

"You know you must," he said.

That he was right did not make her feel better. If they were in the trees, they would be safer. More than that, Eris had felt the power of the forest. A part of her suspected she could even use that power if needed. But on the Verilain Plains?

"Was there a keeper here?" she asked.

A bright surge of light exploded in the sky. Thunder followed.

Eris glanced back. Lanterns bobbed above the grasses. They were still far enough away, but they moved closer. Soon they would reach them.

"Eris," Terran urged. The tone in his voice was clear. "You need to get to the trees before the magi get much closer."

"Was there?" she asked, ignoring him. The magi were still far enough away for her to get her answer. Eris looked around, eyes scanning the long grasses of the plains. Occasional copses of trees dotted the plains. The lightning made small shadows stretch atop the grasses. She felt things moving through the blades, the distant sense of life, but it was vague and not distinct, nothing like what she felt in the forest.

Terran sighed. "For something like this, there must have been a keeper." He looked at her, his eyes pleading. "Please, Eris, leave me here."

Eris wondered if the Verilain Plains had much the same power as the forest. It was certainly vast enough. Already she had managed to focus its energy to block the blast of lightning—could she use it for more?

She needed a better connection to the grasses than she had.

Eris took off her boots. Then she peeled off her socks. Her feet sunk into the hard ground.

Immediately she felt the connection, deeper and differently. Closing her eyes, she rested her hand flat on the ground. Her palm cupped one of the bent and damaged grasses. Damaged, but not dead. Life flowed through the blade of grass, connected to the ground where its roots stretched deep, spreading out, connecting to the other grasses and weaving together. Different but similar to what she felt within the forest. Not nearly as deep. There was no sense of permanence as in the forest—the grasses already prepared for the cold of winter and their dormancy—but there was strength here just as in the forest.

Eris delved into the roots.

She did not know what it was that she did, only that she followed the stream of life she felt within the grass, tracing it into the ground and below, chasing the thin tendrils as they twisted from one blade of grass to the next. Where the forest seemed this vast power that was very much alive, its roots storing the memories of the keeper who had guided their growth, the grasses were more indistinct.

Would they allow her to use their power?

Eris felt the question go out from her and spread across and throughout the roots. A soft breeze fluttered her hair, and like a sigh, she thought she heard the answer.

With this deeper connection made, she could tell where the magi trampled through the grasses. Unlike in the forest, the awareness remained vague. She was too far away to do anything to stop them…but she could slow their progress.

Sending out the question, she waited for the response.

The wind kicked up, suddenly stronger, pulling the grasses

upright around them. The rain blew harder and swirled around them. The grasses stood tall, pulled proud and strong around the magi, the blades of their leaves sharp and cutting, slicing through the clothing and flesh of the magi as they passed through. Blood dripped from hundreds of wounds, watering the ground, and the needlegrass of the plains seemed to sigh in contentment. Their progress was slowed to a crawl as they struggled against grasses now fighting their way.

And then the magi stopped.

Eris did not need to wait to know what would happen next.

Overhead, thunder began to rumble more steadily. Lightning flashed angrily in the sky. Streaks shot down but dissipated before reaching the ground, fizzling out with flashes of blue and orange light. Still the grasses stood tall, pushing against the magi.

Already the stored energy of the plains strained against the violence of the magi. How much longer could the grass withstand? How much power was stored within their shallow roots?

"What did you do?" Terran asked.

She shook her head. "Slowed them, I think."

He smiled, the lopsided expression she had seen so often on his face in the garden returning. "Angered them is more likely."

"I don't know how long it will hold," Eris admitted.

"Now they will know you are here."

She shook her head. "Not me. Just that there is another keeper."

Terran frowned at her. "What do you mean?"

"Adrick would not suspect it was me. He will think there is another keeper. It's why they fear the north, I think."

Terran nodded. "When the gardens were destroyed, my grandfather said many went north. The south was too dangerous. The Conclave had already claimed Saffra. But the north was free."

"So, they'll fear another keeper has come to help Lira. Maybe they'll think it's the same keeper for the Svanth Forest and blame it as his reason for failing before."

"But there is not a keeper of the forest. There hasn't been for years."

"Would the Conclave know that?"

He shook his head. "I am not sure what they know about the keepers. You probably know more than I do about the magi."

Eris looked across the plain toward the lanterns, wishing she was anywhere but standing stranded out on the open plains, the magi pressing toward her filled with their angry violence while Lira was trapped in iron shackles that she could not escape from.

"Why does iron prevent her from using her powers?" she asked Terran.

He shook his head. "Another question I can't answer. I know little about the power of the keepers, Eris. I can tell you much about the gardeners, can list the names of gardeners who've lived over the last few hundred years, have learned names of plants I haven't seen. But what the keepers do is different."

Were she able to somehow help Lira, to free her from the irons, she wondered if together they might be able to do more than simply escape the magi. Out here upon the plains, so near the power of the forest, could they stop the conclave entirely?

Not while Terran was injured.

She looked over to him, the way his face twisted in pain, and wished there was something she could do, something more than simply leaving him while she ran off to try and rescue Lira.

The magi struggled against the grasses, moving slowly but steadily toward them. Given enough time, the magi would reach them—would reach Terran—and without getting him up, there was little she could do to stop it. She felt them moving, having abandoned an attack on her for now, though the angry clouds overhead and the steady flashes of lightning told her they still tried.

Eris crouched next to Terran and took his broken ankle in her hands. If she could somehow do something…anything…they could move back toward the forest and figure out a way to reach Lira.

"What are you doing?" Terran asked.

He tried to pull away, but she held tightly to his injured foot. With the pain he must be feeling, he didn't fight against her very hard.

"Relax," she said.

"Eris—you don't know what you're doing. I said I don't know much about the keepers, but I know there are limits to their powers. You need whatever power you can salvage to save the mistress. Save Lira."

"I'm *not* going to let them have you."

With one hand on his ankle and the other touching the ground beneath him, she reached for the connection she had felt before, the thread of life working through the blade of grass. When she touched it, she pushed down along it, reaching out her awareness to the vast expanse of the roots, before finally sending her request. *Heal him.*

Eris waited, hopeful. The plains had seemed to try and help when she sent her last request, but this time she felt nothing. Emptiness.

Had the energy of the plains been wasted already?

Again she tried, sending out a desperate request. *Heal him.*

There was no sense of energy, no healing surge. No answer.

Thunder rumbled again. Eris opened her eyes and looked over to Terran. "I'm sorry…"

Terran reached across his legs and took her hand. There was warmth in his hand, and he held hers gently. "You need to go. Do what you can to save Lira." He swallowed, his deep brown eyes threatening to overwhelm her. "And if you can't, promise me that you will run to the palace. Don't do anything foolish."

Eris glared at him.

Terran just squeezed her hand. "Thank you for trying."

When he let go of her hand, it felt like a goodbye.

Eris stood, wiping a soft tear that came to her eyes. She took a deep breath, wanting to say something more to Terran, but there was nothing more she could say.

Leaving him here on the plains felt like a betrayal. Even if the magi did not find him, his ankle was injured and damaged enough that infection would set in. Without a healer—and possibly even with one—infection would likely to spread to his blood, leaving him just as dead as if the magi caught him.

"I'll come back for you," she said.

He nodded. The grim look on his face told her that he didn't think she would reach him in time.

Eris started away from him, running toward the trees. Tears streamed from her eyes, anger starting to work through her at the fact that she was forced to leave him. Through the distant connection to the grasses, she sent another request. *Protect him.*

She thought she heard the grasses sigh in response.

CHAPTER 28

*E*ris hurried through the grasses. The tall needlegrass bent away from her, creating a pathway for her to move. It never opened up more than a few steps in front of her, keeping her concealed as she moved. She ran toward the trees. The power of the forest would be able to protect her from the magi. The magi feared it, knew there were protective enchantments in place to keep the forest—truly a garden no different than what Lira grew in the palace—safe. The Conclave had failed to break its barriers, but this time had a different plan. Eris could reach it, might even be able to use the power stored there, but it would do nothing to free Lira.

She stopped and looked around. Dark clouds smeared the sky. Lightning flickered within the clouds, and occasional streaks shot toward the grassy plains, falling short before they struck. Thunder rolled around her. Away from the forest, deeper in the plains, the small lanterns moved as tiny lights in the distance.

Thankfully, they moved away from where she had left Terran. Eris could felt his presence, knew where he lay, broken and injured on the plains, grasses pulled tight around him in a protective circle. At least she did not have to fear them finding him.

But Eris felt afraid for a different reason, one separate from what could still happen to Terran. When the magi reached the forest, they would be able to break through the barriers. With Lira captured, nothing would stop them from working their destructive magic. Then, the barrier that was the Svanth Forest, the one garden that had held the magi at bay when others failed, would fall.

Had Lira been more willing to teach her, she would already know what she needed to do to protect the forest.

How much of this could have been avoided had Lira simply explained to her what she was? Eris might not have been captured, she might have been able to help Lira protect the palace, had she known she had the potential to be a keeper.

And how long had Lira known? Long enough to summon Terran. He had been working in the gardens with Nels for... months? Could Lira have explained things to her, helped her reach her potential faster?

Eris could not shake the sense that Lira had not even *wanted* to teach her. She preferred sending her away, back into the garden to wander, always searching for flowers, to the point where Eris feared Lira was a traitor. And when Eris finally found one that seemed to suit her, Lira still had been unwilling to work with her.

Unlike her sisters. *They* had been allowed to learn from Lira. Were they keepers, or did she simply share her knowledge with them because the queen asked it of her?

And why not with Eris?

Lira could have stopped all of this had she simply worked with Eris. Jasi would not have been captured, carried and tortured, dragged away from her new husband. Terran would not have come after her and been injured, leaving him broken and surrounded by the grasses, likely to die. Eris would not have been stranded, standing in these grasses, helpless.

She closed her eyes and let out a stuttering breath. She could leave Lira, find Jasi, and return home. But that wouldn't save Terran. Wouldn't save the forest.

Without Lira, she would never learn what it meant to be a keeper.

If she did nothing, everyone she loved—her parents, her sisters, her brother...even Terran—would fall before the magi. She'd seen what they were willing to do for power. How could she turn away when she had the potential to help?

How could she turn away now when she finally felt she mattered?

But why her? She could do nothing.

As it was, she was left with memories of a dream, memories which did nothing other than speak a promise of the power of the keepers. With more time, she might be able to read through the stories woven into the roots of the forest by the first keeper, but there was not the time. If the forest was destroyed, there would never be the time.

That left saving Lira as her only option.

Eris wanted to scream. If only Terran had not been injured.

Before, she had done all that she could to run *from* the magi. Now, she would be running *toward* them. If she was caught, if the magi took her and chained her alongside Lira, what then? What would happen to Terran, to her sister, to the forest?

They would be no worse off than they were now.

The realization reassured her. She would not simply wait for something to happen. Eris was tired of waiting, tired of things happening to her, tired of the magi trying to hurt her or those she cared about.

It was time she had answers.

Her eyes snapped open, and she started toward the magi. She

moved quickly, following a direct path. Whatever else she did, she decided, she would see to it that the magi regretted bringing her out here to the Svanth Forest. Now that she knew she had the capability to be a keeper, whether or not she could use that ability, the magi would feel her anger.

She ran through the tall grasses. The needlegrass bent down momentarily, long enough to let her pass, before springing back into place. The ground blurred past her. With each step, memories of what she had been through rolled through her mind.

Anger filled her. She did not push it down.

Anger that she had been captured and tormented, anger that the magi attempted to destroy the forest, anger that Lira had been captured, anger that Lira had known what Eris could do but had not shared, and anger that Terran was injured and could not be with her. The anger sent her nearly flying along the ground.

Eris was aware of nothing other than the sense of where the magi stood. Even moving as quickly as she was, she felt their presence like a blight on the plains needing removal. Distantly, she was aware that storms raged around her, thunder and lightning rolling and crackling from the magi. Rain spit from the sky.

Then she reached the magi. Eris threw herself to the ground to keep from sight. The grasses moved around her, as if sensing her mood, twisting so they did not cut at her arms. She felt the presence of the magi as they came toward her, now cutting their way across the grass, slicing through the tall blades with a sword or scythe.

That only served to fuel her anger more.

Eris sent a message to the plains. With her anger and frustration, this was less a request and more of a demand, unlike anything she had ever tried. There would be no denying this request.

Stop them.

There was a rustling of wind and the sense of a soft sigh she began to recognize as coming from the grasses themselves. The grasses shifted, differently than before. The movement was fast, surged onward with the energy of her demand, taking on the hot rage that radiated through her and into the twisted roots of the plains. The needlegrasss attacked.

Someone shouted. A long scream echoed from where the magi worked their way across the plains and then fell silent.

She wondered if the injured magi was the one who had tormented her. She would feel no remorse for him.

Eris could not see what had happened. Blood had spilled onto the ground, soaking into the soil. The grasses welcomed it hungrily, feeding, pushing harder, searching for more, doing what they could to please her.

Even the grasses feared her anger.

"Vanis?" someone shouted.

When Vanis didn't answer, they yelled again. "Vanis?"

A moan was cut short. She heard a rustling across the ground, felt the sense of someone moving through the grasses, and then nothing. Vanis was silent.

Had he died? Had the grasses, in their attempt to follow her command, killed one of the magi?

Eris didn't let herself feel remorse. How could she feel remorse after what had happened to her? After what the magi intended for her family. They deserved it for Adrick's betrayal.

Her anger seethed. This was not her doing. Whatever happened was because of what the magi had already done. It was their fault she had been forced to take such drastic steps.

The grasses followed her command, shifting and moving, slicing toward the life trampling through it with vengeance for the blades that had been shorn, cut short so the destruction could move through.

There was another grunt, followed by a soft cry.

Eris could not tell how many magi remained. Could the grasses contain them all?

She would be most pleased if they stopped Adrick next, but none of the lives seemed any different from the next to the grasses. Only Lira stood out as different; Eris felt that the grasses recognized the difference and left her alone, twisting so she went uninjured.

One of the magi began chanting. Thunder started to rumble loudly. Lightning pressed down, flickers of bright yellow light streaking around her, as if circling the plains.

"Was it her?"

Eris heard the shout. The voice was rough but full of panic.

"She barely moves. It cannot be her."

This was Adrick. Eris recognized his voice and felt another surge of anger.

The grass of the plains seemed to feed off her anger, eager to follow her frustration as they darted toward the source of the voice.

"How can you be sure? I saw what happened! The grass attacked!" Davin yelled.

There was the sound of a harsh slap. "Have you ever heard of grass attacking? This is needlegrass. You knew the risks of walking through here. A price must be paid to reach the Svanth!"

Hearing his voice made Eris even angrier.

Him.

She felt it as the grasses sighed and stabbed toward where Adrick spoke.

A soft growl was followed by an explosion. The grasses near where Adrick had been standing were burned away.

"We need the full Conclave for this!"

"You are a fool," the High Seat said. "You think one keeper can stand before five magi of the Conclave?"

"What is this then?"

The High Seat laughed. The sound was dark and angry and flooded over her.

Eris felt a surge of anger in response.

"Only another keeper," he said. "We will find her and destroy her."

"I'm not going out there," Davin said.

Eris frowned. Had he done something to Jasi? Was that the reason her eyes carried such darkness?

Him.

The grasses seemed to understand and stabbed toward the magi who had just spoken. She heard a soft scream and felt another blast. The chanting suddenly stopped.

"Find her!" the High Seat yelled. Eris heard the anger in his voice. "It's time this keeper learns we aren't powerless."

"What do we do?"

"She is here. Somewhere close. I can *smell* her. Burn it. All of it."

There was another explosion. Eris felt the grasses burning away.

The other magi began to chant softly, their voices combining as they chanted their spells. Fire bloomed up near where they had been standing, leaping toward the sky. The smell was horrid.

Heat pushed against her. The air became thick and hot. The storm raging overhead grew louder, lightning flashing continuously. With a sense of horror, Eris realized the grasses of the plains tried to withdraw. With enough time, the Conclave would destroy the Verilain Plains.

New rage, different than before struck her. Now it was more than just her family. The magi wanted destroy the plains, a garden she'd come to understand she was meant to protect.

How dare the magi attempt to destroy the grasses on the plains! Had they not done enough? Wasn't the attempt on the Svanth Forest enough?

She stood. Each hand grasped fistfuls of the grass. Her legs were spread, firmly set into the ground. The dirt squished beneath her feet, and she sunk her toes into it as she sent another demand.

"She is here!"

Eris turned toward the voice. Adrick. Anger and rage bubbled inside her, and she could no long control it. The magi would be punished.

Through her connection to the grasses, she made another demand. Around her, she felt hesitation, fear that the magi would destroy more of the grasses, burn this garden entirely.

Eris would not allow that to happen.

She sent a command.

Wind whipped up suddenly, nothing like the soft sigh she felt in answer when the grasses listened to her. This was different. Forceful and buffeting, the wind matched the anger flowing through her, the rage overflowing within her.

She sent the wind toward the magi.

Grasses bent, leaning away from the wind to avoid destruction. Eris stood firm, feet planted deeply into the ground, earth flowing over her feet, a humming energy moving through her.

Eris plunged into the roots, calling for the power stored in this garden. With a furious anger, she sent her awareness along the twisting roots, pressing and pressing.

The flames pushed back against the wind. Hot and violent.

Eris pushed harder, taking a step forward. Between the flames she saw the magi. Three of them stood against her. The High Seat at the fore, his weathered and balding pate fixed in concentration. Adrick stood to his right. His eyes widened when he saw her. His focus shifted, just for a moment.

The break was enough.

The flames faltered, flicking, struggling to withstand the force of the wind buffeting against them. Eris took a step forward. The wind followed, blowing toward the magi.

Still they stood.

The High Seat's mouth turned into a smile, a darkness crossing his face as if he knew something. The chanting came louder, stronger. Flames leapt, spreading not just toward her, but around, pressing outward, rolling away from the magi in a storm of hot fire.

Much longer, and the plains would be fully ablaze. All the power stored in this garden would be destroyed.

Eris felt the energy the magi worked as a force working against her. With the heat billowing from the fire, her breathing became heavy, the weight of their magic pressing on her and mixing with the heat of the flames.

Eris screamed. The magi would not take her. They would not take her sister. They would not take Lira—the one person who could explain what was happening to her.

And they would *not* take this garden.

She shifted, digging her feet deeper into the ground, burying herself to the ankle. Roots dug against her feet. Again she pressed out, pushing along the twisting roots. Demanding more.

The grasses of the plains tried to respond—the force of her anger was overwhelming—but not enough energy remained. Everything she did consumed what power was stored within these shallow roots.

The wind faltered.

The High Seat smiled. This time it was he who took a step forward.

Heat pressed on her like an oven. It felt as if her flesh were boiling. Lightning crashed somewhere nearby. Chunks of earth flew toward her, slapping against her face. Had she not been rooted so deeply into the ground, she would have been thrown into the air. Thunder crashed on her with a physical force.

She would fail. Her fledgling abilities were not enough, not against the power and focus of the magi. Had only Lira bothered to teach her...

The chanting grew loud, rising over the roar of the wind. Eris could not tell how much longer the wind would blow. The power of the plains faded rapidly. Soon the heat would overwhelm her. Flames would reach her, and she would die.

Eventually, so would Terran. Then her family, the city, the entire realm.

All because she was not enough.

But she *would* matter. How could she not embrace her difference now? She was a keeper.

With one last angry attempt, Eris pushed along the roots of the plains, demanding whatever power was left. The wind picked up for a moment before failing.

Eris fell to the ground. Dirt filled her nostrils. She coughed against the heat and smoke.

Somewhere, she heard the magi laughing. Closer. Almost close enough to touch.

Had she only Lira...had she managed to save her...none of this would have been necessary. Had Lira been willing to teach her she might have been ready, saved by real lessons rather than memories of a long dead keeper, memories that filled the deep roots of the forest, roots that if only she could reach she might be able to summon...

Her heart leapt.

The power of the forest welcomed her, pulling her along, reaching out to her. Stretching out as she did, pushing along the thin life of the plains, she reached the edge where deeper roots abutted. There the energy and life of the forest pulsed with vibrant life. Power she could summon. Power waiting for its keeper.

The teary star was her flower for a reason. The Svanth Forest was her garden, and she was meant to be its keeper.

Eris stood. Now, only a dozen paces away, the magi looked at her. The High Seat wore a look of loathing and condescension. Adrick appeared uncertain. Davin, the only one of the magi whose cloak burned, shifted closer to the High Seat. Flames consumed the needlegrass and raced along the dry plains, pushing away from her.

"I cannot believe she chose you," Adrick said.

The chanting of the other magi and the loud rumbling of thunder punctuated his words. Lightning crashed near her, throwing dirt and burnt grasses toward her.

Eris stood fast. "She didn't choose me." She had to yell over the sound of the flames.

"Release the wind, and you might live," the High Seat said.

Eris shook her head.

"Then you will die. Just like the rest of your family once this last garden falls. These lands will be ours. And they will burn." The High Seat stared at her. His dark eyes were hard. "Had I known a garden hid within the forest, I would have gone there first. The puny garden she grew in Eliara would not be enough to withstand the might of the Conclave. Now the last garden will fall. These lands will join Saffra."

"It is not her garden," Eris said. She did not speak loudly this time but her words carried.

She let the wind pick up, circling so that the flames were sucked up and away from the grasses. With the power of the forest behind her, she found this easy.

The High Seat looked at her. "If it is not hers, then where is the other keeper?"

She shook her head. "There is no other keeper. Only me." She inhaled deeply, pulling in air that smelled of dirt and ash. "I'm the keeper of the forest."

Adrick sneered at her. "You are a poorly trained princess. If this flower mage cannot stop me, there is nothing you can do," he said, pointing to where Lira lay limp on the ground.

Eris sent the wind.

The magi chanted, but the sound died against the power she commanded. It ripped at where Eris stood rooted to the ground, unmoving in spite of the howling gale. She unleashed the power stored in the forest in a torrent. The magi pressed back, even the force of their flames not enough against the angry energy she summoned.

The magi screamed, ragged voices calling out destructive magic. Thunder rocked the night. Lightning streaked from the sky in angry purple veins.

With a flood of power, Eris dismissed the storm.

The force of her wind blew the clouds away from the plains, sending the darkness and rain chasing the thunder and lightning away.

She roared again. Wind howled with her.

The magi fell, thrown by the power Eris commanded, disappearing into the night. Adrick lingered the longest. Hatred shone in his eyes before he disappeared.

The magi dismissed, she commanded the grasses to bring Lira to her.

They slid under her, lifting her and pressing her up on their long blades. With a shifting shimmer, Lira was carried toward her. Eris felt it as a sense of life dragged along atop the grasses.

And then she saw her.

As she reached her, she looked upon the Mistress of Flowers. The flower mage. The keeper.

Any frustration she had felt at Lira for hiding what she could be disappeared as she saw her. With sudden realization, she wondered if Lira had not been trying to protect her, hiding what she was—what she could be—because she knew what the magi would do to her if they knew. Even Lira—an experienced keeper— had finally fallen in the face of their magic.

She looked beaten. Her face bruised. Colorful knots raised on her cheeks bloomed with purple and yellow. Blood stained her mouth and nose; deep cracks split along her lips. Arms and legs looked sliced by hundreds of shallow knives that Eris knew to be the result of the grasses fighting the magi's progress.

She wore nothing more than a tattered gown. Even that was simply remnants, the color so stained with dirt and blood that Eris could not be certain whether it started as blue or green. Dressed as she was, all sense of formality was stolen from her. Dark hair fell across her face. Someone had cut chunks from it and burned other parts. A section of her scalp looked scalded.

Yet her eyes opened as she neared. The familiar brightness burned behind her eyes as she looked at Eris. And then she smiled.

"Eris Taeresin. A keeper at last," she whispered.

CHAPTER 29

The rest of the anger seeped from Eris with Lira's words. The wind suddenly died, returning to a soft breeze blowing against her back, still pressing against where the magi had tried to burn through the plains. Huge swaths of charred grasses remained, a reminder of what the magi had nearly accomplished.

Eris still felt the connection to the forest, could still call upon the energy stored there, though the connection was different than what she had managed with the grasses of the plains. The grasses seemed to welcome her commands, willingly served as she demanded, only withdrawing when the heat and flames from the magi threatened to overwhelm. The forest was different; Eris could tell demands would not work. A more subtle touch was needed, and though she had been allowed to use the energy to confront the magi, there was no guarantee such requests would be answered the next time.

Freeing herself from the ground, Eris stepped toward Lira, the grasses cushioning her feet. She knelt next to her and took her hands. Iron shackles held her wrists. A single long pin locked each side, and Eris pulled it loose, freeing Lira from the chains.

Lira looked up at her, a haunted look on her face.

"Why didn't you tell me?" Eris asked.

Lira sighed, letting her breath out in a soft whisper that sent the grasses around them fluttering. "Would you have believed?" Lira asked. "Would you have truly understood had I told you?"

"You meant me to find out like this? I spent weeks wondering if you were a traitor!" Eris looked around at the plains spreading out around her, at the distant forest. Blackness met her eyes. The scent of char and smoke filled her nose and mouth.

Lira shook her head sadly. "Not like this," she whispered. She took a deep steadying breath. "I sensed great potential in you very early, but different than any I had ever encountered. I could not unlock it. That has never been my gift. Were there still others..." She trailed off, a note of sadness creeping into her voice. "But there is only me. The others have scattered, leaving this land unprotected, the gardens destroyed. And you untrained."

She squeezed Eris's hand. "I am sorry I did not know how to teach you. Once, there would have been keepers for you to learn from who understood your particular skills. Mine differ from yours." She coughed. "That is why I had you search for your flower. Finding one's flower helps to know what type of keeper you can be."

"And the teary star?" Eris asked.

Lira shook her head. "Unusual. I placed the vine in the garden thinking only to test it. It came with me after I planted my garden years before." She swallowed. "I've never known a keeper to pair with that particular flower. It's why you were drawn to the forest. Why you were able to use its energy. Had it not been for you, the magi would have destroyed this last great garden. Then nothing would have stopped them from taking Errasn."

"It's not the last," Eris said.

Lira frowned. "Once there were dozens of gardens. The great Gardens of Elaysia. Each as different as their keepers. Now only the Svanth Forest remains."

"Not just the Svanth," Eris said. She did not know much about the great gardens, but what she felt upon the plain was clear. "The Verilain Plains are just as much a garden as the Svanth Forest. Different, but nearly as powerful. Without the power stored in the plains, I doubt I would have been able to withstand the magi attack."

Lira looked around her. She touched the earth, making a shallow mark, and pushed out a soft breath, little more than a sigh, worked into the wind. She leaned forward, hand touching the ground, lightly gripping one of the blades of grass. A pained expression was written on her face.

"How did I not see this?" she said softly. "How is it you learned?"

Eris shook her head. "I don't know," she answered. "Just like in the forest, I found I could trace along the roots. Where the forest is deep and massive, the plains are shallow but expansive." She shrugged, unable to answer it any better than that.

Lira smiled slightly, brushing a strand of loose chestnut hair away from her head, leaving a patch of burned scalp visible. She shifted to her knees and pushed up from the ground, wiping her hands across what remained of her dress. "You speak of chasing the roots. An unusual gift, even in a keeper. Perhaps that is why I could not help you when I first recognized your gift."

Eris shifted her feet. "I thought you didn't want to teach me. That I was too much trouble for you. Nothing like my sisters."

Lira laughed a rich and full laugh. "You might be trouble, Eris Taeresin, but it was not that I didn't want to teach you, only that I couldn't help you make the first connection. You had to do so on your own." She held Eris's eyes. "I *had* hoped you would discover your own power more easily. Only then did I think I could I teach. It is…unfortunate…the magi chose now to attack."

Eris breathed out a soft laugh, relief that Lira had not avoided trying to teach her filling her. Distantly, she felt the pull of the forest, a quiet understanding that much of what she wanted to know could be found in the story woven into the roots of the trees.

"Can you walk?"

Lira took a few tentative steps. She wobbled, but remained upright. "I think so."

Eris guided her forward. The needlegrass bent away from her without her even needing to be asked. Lira watched without comment for a moment.

"You don't wish to return to the palace?" Lira asked.

"There's something we need to do."

She imagined Terran lying in the field, just waiting, hoping she would return, pain overwhelming him. Hopefully infection had not set in yet and he could still be saved.

Eris sensed where Terran rested in the long grasses and started toward him.

As much as she wanted to hurry, Lira moved slowly, gingerly walking through the grasses as if afraid they might slice through her flesh. Probably they had, Eris realized. She was surprised to realize she no longer feared the grasses attacking her. She sensed…respect… from the grass, drawing away so as not to injure her as she passed.

"And now?" Eris asked. "What happened to the magi?"

Lira turned and looked south. "They have gone, but not for good. The High Seat, at least, will have survived. Possibly the others. They will retreat to Saffra, rebuild their strength."

Eris wondered what would happen when the magi attacked again. "What of me?"

Lira shook her head. "I will teach you what I can, but I am afraid not much that I know will be of use to you."

"But you can use the power of the Svanth Forest as well!"

"Not the forest," Lira said. "Different, I think, than you." She looked toward the west. The sun was just starting to rise, orange light crept along the horizon, the darkness of the night fading. All traces of the dark clouds the magi brought with them had scattered. "When the magi learned of the true strength of the gardens, they attacked, destroying what had once provided a layer of protection. And when my garden was destroyed, part of me went with it," she began, her voice soft. "The surviving keepers departed. Most went north. Only I remained, retreating into the forest, planting a new garden on the fringe where enough sunlight still came through the canopy to help my flowers grow. This garden was different than the one I lost, but over time just as powerful."

"I don't understand how that is different," Eris said.

Lira smiled. "Think of your connection to the forest, Eris. Mine is a connection to the flowers I planted, a particular garden within the forest, one the forest *allows* to grow. Yours is…"

Eris nodded, understanding finally coming. "Mine is the entire forest." And she realized she could feel the small garden Lira planted. Compared to the rest of the forest, the garden was tiny. "How is it that I can do this?"

"That is for you to learn," Lira said.

Eris thought for a moment. Is that what she wanted for herself? Did she want to become a keeper? "Did you find Jasi?"

Lira nodded. "It's how they caught me. I left the palace after their initial attack. There wasn't much left for me to work with… Nels will have it repaired quickly, but I needed a better connection." Her eyes went distant as she looked toward the forest. "I found Jasi. Your brother, too. He was injured but will live. He took her back to the palace. They're safe now."

Eris sighed, relieved. Safe—at least until the magi attacked again. And now that she'd seen what the Conclave would do for power, she had no doubt the magi would try again. Jasi would ensure their father listened. And she felt relieved Jacen lived. But how had he gotten free from the magi?

Unless...

She shook away the thought. There was no way Jacen was involved in this.

"Are my sisters keepers as well?" she asked after a while.

Lira shook her head. "They don't have the skill. They have some eye for arrangements, and there is a certain power in that. In time, they might learn to communicate using messages written in the flowers themselves, a language long guarded by the keepers and gardeners. But they will never be keepers."

Eris closed her eyes, letting her sense of Terran lying unmoving draw her forward. For so long she had thought herself different from her sisters—and she was. She didn't have the same interest in sewing and dancing and gossip as her sisters. But for the first time, she felt good about that difference.

"What if I choose not to use this ability? What if I don't want to be a keeper?"

Lira only nodded, as if understanding. "Being a keeper is a difficult burden. The Conclave seeks to destroy us, fearing what we can do in their quest for power. Those keepers who remain have hidden. Like them, you may choose to ignore your abilities. As you have never developed them fully, I suspect in time they will wither. With them, so will a part of you." Lira turned to her, a focused expression on her face. "Or you can embrace this part of yourself, know that you are part of something greater, use your abilities to protect the realm and your people."

"Is that what you do?"

Lira sighed softly. "Not at first. At first all I wanted was revenge." She nodded. "Yes, revenge. When my garden was lost, so too was my paired flower. No more will rivenswood bloom. Wood from which the very throne your father sits upon is now lost forever. I still feel its loss strongly."

"I thought your flower was parisander."

"A poor substitute, but it is all that I have."

"You said 'at first'."

Lira nodded. "As the palace garden grew, as Nels helped me replace what I had lost, I began to see the beauty of the flowers once again. In time, I no longer sought revenge, but to help protect Errasn from the magi. I don't know the motives of the Conclave, but it is not for peace."

"They want the throne," Eris said. But it was more than that, she suspected. They wanted to destroy everything that grew, turn Errasn into a desert like Saffra.

"And had you not stopped them, they might have gained it."

"What now?" Eris asked.

"The Conclave isn't defeated. But they know there is another keeper. One powerful enough to overwhelm five of their magi, including one of their greatest. They will not attack soon."

"But they *will* attack again."

Lira nodded slowly. "That is their nature."

Eris thought about what she would do. She could return home and become the princess her father wanted. That meant marrying and becoming more like Jasi. Or she could embrace her difference, accept that she was born to be a keeper.

For so long she had not known her place in the world. Not firstborn, destined to be king like Jacen. Not desirable like Jasi and Desia, destined to unite the realm. And unlike Ferisa, she did not have the necessary faith to serve the Sacred Mother.

Before she had time to say more, they came upon Terran lying on the ground. A mound of grasses pressed down atop him, hiding him from view. Yet Eris felt him lying there, barely moving but breathing still. With a silent command, she told the grasses to move, and in less than a breath, they spread apart, splaying wide on a soft gust of wind.

Terran looked up at her. His face had gone pale and ashen. His mouth was dry, and he ran a tongue over his lips to wet them. A soft sheen of sweat covered his face. His body shook, whether in tremors or with chills, Eris knew neither was a good sign.

"You need to get..."

He trailed off when he saw Lira.

She looked at him with an expression of sadness. "I cannot heal him, Eris," she whispered. "I am too far removed from my garden. What connection I have is weak."

Eris could not look away from Terran. He tried to hide the terror on his face but failed.

"Terran—"

He shook his head. "You did what you could."

But Eris knew she had not.

She knelt in front of him and again took his ankle between her hands. The skin was hot, burning against her. She resisted the urge to pull her hands away. Terran shook his head, but she ignored him.

Setting her feet in the dirt beneath her, she raced along the connection of twisting roots of the plains toward the stored energy of the forest. The energy stored in the grasses already returned even after all that she had done to use it. The grasses had been unable to do anything to help heal him, but the power stored in the Svanth Forest would not be limited.

As she reached the roots of the forest, she delved into them, pressing along the twisting pathways that raced toward the heart of the forest where the tall Svanth trees lived. An awareness of the trees filled her. Eris sent out a request. *Help me.*

Countless heartbeats seemed to pass as she waited.

The forest seemed to consider her request before finally releasing a surge of power through her. Eris was not sure what happened. Terran gasped.

Opening her eyes, his ankle was no longer swollen. Bone piercing his flesh had mended, the skin drawn closed as if never injured. The heat she felt in his ankle was gone. Even his color was better. He shivered, but it was nothing like before, more the tremor of someone awakening from a deep sleep.

She sent a message of thanks to the trees. A request came as an answer. *Come.*

Lira touched her on the arm, and Eris started, turning to face the Mistress of Flowers.

"We should return home. Your parents were safe when I left, but your father will need convincing."

"Jasi will help. She saw what happened here."

Eris looked over the plains, toward Eliara and the palace, where Jasi would need help recovering from what she'd been through. Likely Jacen, too. She turned to where the sun had started to creep over the top of the forest. Eris couldn't return to the palace. Not yet. Returning meant she'd never learn what her difference meant, and she'd always wonder what could have been.

Lira looked at her then looked at the forest, and nodded. "You will return?"

"Eventually." There was so much she could learn from the forest. Much it wanted to show her. That was part of the request. She didn't understand the other parts but knew that, in time, she would learn.

"When you do, I will be ready to teach," Lira said.

"I would like that."

"Keep her safe?" Lira said, looking down at Terran.

He stood slowly, the color returning to his face. "I will."

Eris spun, turning to Terran. "You will come with me?"

He shrugged, his lopsided smile returning. "I am a gardener."

A wide smile turned her face, matching his. Eris wouldn't have to be alone. Terran would come with her. More than that, she finally knew what she was meant to do. Different than her sisters, Eris now felt okay about those differences. She would never have been happy as some lord's wife, used as a means to tie the kingdom to the north. But this?

She gazed toward the Svanth Forest as Terran took her hand. Her smile widened. The trees called her back, wanting to guide her, to teach her. This was what she was meant to do.

Eris turned to Terran. He watched her, expectantly. Finally, she spoke. "And I am a keeper."

Buy Book 2 of the Lost Garden: The Desolate Bond or get the entire Lost Garden trilogy.

Newly named keeper of the forest, Eris Taeresin struggles to understand what her new role – and new powers – mean for her. A keeper can use the energy stored within the forest, can learn from ancient lessons woven into deeply buried roots, but Eris doesn't fully control it. As she fails to use that power, she begins to wonder if she really is a keeper of trees. With the Conclave of Magi attacking along the southern border, Eris must learn the key to her abilities or everything she knows will be lost.

To help, she decides to return home to learn from the Lira, the Mistress of Flowers, knowing it will put a strain on her growing relationship with Terran. There she discovers her mother is dying and Lira cannot save her. As Eris works to learn whether her connection to the forest can save her mother, she discovers a mysterious message hidden in flowers around the palace. Before she can decipher its meaning, she is betrayed and taken from the palace.

Eris must discover the key to her abilities in order to save herself, help her mother, stop the magi, all without losing Terran, but can she do so in time?

Looking for another series? Grab Shadow Hunted, book 1 of the Collector Chronicles.

Carthenne Rel is born of shadow magic. Gifted with the power to control the flame that burns within her. A master strategist. All will be tested by the mysterious Collector.

As she travels south, wanting to solidify her growing network, word of attacks in the south leads her to a distant city with a strange past. While searching for answers and attempting to establish a presence as she has in countless other cities, she finds power that rivals her own and a challenger who might be not only more powerful than her, but an even more cunning strategist.

Carth must save her friends—and the city—before the plan set in place by the Collector succeeds.

Check out the first in a new series: The Dark Ability.

Exiled by his family. Claimed by thieves. Could his dark ability be the key to his salvation?

Rsiran is a disappointment to his family, gifted with the ability to Slide. It is a dark magic, one where he can transport himself wherever he wants, but using it will only turn him into the thief his father fears.

Forbidden from Sliding, he's apprenticed under his father as a blacksmith where lorcith, a rare, precious metal with arcane properties, calls to him, seducing him into forming forbidden blades. When discovered, he's banished, sentenced indefinitely to the mines of Ilphaesn Mountain.

Though Rsiran tries to serve obediently, to learn to control the call of lorcith as his father demands, when his life is threatened in the darkness of the mines, he finds himself Sliding back to Elaeavn where he finds a black market for his blades - and a new family of thieves.

There someone far more powerful than him discovers what he can do and intends to use him. He doesn't want to be a pawn in anyone's ambitions; all he ever wanted was a family. But the darkness inside him cannot be ignored - and he's already embroiled in an ancient struggle that only he may be able to end.

ALSO BY D.K. HOLMBERG

The Lost Prophecy

The Threat of Madness

The Warrior Mage

Tower of the Gods

Twist of the Fibers

The Lost City

The Last Conclave

The Gift of Madness

The Great Betrayal

The Teralin Sword

Soldier Son

Soldier Sword

Soldier Sworn

Soldier Saved

The Cloud Warrior Saga

Chased by Fire

Bound by Fire

Changed by Fire

Fortress of Fire

Forged in Fire

Serpent of Fire

Servant of Fire

Born of Fire

Broken of Fire

Light of Fire

Cycle of Fire

The Endless War

Journey of Fire and Night

Darkness Rising

Endless Night

Summoner's Bond

Seal of Light

The Shadow Accords

Shadow Blessed

Shadow Cursed

Shadow Born

Shadow Lost

Shadow Cross

Shadow Found

The Dark Ability

The Dark Ability

The Heartstone Blade

The Tower of Venass

Blood of the Watcher

The Shadowsteel Forge

The Guild Secret

Rise of the Elder

The Sighted Assassin

The Binders Game

The Forgotten

Assassin's End

The Lost Garden

Keeper of the Forest

The Desolate Bond

Keeper of Light

The Painter Mage

Shifted Agony

Arcane Mark

Painter For Hire

Stolen Compass

Stone Dragon